AGAINST THE CURRENT

J. ALSPAUGH

LITTLE LAMP PUBLISHING

Published by Little Lamp Publishing
Oklahoma City, OK

Design by Julie Alspaugh

Printed in the United States of America

First Printing, 2026

ISBN-978-1-966775-11-9

Library of Congress Control Number: 2026911518

DEDICATION

This book is dedicated to Fred and Carol Levy and the many others who look beyond themselves to invest in others and help them to become what God designed them to be.

CHAPTER 1

Twelve year old Brent Macintyre stood in the alley undecided. Not because he was afraid the police were gunning for him, but because he knew they were there for his dad.

Guns barked not far away, and someone cried out.

Still Brent did not move. He could not move. He felt numb, unable to think.

A male voice was shouting commands out on the street, loud and bold. More gunshots echoed through the night. Had they killed him?

Brent knew he had to snap out of it. He had to think about something else. He forced himself to remember the last time he had seen his dad at home. The big, dark haired man was leaning back in his chair beside the kitchen table. He was talking about the money they would have if the job went through. Talking about all of the things they could do together as a family. Most importantly, Brent's dad was happy. That was an emotion that seemed out of place in their home.

Brent didn't know much about what his dad did for work, but he did know that when Roland Macintyre's business suffered, the nervous angry tension became a part of his family's daily life. But last night, Roland had been happy, laughing and planning for the future. Twelve year old Brent remembered the thrill of hope that had surged through him as Roland Macintyre promised Brent anything he wanted. His mom had turned from the dishes she was washing to look over at Brent, her fearful eyes holding a silent warning. How he wished he had understood what her look had meant.

More gunshots shattered the memory Brent was trying to solidify in his mind. He did not want his last memory of his dad to be the big man sprawled out on the pavement with officers swarming around him. And yet, he could not seem to walk away.

"What are you doing here?" It was Slinger, one of his dad's close business partners. His dusty blond hair was disheveled, and his face gleamed with sweat. One hand was hidden in the pocket of his leather jacket.

Brent blinked at him, stunned. "Did they get my dad?"

"You tipped the cops, didn't you?" Slinger was coming toward him, his face hard. "You turned the lights on in the bank when the cop was passing, and then you made a run for it."

"I wasn't even in the bank." Brent backed away, his eyes darting from Slinger's right hand to the man's hard face. Something was different about him, but Brent could not place it. An overwhelming urge to run surged through Brent. He steadied himself, knowing that if he ran he would not get far. "I didn't talk to the police, Mr. Slinger."

The man's frown deepened. "You followed Macintyre here, didn't you?" Slinger accused, stopping a few feet from where Brent stood.

"I followed Dad, but I didn't know what he was going to do. I didn't know about the bank."

The fingers on Slinger's right hand twitched, and Brent was silent. He knew his dad's partner was lightning fast with the gun hidden under his jacket.

"You expect me to believe that?" Slinger stumbled a little, but righted himself almost instantly.

For the first time, Brent realized Slinger was leaning slightly to the left.

"They shot you," Brent observed in shock. "You gotta get help." This was not the first time Brent had seen someone who had been shot. His dad was notorious for bringing wounded strangers home to get fixed up. Brent remembered with a shudder the older man who had died in their living room.

"Did they get my dad?" Brent no longer felt afraid. Emotions swelled, threatening to suffocate him. "You are a coward, Slinger. A lousy coward!" Brent shouted. "You are just as guilty as dad, and you left him out there to face the law alone!"

"I don't see you out there helping him," Slinger spat back. "It's too late for Roland Macintyre, Kid, but not for me," he grimaced, leaning slightly forward to make his pain more bearable. "It's your lucky night," Slinger went on, his voice tense. "Normally I don't like to leave witnesses, but tonight you're going to help me get away."

"In your dreams!" Brent was trembling uncontrollably. "I'm not helping you. You knew what he was doing. You should have stopped him."

"Stopped Macintyre?" Slinger shook his head. "Nothing could stop him. Nothing but his traitor son and a 9mm. You killed him, Brent. You led the police here and helped them kill your own dad." Slinger pulled out his gun in one smooth motion. "Now, do you want to help me, or join him?"

Brent did not have to decide. An officer rounded the corner. Gun in hand, Slinger spun to face him. Before Slinger could pull the trigger, the barrel of the officer's gun lit up, and Slinger's body crumpled to the ground at Brent's feet.

"Brent? Brent Macintyre." The teacher's tone was annoyed.

"Yeah?" Brent dragged his eyes from the window to give his teacher a bored look.

"Name the capital of France." She was a narrow, strict

woman with graying hair and a pinched face. Her folded arms and severe expression challenged Brent to prove he had been listening.

"Nepal," Brent answered defiantly.

The other kids laughed and glanced at one another. Brent was the dumb kid in class. Always good for a laugh, but nothing more.

"That is incorrect."

"That's news to me!" Brent shot a sly look at his classmates. "When did they change it?"

Silencing the class with a look of her own, Mrs. Heading went to the board and tapped her pointer on France on the map. "Perhaps you would like to come up and study the countries again since you found the window more entertaining than my lesson. Come up here and stand in front of the map until the end of class. You are too old for silliness like this, Brent. You will end up like your father if you don't start applying yourself."

None of the kids dared to make a sound as Brent pushed his seat back from his desk making sure it scraped loudly on the floor. He walked purposefully up to the board and stood before it. His feet slightly apart, his hands in his pockets. Defiant, even as he obeyed.

Some of the kids whispered to each other, but they were quickly silenced by the teacher's firm glare.

"May I remind you that the summer school term is over in two days? After this, you will be transitioning into classes with other students who were ahead of you last year. You will be facing another level of learning. Many of you have applied yourselves and will find the next level to be merely a stepping stone. Others..."

Though he was not facing her, Brent could feel her eyes on him as she paused to emphasize her words.

"Others have made little progress and will find the transition much more difficult. Apply yourselves here and soak in as much as you can. I am doing my best to prepare you."

"Apply yourselves, you sponges!" Brent's whispered admonition caused a ripple of giggles through the class.

Brent smiled at the map.

"Do you want to end up like him?" Mrs. Heading demanded, at her wits end. "Like his dad?"

Brent turned from the map to look at his teacher. "Mrs. Heading, you might be pleased to know that my dad graduated with honors. He was a very well educated man. Education does not make a man, it is merely a tool to help direct him."

She blinked at him in shock. The class blinked at him in shock. For a full thirty seconds, no one moved.

The bell rang, signaling the end of the day, and the kids scrambled to get out of the class before homework could be assigned.

Mrs. Heading had been so caught off guard that she could not recover herself. She sputtered and blinked hard as if she might cry. Then, without a word, she gathered her things and left the room.

Brent, hands still in his pockets, turned to face the empty classroom. Two more days and summer school would be over. One week after that and the regular school year would begin.

He sighed heavily. Four months had passed since his dad's death. The whole school knew about it. For almost fifteen years the police force had poured thousands of dollars into breaking up a notorious and very successful crime ring. The corruption snaked through various cities, always changing and moving, never able to be tracked or pinned down.

In that one fateful night at the bank, Roland Macintyre was killed and his secret life of crime came to light. Now, everyone in town knew that it was Brent's dad who had been the mastermind behind the most successful crime syndicates of the century. He wanted to move, but the police had different ideas. By the time they were done investigating, pressing charges, and confiscating property, Brent and his mom had no money to start over in another town.

Every day, Brent walked to school, acting as if he did not notice people's looks of sympathy and anger. Some whispered behind his back while others, who were hurt more directly by the work of Roland Macintyre, ranted at Brent mercilessly. He had listened to his mother cry alone at night, her sobs coming through the thin door that divided her room from the room where Brent slept.

With a sigh, Brent retrieved his books from his desk and shoved them into his backpack. Were the townspeople right? Was the life of a criminal really the only life for him? Would they treat him differently if they knew his secret?

CHAPTER 2

"Mom, I'm home!" Brent called pushing open the door to their ground floor apartment. A plump gentleman in a tight suit sat on their couch. He had a shiny briefcase balanced on his knees.

Brent stopped with his hand on the doorknob. His eyes went to his mother's face. She had been crying. In the months since his dad's death, Brent had seen her grow thin and pale with worry. He knew that the strain of trying to scrape together enough money to pay the rent while living under people's judging looks weighed heavily on her. Already, they had sold their well-furnished little house outside of town and moved to this modest little apartment just up the street to try to make ends meet after Roland's death.

Closing the door, he set down his backpack and waited for her to explain.

"Brent, we are going to move." She tried to sound cheery as she wiped her eyes. "We don't really need an apartment this big."

Brent's eyes moved over the room. It was tastefully furnished thanks to his father's career. Even after four months, the legal system was still scrambling to follow up on the growing number of leads the death of Roland Macintyre had produced. The professional criminals were laying low, waiting for the investigations to blow over. However, the amateur crooks were not as patient. They got scared. And trying to do one more job to get enough cash to run, they were caught. These men and women were quick to betray others in the racket to lighten their own sentences. Each time this happened, another layer of corruption was discovered and had to be ratted out. All this kept the police busy, allowing Brent and his mother to live in relative peace as long as they stayed in town.

They had been able to take most of the functional furniture with them when they sold the house. Now, they would have to move again. The thought made Brent's heart heavy. He glanced at his mom and knew what he had to do.

"Sure, Mom." Breaking the awkward silence, Brent met his mom's tired eyes. "This apartment is too big for the two of us." Brent was doing his best to sound cheerful. "We could do better with less space. We can sell the bigger furniture since we will not be needing it."

A moment of silence followed.

"If I hadn't heard it myself, I wouldn't believe it," the stranger said in awe. "I've got a boy about your age, and he would have blown the roof off if I had given him news like this."

"Your boy obviously struggles to grasp the common transitions of life." Brent's expression was not friendly. He knew the man's pudgy, look-a-like son, Marvin, from school. He was spoiled and unkind. "When do we need to be out by, Sir?" Brent took a chair from by the table and moved it a few feet to sit beside his mother who was crying again.

"As you know, the court recently made a ruling regarding your dad's funds. All of the stolen money has been confiscated and returned to the government. It will be used to make restitution for the crimes committed against various businesses here and in other towns where your father worked."

"I understand. When is the deadline?" Brent asked again.

"If the rent isn't paid by Monday, you will need to be

out by then."

Brent could see the man felt uncomfortable saying it.

Violet wiped her eyes, sniffling softly. Brent said nothing.

"I could give you to the end of the week," the man added without being asked. "No more than that. I have a family to feed too." The man rose, buttoning his suit over his ample stomach.

"Thank you for the extension, Sir." Brent rose and held out his hand. "That will be very helpful."

The man shook Brent's hand weakly and hurried out, closing the door behind himself.

"Oh, Brent. I'm so sorry." Violet Macintyre put her face into her hands and wept.

When she had married Roland Macintyre, he was a young, eager business man. He had big dreams of success and was ready to conquer the world with his shy, beautiful bride beside him. Years passed, and times were lean for the couple. Roland's business did not grow as he had planned, and his next big dream was always just out of reach. Then things started to change. Roland started with a new company and began bringing home cash bonuses. When they moved to a neat little house just outside of town, Violet had suspected Roland had not gotten the money honestly. But, by then, they had a child to care for, so she said nothing as the money continued to come in. As the years passed, Roland started sneaking home men with gunshot wounds or who needed to hide out after a run-in with the police. She would patch them up without questions, pretending she did not know what Roland was doing. Now, she had to face the facts. The money they had did not belong to them. Now that Roland was gone, there would be no more coming her way. The only bright spot was the fact that the police were not putting her in jail as an accomplice. She had not known the scope of what he was doing, but she knew her silence had cost many people their lives or fortunes.

"It's okay, Mom." Brent put his hand on her shoulder "We'll get through this." Standing, Brent looked around the room. There was one perk to moving. He would be glad to be rid of the furniture that brought back memories of his dad.

"Dr. Nee? Do you have a few minutes?" Mrs. Heading entered the classroom without knocking.

A middle aged Asian man looked up from the textbook he had been reading. His dark eyes curious. "Yes, Ma'am? What can I do for you?" Setting aside his book, he gave her his full attention.

"I am Mrs. Heading. I teach 6th grade geography and world history."

"It is a pleasure to meet you, Mrs. Heading. Will you have a seat?" He rose and moved a stack of books from the nearest chair, setting them on the edge of his desk.

"No, I'll stand. Thank you," she responded primly. "What I have to tell you will not take long."

Dr. Nee politely remained standing.

"As you know, summer school has come to an end, and regular classes will begin in a few days. You are new here, so I think it is my duty to warn you about one student in particular."

"Do you not think it would be better for me to meet the students and form my own opinions?" Dr. Nee asked with a humble air of authority.

"Normally, yes. However, Brent Macintyre is not like other students."

"I have heard the name Macintyre before," Dr. Nee looked thoughtful, trying to recall the connection.

"Roland Macintyre was a criminal mastermind who

lived right here in this very city." The gossip was old, but Mrs. Heading enjoyed telling it to someone new. "Macintyre came and went right under the nose of the police for years. He seemed like such a nice man." She remembered with a sad shake of her head. "Some people said he had a bit of a temper now and then, but never once did anyone suspect he was the one behind all the crimes and killings across the country."

"What happened to him?" Dr. Nee asked.

"He was gunned down. They caught him robbing a bank here in town. No one knows why he did something so careless after so many years. He killed one of the cashiers in cold blood. The other banker, the one who survived, was my sister-in-law's nephew's boss."

"Ah, I see." He tried not to look too amused by her lengthy connection to the man. "Do you remember how they caught up with Macintyre?" Dr. Nee asked.

Flustered, Mrs. Heading put a hand to her forehead. A habit she had developed after having Brent in her class all summer. "I don't remember all of the details. It happened several months ago. All I came to say is that Brent is a troublemaker, like his father. You will need to keep an eye on him in your class."

With that, Mrs. Heading turned on her heel and stalked out of the classroom.

Collecting the stack of books once more, Dr. Nee carried them to the shelf. Pausing as he passed the classroom door, he smiled. "Perhaps I will keep an eye on Brent, Mrs. Heading."

CHAPTER 3

"That's the last of the furniture we are selling." Brent wiped his forehead on his sleeve. "It sure is hot out there."

Violet Macintyre took the money her son held out to her. "That gives us enough to cover the first month's rent." She smiled at him, but Brent could still see the haunting worry in her eyes.

"Mom, let me get a job." Brent pleaded. "I'm thirteen now. I don't need school anymore. I know enough to get by. And if I don't know something, I can just look it up and learn it."

"Absolutely not. You can get a part time job after school if you keep your grades up. I'm not going to have you waste your life on some low paying job they give to uneducated people."

"Would you rather I get a high paying job like Dad's?" Brent said it in jest, but there was an underlying challenge in his tone.

Violet's severe expression silenced him. "Don't you ever say that!" She grabbed his arms roughly. "Don't you ever say that, Brent. Don't you ever do what your dad did. Promise me, Brent." She was looking desperately into his eyes. "Promise me you will not take that path."

Brent was startled by her outburst. His mother was usually a timid, soft-spoken woman. Now, her eyes blazed with passion as she gripped him.

"Promise me," her commanding passion was melting

into desperation.

"Mom, you..."

"Please, Brent. You are all I have left. I don't want to go out some night and identify your body in the street."

"Will my saying it really make a difference?" Brent thought of the kids' jeering faces and Mrs. Heading's firm scowl.

"You are young, Brent, but I know I can trust you. You are a man of your word. A good man."

Brent didn't know how to answer. He tried to pull out of his mother's grasp, but she did not release him.

"I need to hear you say it, Brent."

"I won't let you starve, Mom." Brent didn't meet her eyes.

Tears slid down her cheeks. "I would rather starve than see you follow in your father's footsteps. I could not bear it again." She looked intently at her son, and the silence dragged on. Finally, she spoke again, her voice soft. "Will you promise me that whatever happens, you will tell me the truth?"

Looking away, Brent considered his options. His eyes moved back to his mother's tear stained face. "I will promise you that. But you must not ask me about this again."

A slight frown flitted across her face, and she nodded. "Thank you." She held onto him for a moment more, drawing him into an awkward hug.

When he was free, Brent stepped away, shoving his hands into his pockets. "Don't worry about it, Mom. We'll make it work."

The sorrow in her eyes cut him to the heart. He couldn't promise he would not break the law. Not now. They had no money and nowhere to go. Everyone treated him like a criminal, and he wondered if that was the only path he could take.

"This is the only apartment I've got available." The landlord, Ms. Wordsworth, was a rough looking lady. Her forceful way of speaking gave Brent the impression that people did not intentionally cross her. The apartment was cramped and needed a good cleaning. A single counter was crammed up beside the refrigerator which was halfway into the kitchen space and halfway in the main room. The couch they had not sold would fit at one end of the room and double as Brent's bed. Once they brought up the little table and two chairs, there would barely be room to get around them. The tiny bedroom had only about a foot to spare between the twin bed and dresser his mother would use. Brent looked at his mom and saw deep sadness in her eyes. She did not know what her husband had become, or that it was Brent who had caused his death.

Brent's mind moved uninvited to the night his dad was killed. Brent had followed his dad, eager to see where the money was coming from that had made his dad so happy. Peering through the bank window, he saw a side of his dad that he could never forget. Roland Macintyre stood over a man who had obviously taken a beating. Roland was barking orders, his face hard and cruel. Slinger was there too, gun in hand. Brent had watched in horror as his dad drew his gun and shot the man cowering on the ground. The second bank teller scrambled to open the safe, pleading for his life in terror.

Brent could see it all clearly in his mind. How many times had he dreamed about the same scene? How many times had he worked through every detail, trying to find something he could have done differently? After his dad had killed the man, Brent remembered stumbling away from the window in shock. His shoulder had struck the dark pole of the decorative streetlight outside the bank. The light did not shine tonight. It stood like a dark sentinel, silent and uncaring.

Brent felt sick. His world had been shattered the instant the bullet left his dad's gun. He had known that he would never be able to look his father in the face again without seeing the murderer he had seen that night through the window.

A police car turned onto the street a few blocks up, the officer inside routinely glancing at the buildings along his quiet route. Brent remembered looking around for a way to help the remaining bank teller and draw the officer's attention to what was happening inside the bank. Without thinking, he had looked up at the dark light bulb of the streetlight and willed it to light. What he was doing made no sense, and yet somehow, to him, it did. Concentrating, he had felt a surge in electricity. Backing away, Brent kept his eyes on the dirty white orb at the top of the pole. As the car approached, the streetlight outside the bank flickered to life, drawing the attention of the lone cop in the police cruiser. Another streetlight, and the lights inside the bank came on, and Brent remembered running for cover into the alley.

"Brent?"

His mother's hand was on his arm, drawing Brent from the vivid memory and back into the tiny apartment that was to be their new home.

The memory had been so real that Brent had to look around the room to remember where he was.

"Are you okay?" Violet asked keeping her hand on her son's arm.

He nodded, waiting for the sick feeling to subside.

"Teenagers are like that Mrs. Macintyre," Ms. Wordsworth prattled on. "They call it 'zoning out'. It's just plain rude if you ask me. You got stuck with a boy, so you got your work cut out for you. They are nothing but trouble. I've got two of my own, and they are driving me crazy. All you can do is put up with them until they come out of it. They hang around doing nothing and wanting everything they can't have."

Brent glanced apologetically at his mom who smiled back.

"So this is it. What you see is what you pay for." Ms. Wordsworth looked around the little room and put her fists on her hips. "The rent is due on the first of the month, rain or shine. That means if I don't get it, you are out on the street. I don't run a charity. You won't find another place in town for the price you are paying. Besides, I don't think many people would rent to you anyway."

"What is that supposed to mean?" Brent knew his father's reputation would follow them, but he wanted to make the landlady say it out right.

"Your mom gets my drift," she held out her hand to Violet. "First payment is due before you move in."

Violet dug in her purse and counted out the precious bills.

The lady eyed the remaining cash skeptically. "Remember, your next payment is due on the first."

"Thank you, Ms. Wordsworth. I'm sure that won't be a problem."

Ms. Wordsworth looked them over one more time before leaving the room. They stood listening to the stairs creak as she returned to the first floor.

"I'll see if I can get someone to help us bring over the table and couch tomorrow." Brent closed the door and looked at his mom. He was the man of the house now. "It isn't much, but we can make it work."

Violet nodded. They would be brave for each other.

CHAPTER 4

"Excuse me, young man?"

Brent let down the end of the couch he was holding and looked around. He spotted a dark haired, narrow-eyed man in the car that had pulled up to the curb. Wiping sweat from his eyes with his sleeve, Brent went to the car.

"Yes, Sir?" Brent was breathing hard.

"I am Dr. Nee, a new teacher at the middle school. I saw you have been quite creative moving that couch and wondered if you could use some help?"

Brent used his sleeve to wipe away another bead of sweat that trickled down his hot face. He looked back at the couch. The legs on one end were tied with rope to Brent's roller skates allowing Brent to drag it along the sidewalk by holding up the other end and pulling. "Makes for a good laugh, doesn't it." He was grateful for the excuse to take a break.

"I found it quite ingenious, actually." Dr. Nee's smile was friendly. "So ingenious, in fact, that I would like to help you."

"Why would you help me?" Brent asked, with a hint of bitterness. "No one else is interested."

Dr. Nee got out of his car and came over to where Brent stood. "Because you need it." He was a short man whose head only came up to Brent's shoulder.

"Look, they might stop and help people over in Asia," Brent began.

"China," Dr. Nee corrected, still smiling.

"Okay, China. But people don't do that here, not to my family at least."

"Why is that?"

"I guess you don't know who I am," Brent observed.

"I don't believe we have met," Dr. Nee agreed.

"I'm Brent Macintyre." Brent waited for a reaction, but there was none.

"It is nice to meet you, Brent." Dr. Nee shook Brent's hand cordially before turning his attention to the couch.

"You haven't heard of me?" Brent pressed, walking around where he could see the strange new teacher's face.

"Have you heard of me?" Dr. Nee asked, testing the weight of the couch.

Brent frowned. "I don't think so."

"Good. Where are you taking this couch?"

"Are you a criminal?" Brent eyed him warily.

Dr. Nee laughed. "No, are you?"

"Not yet."

A strange expression came over the teacher's face. "Be very careful, Brent, that you do not allow the expectations of others to turn your life in a way it was not designed to go."

Brent frowned. "You have heard about my dad."

"And you have heard about my school, so we are even." Dr. Nee wiped his forehead. "It is a hot day today. Shall we move the couch, or would you like to discuss my credentials further?"

Eyeing the new teacher curiously, Brent knew he had no other option. "I'm taking it to an apartment on South 26th Street."

"Isn't that across town?"

"Yes," Brent sighed wearily, realizing how much farther he had to go.

"Why don't you rent a truck?" Dr. Nee asked.

"I told you. You don't know who I am, so you don't

understand."

Dr. Nee nodded. "True, true. But one must never break one's back when there is a way to avoid it."

"Is that some kind of proverb?" Brent went to the far end of the couch and grunted as he lifted it once more.

"It is now," Dr. Nee smiled. "Put the couch down and sit on it. I will return in ten minutes. Is there more furniture you have to move?

Putting the couch down again, Brent slumped into it, feeling the weight of the impossible task. "Yes. I can't do it though. It's too heavy, and I don't know how to move it." He blinked hard and did not meet the teacher's eyes. "We sold Dad's tools, so I don't have a screwdriver to take it apart."

"Wait for me here." Dr. Nee returned to his car and pulled away from the curb.

Brent stayed on the couch, lounging comfortably and grinning at the staring people who passed. He grew uneasy as the minutes ticked by.

An officer approached, stopping a few feet away. He hooked his thumbs into his belt.

"Look, Son, this is a good joke, but I'm going to have to ask you to move your couch off the sidewalk."

"I'm trying to move it, I mean, someone was going to help me." Brent scrambled to his feet. "He went to..." Suddenly it occurred to Brent that the stranger could have been leading him on. What if the man had no intention of coming back at all? Here Brent was sitting on the sidewalk on a couch like a crazy person just because some stranger said he should. "I thought he was coming back." Brent finished lamely. "I'll move it."

"Aren't you kind of young to be moving furniture like this? You are what, fourteen?" The officer had seen the realization and disappointment in Brent's expression.

"Thirteen."

"Pretty tall for your age, huh. I wish I had your height," the officer confided with a grin. "Where are you taking it?"

"I have to get it across town." Brent pushed his short hair off his forehead. "I really thought he would come back. Stupid of me to trust a stranger."

"Maybe not." The officer pointed to a moving truck that was coming toward them. "Is that him?"

They watched as the moving truck pulled up to the curb. Dr. Nee's car pulled up behind the truck. He walked around to the passenger's side, and they had what appeared to be a heated discussion. In the end, the driver and another man got out and loaded the couch into the truck. Dr. Nee waved Brent over to his car. "Come, we will get the other items and make one trip."

Brent thanked the officer and ran to climb into the car.

"Dr. Nee?"

The teacher looked up to see Brent standing hesitantly in the doorway of the classroom.

"Hello, Brent. Come in."

Obeying, Brent looked around the classroom at the new posters and equipment Dr. Nee had added. "Are you teaching about electricity?"

"Among other things, yes," Dr. Nee answered with a smile. "Are you interested in learning about electricity?"

"I think it would be interesting to know how it works." Brent's gaze was on a poster portraying streaks of lighting against a night sky. He drew his gaze back to the teacher. "What else are you teaching?"

"You will have to wait and see," Dr. Nee laughed. "Now, did you come to have a sneak peek of the classroom? Or was there something else on your mind?"

Brent shoved his hands into his pockets. "I wanted to thank you for helping me yesterday. I was in a pickle and didn't have a way out. That was really good of you to stop. My mom said to thank you, too."

"Please tell her she is very welcome. As are you. I am glad to have been able to help."

"I tried to hire a truck, but no one would do it. I guess my dad's work impacted a lot of local businesses around here." Pulling twenty dollars from his pocket, Brent laid it on the teacher's desk. "If it cost more, I can earn it and pay you later. I'm still looking for a job, but I'll find one."

"That's what I like about you, Brent."

"What?" Brent met his eyes, intrigued that a teacher would actually admit to liking him.

"You are self-motivated, and very creative." Dr. Nee picked up the money. "I would like for you to keep this. Sometimes it is better for someone to help without being paid in return. It builds character. The fact that you brought this," he held up the bill, "and were willing to reimburse me, was reward enough for me." He held it out to Brent and saw the boy's inner struggle. They obviously needed the money, but the boy still had a sense of pride despite the reputation his father had left him.

Dr. Nee smiled, breaking the tense moment. "You were entertaining enough out there, pulling the couch on roller skates, that I feel I should pay you." Reaching over, he placed the twenty dollar bill into Brent's hand. "What made you think of such a creative idea?"

Brent did not protest, he folded the bill uncertainly. "I didn't know how else to get it to move."

"But how did you get it out of your house in the first place? The doorway was too narrow for it to go through on the skates."

Brent grinned and shoved the money into his pocket to

free his hands. Forgetting himself, he launched into a detailed description of how he had wrestled the couch through the narrow doorway.

Dr. Nee watched him, laughing at the boy's reenactment of the process. This was a young man whose heart was still soft enough to be molded into a great man.

CHAPTER 5

"Look, it ain't much, and it doesn't take brains to do it, so I can't pay you a brain surgeon's salary." The shop keeper hobbled down the rickety wooden stairs to the basement. "Besides, you being a minor adds extra regulations."

"How much can you pay?" Brent followed the old man at the same painfully slow pace.

"You got any other job offers?" the man turned and adjusted his glasses to look at Brent.

"I don't think that should impact what you pay me, Mr. Leno," Brent answered boldly.

"Ever hear of supply and demand?" Leno chuckled at his own joke. "No one wants you working for them. Having the kid of a Roland Macintyre around would be bad for honest business. I, on the other hand, have what you need. A secluded job where you can work out of sight of the customers. Not a full-time job, mind you. And I'm not making any promises on how long it will last."

"Okay, so what do you pay your secluded workers?"

"Three dollars an hour."

"What?" Brent looked around the dingy basement.

"Take it or leave it. I've got what you need, not the other way around." Leno leaned on a table of junk to catch his breath.

Brent was skeptical. "What do you expect me to do for three dollars an hour?"

"Just turn the crank." Leno gestured to a small generator

that looked as old as its owner.

"What does it run?"

A funny look crossed the old man's face, and Brent frowned.

"Not to worry, Brent." Leno gave a breathy, soundless laugh. "It runs the ice cream freezer out on the street. I have Jimmy put the treats out there after school for the kids. I can't leave them out there all night or they will get stolen, and I don't want to pay to have the freezer running all through the day. You turn the crank here," Leno tried to demonstrate, but could not get the handle to move. "Anyway, you turn it, and that generates the power to keep the generator running. It is an invention of my own. Keep in mind, if the ice cream is soft in the freezer, I'll know you aren't doing your job. That's accountability. That's what young people need these days."

"It can also be helpful if you give them money." Brent was rewarded by a wheezing laugh from Leno.

"You are a funny kid. I like that. I'll raise you to four dollars an hour after the first week if you are a good worker and show up on time."

"Make it five and I'll keep it a secret that I'm working here," Brent bartered.

Again he saw that strange gleam in the old man's eyes. "Done!"

He offered his shriveled hand, and Brent shook it gently.

"Give that crank a whirl so I know you know how to work it," Leno instructed.

The crank was stiff from lack of use. Looking around, Brent located a little bottle of oil which he applied with Leno's permission. After a few rotations the handle turned easily.

"Five or six rotations a minute will keep the generator running. Any less and it will have to be started again. Give it a few cranks and pull that string there."

"Like a lawn mower."

"Something like that."

"Wouldn't it be easier and cheaper to add a gas tank so it could run on its own?" Brent asked turning the handle. He pulled the string and the generator purred to life. "It is a lot quieter than I thought it would be."

Leno looked pleased. "I have your word that you will keep it a secret that you are working for me?"

"As long as I am getting five dollars an hour. I'll keep it to myself. If anything changes, I'll come to you privately and let you know I'm moving on. I appreciate you giving me this job."

The generator died, and Leno raised an eyebrow.

"I thought today was an orientation. You said I would start tomorrow."

"You are right. It was good for my heart to hear that thing running again. I'll expect you to be here from three to six every day. Your school lets out before the elementary, so you shouldn't have any trouble getting here on time." Leno hobbled back to the steps. Stopping on the first one, he dug in his pocket and handed Brent a key. "Let yourself in by that side door there. And make sure no one sees you."

Brent turned it over in his hand, "This is an odd key."

"It is a special lock," Leno answered over his shoulder, as he continued up the stairs.

"Where will you leave my pay?" Brent asked from the bottom of the steps.

"I'll slip it into this old satchel hanging by the door. My heart can't take these stairs anymore."

"Thank you, Mr. Leno."

"Don't mention it." The look the old man gave Brent said much more than his words.

"Hey, wait up."

Turning, Brent saw Jimmy hurrying up. "Hi," Brent said hesitantly.

Jimmy had started at their school a few days into the semester. He seemed confident of himself, but already he was hanging out with the group of boys that other kids didn't mess with.

"I saw you coming out of the alley there." Jimmy pushed his thick red hair off his forehead. "You'd better watch out. Mr. Leno owns this store, and he's pretty particular about kids hanging around. Especially in the alley."

"Thanks." Brent knew he would have to be more careful. They stood sizing each other up. Brent was tall for his age, dark haired and dark eyed. His lean frame had become more noticeable since his dad's death, but the errands he did around town to pick up spare change, kept him in good shape. Strong and quick, Brent had no intention of letting this new guy bully him.

He walked away, but Jimmy fell into step beside him. Jimmy was about an inch taller than Brent. The teachers called him a red head, but his dark auburn hair looked more brown than red to Brent. He could tell Jimmy worked out, and had seen him picking fights with some of the other guys on the track during P.E. class. Brent was not concerned. He could hold his own.

Jimmy seemed to guess what Brent was thinking. "Some of the guys at school said your dad was a major crook around here not too long ago."

"So?" Brent didn't stop.

"So is it true?"

Brent turned on Jimmy, "What does your dad do for a living, Jimmy?"

"What? Uh." Jimmy stepped back, stunned by the sudden question. "My dad's dead," he blurted with an angry frown.

"So, mine is too." Brent glared at him, daring him to push

the subject. "Let's leave it at that."

Considering Brent for a moment, Jimmy seemed to have made up his mind about something. "You think you can throw your weight around, huh?" Jimmy sneered. "We'll see what you are made of soon enough."

Brent bowed his head over his test paper and tried to concentrate. Another wave of energy pulsed through the room. Brent looked around, no one else seemed to notice.

"Brent? Is there a problem?" Dr. Nee was watching him closely.

"No, Sir. I didn't realize we were testing today. I would have worn my nice shoes."

A few of his classmates stifled their amusement.

"Please continue with your work," Dr. Nee told the class.

The lead of his pencil scraped out the words, filling the line.

There it was again. Another pulse of energy. Brent forced himself to keep his head down, but his pencil froze. Brent re-read the question, struggling to focus.

Another wave. Brent glanced up and met Dr. Nee's eyes. The teacher was looking right at him, studying him.

Frowning, Brent returned his attention to his test. What was happening? Was there some kind of power surge in the building? His ability to feel changes in the electricity of a room was something Brent had never shared with anyone. He stole a glance at the teacher, but Dr. Nee's focus was on the book that lay open on his desk.

Brent studied him, guessing the teacher was in his late thirties or forties. Why was he called 'doctor' anyway? Was it because he was an actual doctor, maybe in a war somewhere?

"Brent." Dr. Nee's voice jarred Brent's drifting thoughts back to the present. "I suggest you focus on your test if you would like to get a passing grade in my class. This test is to determine your current level of knowledge."

Jimmy, seated behind Brent, spoke up. "Don't waste your time, Nee. Brent doesn't have a level of knowledge."

The class laughed, and Brent felt his face flush.

"It would be a shame to hold you back simply because you did not choose to focus during a test," Dr. Nee said it to everyone in the class, and the laughter died as quickly as it had started.

"Oh, great, the crook's boy is coming out to play. Guard your pockets." Jimmy had not let up on Brent since their encounter outside of Leno's. He seemed determined to undermine any chance of success Brent had.

"Hey, Jimmy? What's the best thing about a clam?" Brent asked, jogging in place to stay warm in the brisk fall breeze.

Everyone looked at Brent.

"They keep their mouths shut," Brent finished without looking at Jimmy. "You might want to try it out."

A few kids laughed, looking at Jimmy for his comeback.

Before Jimmy could react, the coach blew his whistle and sent everyone jogging around the track.

The coach didn't tolerate any fighting during PE, but Brent was careful to keep his distance from Jimmy just in case.

CHAPTER 6

Brent turned a page of his book and pulled the thick blanket closer around him. He sat with his back against the sturdy wood stand that held the generator. His school books and a couple of used newspapers lay on the floor beside him. The book on his lap was tipped at an angle to catch the light of the single bulb above him. The generator purred contentedly behind him, like a strange metal beast. It was a delicate balance, sending power to the generator and keeping focused on his studies. He had spent hours alone in the dim basement. That gave him plenty of time to test out his interest in electricity. He had learned by trial and error over how to give power to only one object at a time. Even though he could send enough power to the generator to keep it going, Brent still got up every so often to turn the crank for a minute or two in order to give his brain a break and warm up. As he turned, he recited the facts he had read, embedding them deeply into his memory.

In class, he was the clown. No one expected anything of him besides a little trouble, and he usually met their expectations. Despite his reputation in class, Brent loved learning. His mind soaked in facts and figures leaving Brent hungry for more. He had read through the text books from class, discarded newspapers he found in the trash in the alley, and the random magazines he had found in the street. With each addition, he found himself longing for more.

The generator choked, and Brent leapt up to crank it several times. He had to be careful, or he would lose this job. He had joked around with a couple of the other guys at school and found out they were making only a few dollars more than him. His salary alone would pay almost half the rent in the tiny apartment he shared with his mom.

Brent cranked on, thinking about his mom. She was tired and thin. She had started out cleaning houses, but there were only a few people in town who would trust her to come inside their homes. Since then, she had added mending and ironing which she could do from their apartment. Perkin's Cleaners paid her to do mending for them, and a good word from Mr. Perkin had brought her a few well to do customers who came to her directly. Brent had strung a rope across the main room for her to hang the ironed clothes on. That also served as a makeshift curtain between the couch he slept on and the rest of the room. He would lay there, listening as she worked late into the night to finish the mending given to her.

His mom deserved better. Sighing, Brent thought of the little pouch he kept tucked up in a tear under the couch. He had worked for Leno from August to December. Christmas was next week, and Brent had the perfect gift picked out for his mom. Once he got this week's pay, he would have enough to get it.

Hearing a thump by the door to the basement, Brent scrambled to shove his books back into his bag. He cranked the handle a few more times before slipping into the tight space between the generator and the wall. He crouched there, clutching his book bag to his chest and sending power to the generator to keep it purring. He could not afford to let it stop. A week or so ago, a clerk had slipped down into the basement to grab a break from Mr. Leno. Brent had hid until the guy was discovered. Mr. Leno had bellowed and raged at the young man until Brent was afraid the old man's heart would give out. The next day at school, Brent had overheard Jimmy complaining about having extra work since Mr. Leno had fired his other clerk.

Someone banged on the door, and a shouted command was muffled by the thick outer door. Brent remembered the police commands he had heard the night his dad was killed and shuddered in his hiding place.

The door crashed open and men's voices filled the basement. Brent turned out the light above them, and the men instantly fell silent. Brent frowned, inwardly berating himself for making such a dumb move. He had hoped to slip out in the confusion, but these men were too well trained. It would be impossible for Brent to make a move even in the dark without being heard.

A hushed command was given, and flashlight beams lit the dingy room in every direction.

"There's the power source," a man pointed out. Several lights came toward Brent's hiding place.

One beam shone into Brent's eyes, making it impossible for him to see.

"Don't move." The voice was commanding. "Sergeant, I've got a teen hiding near the generator."

A few more beams lit up the corner where Brent was wedged.

"The rest of the basement has been cleared," a younger man's voice reported from behind them.

"This is the police," the commanding voice informed Brent. "Come out slowly and keep your hands where I can see them."

Brent found it difficult to squirm out of the tight place while keeping his hands up. "Hang on, don't shoot. I'm kind of stuck in here. You guys nearly scared me to death."

An officer moved in from the side, keeping out of the line of fire. Reaching out, he pulled the book bag from Brent's lap so he would have more room to work his way out.

Brent heard the sound of a zipper and knew the officer was checking the contents of his bag. "Hey, that's mine. Don't you need some sort of search warrant?" Brent asked getting to his feet.

"We already have one." The officer who had taken his bag moved in behind Brent and did a quick pat down to make sure he was not carrying a weapon. He felt something in Brent's pocket that stopped him.

"Empty your pockets on this table," the officer instructed. "How long have you been working down here?"

Brent shrugged. With the light beams in his face, he could not see who was speaking to him or how many people were in the room.

"Your pockets." The officer tapped the table top.

Brent obeyed. Moving slowly, he pulled a few coins from his left pocket.

"Now the other one," the voice instructed when Brent hesitated.

When he put his hand into his right pocket, Brent felt the key. He knew now that Mr. Leno had given him a skeleton key, a key used by thieves to get into places they would not otherwise have access to. Moving his fingers carefully, he dropped the key back into his pocket as he pulled out a pencil stub and a few scraps of paper. He didn't know what they were looking for and hoped there was nothing on the papers to incriminate him.

One of the flashlight beams stayed trained on the things he was laying out on the table. Several more stayed on Brent's face.

"Is that everything?" the man in charge asked.

Brent knew his face gave him away.

The officer's tone changed. "If you work with us, we can work with you. If you withhold information, it will reflect on your record and make things tough for you."

Keeping his eyes diverted from the blinding beams, Brent stood with his feet apart and his hands in his pockets as he had so many times in Mrs. Heading's class that summer.

"How old are you?" a different voice asked. There was a gentleness in the tone.

"Fourteen," Brent answered fingering the key in his pocket.

"What's your name?"

Brent felt his shoulders sag. This is where they would have him.

"I'd rather not say." Brent knew he could not delay them forever. "Don't I get a lawyer or something? Or is that just in the movies?"

"Have you ever been in trouble with the law?" the officer asked, moving on from the delicate subject of Brent's identity. Brent knew he would circle back to it.

"No." Brent relaxed a little. "Actually there was one other time. See, I had this couch on the sidewalk…"

The officer interrupted, "I thought you looked familiar."

Brent let the light above them come on, hoping to divert their attention. Several men shut off their flashlights leaving Brent blinking in the dim light. He still could not see through the bright spots left on his vision from the officers' lights.

"You are Brent Macintyre, aren't you?"

Brent silently kicked himself. His attempt at humor had backfired badly. "What is all this about?" Brent asked, avoiding the confirmation of his identity.

"Do you know anything about this generator?" the kind officer asked.

"You must be a professional negotiator," Brent observed. "You are much better at getting information than that other guy." He could see them now. Two officers stood a few feet from him, and a third was off to his right. The generator behind him continued to purr. Brent powered it almost subconsciously now. A fourth officer stood by the door that led into the shop above, and Brent could only assume the younger officer he had heard was still stationed by the door to the alley.

"My name is Officer Cane," the kind officer informed Brent, drawing his attention back to himself.

Brent recognized Officer Cane as the one who had talked to him about the couch at the end of the summer.

"Your mother must have been thinking ahead to give you a name like Officer," Brent quipped.

"It's okay at school, Brent, but not here," Officer Cane informed him firmly. "We need to see everything that is in your pockets."

"What are you looking for?" Brent asked, his hand closed around the key. Once they had that, they could pin him with whatever crime had been committed. He had given his word to Leno that he would not tell anyone he was working for him. Remembering the greedy gleam in Leno's eyes and his eagerness to meet Brent's price under those terms, Brent knew he had been set up.

"Do you know what that generator is powering?" Officer Cane was avoiding his question.

Brent bit his lip. If he said the ice cream freezer on the street, would that be breaking his agreement with Mr. Leno?

"Alright, tell me this, Brent. Do you know what it powers, but can't tell me? Or do you not know?"

Realizing he was biting his lip, Brent stopped. He did his best to keep his emotions from his face. He was up against a wall. There was no way out. Whatever it was, he had been foolish enough to play into it, and he would be the one to take the blame.

"Brent, we can't help you unless you help us." Officer Cane had his thumbs hooked into his belt and stood relaxed and easy.

It was clear that Cane's partner did not trust Brent. He stood ready with his hand on the butt of his gun.

"I am the class dummy," Brent hated the swell of emotions that struck him. "I didn't think." His face twisted as he fought the anger inside. He was not angry at Leno, or Office Cane. He was angry with himself. "I don't know what this generator powers. I only know what I was told. And," Brent pulled out the skeleton key and tossed it onto the table. "I only have what I was given." He shook his head, taking a deep breath to steady himself.

Officer Cane stepped forward and picked up the key. "You know that this is a skeleton key, used to pick locks, right?"

Brent nodded miserably.

CHAPTER 7

"Did you know that when it was given to you?" Officer Cane was watching Brent's face for the answer.

Feeling a slight twinge of hope, Brent met his eyes. This man did not treat him like a criminal. "I knew it was a strange key, but I'd never seen a skeleton key before."

"And you can't tell us who employed you or gave you the key?"

Brent shook his head, "No. I should have thought it through. I should have known I would be the one thrown under the bus."

Officer Cane's partner moved forward, but Cane put up his hand to stop him. "Why do you think we are here, Brent?"

Brent was moving around now, running the fingers of both hands into his short hair. "Whatever it was, I wasn't in on it. I didn't know it was happening. All I did was keep the generator going."

"Speaking of that," the officer who had searched his bag moved forward and put his hand on the crank handle. "How is it running now?"

"I found a way to crank it and keep it going," Brent answered. The generator choked, and Brent turned the handle a few times just for show. He wasn't about to explain to them that he was the one creating the electricity. "Should I let it stop?" He looked from one officer to the other.

Officer Cane said something into his radio and a garbled

response came back almost instantly. He nodded, "Go ahead and let it stop."

Brent checked his watch. It was two minutes until six. He wondered if maybe, somehow, he could still get paid.

"It will take a couple minutes," Brent shifted uncomfortably and did not meet their searching eyes. "What is it powering?"

"Brent, I'm Officer Brandon. I saw you had a newspaper in your bag. Have you read it?"

"Yes, but I didn't steal it. I got it out of the trash out back."

"No one accused you of stealing it. Is the back door the one you use the key on?" Officer Cane asked. "I'm assuming you don't come through the store."

"Yes."

"Brent, did Vincent Leno hire you?"

"I told you, I gave my word." Brent let the generator cough and die. Silence filled the room.

Officer Brandon cleared his throat. His ebony face was serious, but the lines around his eyes betrayed an underlying kindness. "Did you read in the newspaper about the counterfeit money that has been discovered around town and in the surrounding cities?"

Brent nodded with a confused frown.

"I don't know how to break this to you gently, Brent. You are the one who has been powering the machine they are using to make counterfeit money."

For a moment, Brent did not move. His hands felt clammy, and his stomach churned. He looked at the officers; their faces were serious. Panic welled up inside him. All of the things his teachers, classmates, and neighbors said about him ending up as a criminal flooded his mind. He put his hand on the frame of the generator to steady himself.

Officer Brandon moved in and gripped his upper arm. "Take a deep breath and pull yourself together," the officer instructed.

Brent wanted to rage and shout like his dad had. He wanted to hurt someone to try to ease the pain that was crushing him inside.

Officer Brandon shifted to a better position as he felt the muscles tense in Brent's arm. "Get yourself under control," he warned, his voice low and firm.

Closing his eyes, Brent took a breath and thought of his mom's pleading teary eyes. He had tried so hard. A moment later, Brent opened his eyes again. Clenching his teeth, he forced his shoulders and arms to relax. No matter what happened, he refused to act like Roland Macintyre.

Officer Brandon let go of Brent's arm. "We are going to have to take you in for questioning."

"How can someone be a criminal without knowing it?" Brent's mind was reeling. What would his mom think? What about Dr. Nee who spoke so grandly of a bigger purpose and how Brent could be a great man someday? It was all a lie.

"Brent?"

Brent nodded. "I know. I'll come without a fight."

"You have the right to remain silent. Anything you say can and will be used against you in a court of law."

The basement door to the shop opened, and Leno stood above them accompanied by an officer.

Officer Cane moved to the bottom of the stairs. "Leno, did you hire this young man to work down here?"

Leno adjusted his glasses and peered down at Brent for a moment before shaking his head. "No. I never hired him. I've seen him around some in town, but I don't know what he is doing down here. I keep that back door locked to keep kids like him out."

Brent knew there was nothing more to be said.

———

"He is in here, Mrs. Macintyre." The officer opened the door, and Violet walked into the bare little room where Brent sat waiting.

Brent kept his eyes on the floor. His shame grew as his mother's worn and patched shoes came into his line of sight.

"Hi, Brent," she said softly.

Brent did not answer. A single tear started down his cheek, but he stopped it with a swipe of his hand.

Violet knelt before him, taking his hands in her little calloused ones. She looked up into his face. "Brent, were you working with the counterfeiters?"

His eyes focused on hers, and she saw a little glimmer of hope in her son's eyes.

"No."

It was whispered so softly she could barely hear it, but it was enough.

She smiled, blinking back her own tears, and squeezed his hands. "Let's go home."

"Brent, we missed you yesterday. Where were you?"

Brent knew by Jimmy's mocking tone that he knew where Brent had been. The police had questioned Brent the night they discovered him in Mr. Leno's basement. They had asked his mom to bring him back the following day for more questions and paperwork. With flushed cheeks, Brent remembered the shame he had felt when his mother came to the police station to identify him and sign the paperwork to get him out. He had wished the ground would open up and swallow him. Now, facing Jimmy and the other classmates made him wish for it again.

"Yeah, Brent, what were you working on?" Marvin joined in.

"I heard he was working for that counterfeit ring in Mr.

Leno's basement. Mr. Leno had no idea he was sneaking in down there. This crook used a skeleton key to get in," Jimmy jeered sliding into his seat. "I bet his dad gave it to him before the police caught up with him."

"Settle down, boys." Dr. Nee entered the class, his face serious. He had heard the last of their conversation from the hall.

"Jail bird," Jimmy called softly.

Normally, the class would have laughed or joined in the jeering, but this time the room was deathly silent.

Jimmy looked up to see Dr. Nee standing over him.

"Jimmy, you will find the principal is waiting in his office for you."

"Aw, come on, Mr. Nee." Jimmy leaned back in his chair. "It was just a joke."

"The class did not benefit from your joke, Jimmy. Remove yourself immediately."

"What? Is Macintyre your pet student now? I've noticed how you treat him." Jimmy stood up. Like most of the boys in the class, he was already several inches taller than Dr. Nee. "What are you going to do about it if I don't go?"

"Try me and see."

A chorus of "oooh" rippled through the class unchecked. They looked at each other with wide eyes. Never before had a teacher responded to a challenge like that. Jimmy was unsettled by the teacher's calculated calmness.

"I'll go," Jimmy finally said. "But just because I don't want to be near the jail bird." Though his tone was jaunty and light, the others could see the hint of fear in the red haired boy's eyes. "I'll tell the principal how you have been favoring Brent above the rest of us."

"You have made a wise choice," Dr. Nee informed him, stepping aside to let him pass.

Once he was gone, Dr. Nee turned to Brent. "You missed

the discussion on chapter ten and the assignments that were given out yesterday. Your homework will be due tomorrow like the rest of the class. If they are late, your grade will be docked accordingly."

Brent nodded. He wished he had a little of that teacher's pet favor Jimmy had accused him of.

"Class, I have an announcement." Dr. Nee waited until he had their attention. "I will not return as your teacher after the Christmas break."

The class erupted in surprised chatter and groans as they processed the unexpected news. "This was a substitute position. I am being transferred to teach at the high school. You will have a new professor in January. Stick to your studies and make something of yourselves. You will have me again when you reach 9th grade, and I will expect you to know the basics well by then."

Brent looked up wearily from his desk to find Dr. Nee studying him intently. It was Dr. Nee who broke eye contact first. He stood and called the class to order for their lesson.

Brent glanced at the other students. Dr. Nee's words came to mind. "Stick to your studies and make something of yourselves." Brent rolled his eyes. As far as he was concerned, he didn't have a choice in what he became. Officer Cane had helped to lighten Brent's sentence, but he still had several months of community service ahead. The worst part for Brent was that the little stash of money he had saved turned out to be made up of counterfeit bills. In one night, he had lost his reputation and his dreams.

"We are teenagers, Brent. This is what people expect us to do," Jimmy informed him. "We bum around town. We get to have a little fun. And let our parents foot the bill. There's no reason to rush into a career." Jimmy elbowed him with a grin. "You know that didn't get you very far last time."

Brent shoved him hard. Jimmy lost his footing and fell in the dirt of the empty lot they had been crossing. He scrambled up, mad.

"Can't you take a little joke?" He came at Brent, and they circled, eyeing each other.

Instantly, the call of 'fight' rang through the younger boys who were playing baseball on the other side of the lot. They dropped their equipment and raced over to watch the older boys duke it out.

Brent threw a few punches and got a bloody nose, but his heart wasn't in it. Brent was bored. Wiping his nose with a shirt that was a few sizes too big, he let Jimmy take the win and wandered off toward home.

Brent was fifteen now, going into 9th grade in a few weeks. He would be starting a new school and would, as usual, be on the older end of the class. Jimmy was the only other fifteen year old Brent knew of, and he saw no hope of an actual friendship with that bully. Jimmy seemed to have made it his mission from the first day they met to make sure Brent's time at school was always miserable.

Brent had done okay at school, mostly for his mom, but learning no longer excited him. The counterfeit mishap had taken the interest out of life. If working hard and doing his best ended in false accusations and community service, Brent wanted nothing to do with it. He kept a lame job to help cover the rent and put on a good act for his mom, but he found himself avoiding going home to the cramped apartment. Instead, he wandered the streets aimlessly, making no effort to keep from becoming what Jimmy called a typical teen.

CHAPTER 8

"Brent, please stay after class today. I need to have a word with you."

Jimmy led a few of the others in a chiding "ooo!" and they scrambled out of the high school classroom before Dr. Nee could react.

"Sit down, Brent."

Slouching reluctantly into his seat, Brent waited, tapping his fingers on the attached desktop to show his impatience.

Dr. Nee leaned on a nearby desk and looked hard at Brent. Studying him as he had during the class period.

"So, shoot," Brent prompted when the silence got awkward.

"You have lost something since the 6th grade, Brent," Dr. Nee told him seriously. "I hardly knew you when you came into class today."

"What of it?" There was boredom in Brent's tone.

"You don't look like you have been eating well. Perhaps that is why you wear shirts that are too big?"

With a hollow laugh, Brent looked down at his baggy shirt. "I like being comfortable."

"I do not approve." Dr. Nee's mood had not lightened. "It makes you look careless and frumpy. Your hair is shaggy and uncombed. Your whole appearance tells the world you have no purpose and you do not care."

"Then my whole appearance has got the message right," Brent responded without remorse.

"When you entered the room, you lacked confidence," Dr. Nee went on without breaking eye contact with the teen. "You slouch so much that they could teach the kindergartners the letter "C" with your spine."

Brent smiled a little at the ridiculous statement, but quickly caught himself. "What's it to you anyway?"

"I had hoped to meet you part way on your journey and help you to the next level. Instead, I find you have given up and are drifting backward at an alarming rate. When you were thirteen you had drive and purpose. The whole world was against you, and yet you were staring them down and proving them wrong. Of course, you goofed off in class, but I could see through your act, Brent. You were brilliant." He stopped and corrected himself. "You are brilliant. Your mind soaks up every ounce of information it can get. You have a power that others do not have."

A slight frown creased Brent's face at the last statement. He dropped his eyes to the desk top. What did Dr. Nee know about his power? He and his mom had moved into the two upstairs rooms of a house that belonged to Ms. Cornshaw just before school started. They lived there at a discount because his mom kept house for the widow. She still took in laundry and mending which often kept her up until the wee hours of the morning. It seemed like no matter how much they worked, they were still barely making ends meet.

Even though Brent had told himself that he would never generate power again, he was determined not to go back to the cramped apartment. The last few days, he had started generating power to light the room for his mom to work. It was frustrating because he could no longer power a specific object like he had when he was working for Mr. Leno. Every time he tried, Brent's mind got caught up in the turmoil of emotions that accompanied the memories of that night. He was hoping to cut down on the electric bill they shared with

Mrs. Cornshaw. Had Dr. Nee somehow found that out? How much did this man actually know about him?

"You have a lot going on in that mind of yours, Brent," Dr. Nee observed. "Why would you stop now and let it all go to waste?"

"There's no future for me, Dr. Nee," Brent informed him. "In case you didn't know, I got slapped on the wrist for being involved in a counterfeit ring just before you switched schools."

"I did know. I also know you had nothing to do with it."

Brent's eyes narrowed skeptically. Very few people actually believed that he was innocent.

"Why do you think I accepted the position teaching 9th grade, Brent?" Dr. Nee was reading his expressions which made Brent uncomfortable.

"Your personal life is none of my business." Brent rose. "Great catching up. I gotta get to work now."

"I accepted the position because of you."

Brent paused in the doorway, waiting.

"I have stuck to this post for years in order to be here when you came through. You have incredible potential, Brent. You were soaking up information faster than I could teach it without leaving the class behind. I knew I had taught you all I could and would need to move ahead of you if I wanted to help you any further."

Brent turned, searching the teacher's expression for any sign of falsehood.

"You acted silly in class, but I knew by your answers that you had read the text books for the entire semester before we got to the Christmas break. Brent, don't throw that all away to meet the low expectations of others."

Brent leaned casually against the door frame and crossed his arms. "I'm a teenager now. That's what teens do."

"If you wanted to cripple a generation without violence, what would you do?" Dr. Nee's voice held a new intensity.

Brent frowned. "What do you mean?"

"The culture of teen rebellion is simply a clever lie that has been accepted by our society." Dr. Nee saw Brent's confused expression. "Imagine convincing an entire generation of young people that they are too young to strive for greatness. And then, playing the long game, you let that generation pass the lie on to their children until they believe it. It would not take long to create a crippling spiral that continues from generation to generation. It is warfare so subtle that most people do not realize it has been done." He paused to let Brent consider the idea. "Teens don't have to be good for nothing, Brent. They don't have to be rebellious and rude. At your age you are packed with potential and have the energy it takes to pursue any dream you can imagine. Teens can be powerful men and women of purpose. You can be a man of purpose, Brent. You can change the world if you are interested."

Brent had moved back into the classroom without realizing it. He was soaking in the words of his professor. Longing for them to be true of him.

"Are you interested in that kind of a life?" Dr. Nee's face shone with anticipation.

"Yeah, I am." Brent sat thoughtfully, "but I don't think it's for someone like me."

"I'll coach you, if you are willing." Dr. Nee pulled a business card from inside his suit coat. The simple motion brought the memory of Slinger to mind and sent a chill through Brent. He remembered the way the cop's gun had sounded and saw again Slinger's sudden death. He did not want his life to end that way.

Dr. Nee had seen the change in Brent's expression as the memories converged on him. "You have seen a way of life that brings nothing but pain. You can break that cycle if you are willing to work hard at it."

"I want to," Brent's voice was thick with emotion.

Dr. Nee could tell he meant it. A broad smile spread across the teacher's face. "I was hoping you would say that. I want to be fully open with you, Brent. In your journey to become a man of integrity, you will reach a point where your hard work isn't enough to reach the next breakthrough. When that happens, let me know, and I will tell you the secret piece you are missing."

Brent laughed nervously. "That was strangely cryptic, but okay."

"I told the class earlier that I am willing to stay after school on Mondays to give extra tutoring in electronics to anyone who is interested. No one took me up on that. I think you would find it helpful."

"Okay," Brent agreed. He was ready to try anything.

Dr. Nee looked pleased.

"So, what now? Do I buy new clothes and start acting differently?" Brent prompted when Dr. Nee's pleased smiling continued.

"We will get to that. You need to get to work, so I will not detain you any longer. Your assignment for tomorrow is to make your bed and come to class on time."

An amused smile was Brent's only response.

"Don't worry. It will get harder. For now, only the bed and the punctuality. Nothing else. I will give you your next assignment when you are ready." Dr. Nee stood and extended his hand. Brent shook it firmly.

"Hi, I'm Brent."

Paul, a heavyset man wearing a camouflage ball cap and a navy Bill's Auto shirt, looked up from the wheel he was rolling over to the balancer. He glanced around the auto shop, obviously hoping to see Bill, the owner. Bill was not in the shop.

"Yeah, I've seen you around." Paul selected a comb and slid it into place before hefting the wheel onto the rod of the machine. "You are the Macintyre boy." He glanced up in time to see Brent's face fall. "You don't have to worry about me I don't have nothin' personal against the Macintyres," Paul went on as he tightened the rim in place. "Bill and I fixed up a few cars for your dad over the years. He never had no reason to cross us, and we never had no reason to distrust him. He paid good, and the money was real."

Brent cringed slightly at what seemed to be a reference to his past scandal.

Paul noticed that too and felt bad. "Bill might be around back. If you were looking for him," he offered. Just then, he saw Bill out of the corner of his eye and called him over. "This is Brent Macintyre." Paul rested his elbow on the tread of the wheel and looked Brent over. "He's grown a lot. I bet if you stood up straight, you would be a regular fence post."

Brent grinned, turning to Bill. "I was thinking about getting into car repair and was hoping you would have some tips on how to get started."

Bill rubbed his thick brown mustache. It was well trimmed and accented his buzzed hair. He too wore a branded shirt, but his was a navy polo instead of a t-shirt like Paul's. "What do you want to know?"

"When did you start?" Brent asked, his eyes betraying his eagerness.

A deep, humorous sound came from Bill. "Well, Brent, I'm a little different. I started when I was fifteen. I have a cousin with a big auto shop about five or six hours north of here."

Brent noticed Paul was trying to subtly catch Bill's attention. Paul had caught on quicker than Bill, and knew that Brent was really there to ask for a job. Brent took a couple of steps to his left so he could slouch against the edge of the garage door frame. This caused Bill to turn slightly away from Paul.

Bill went on, unaware of what was going on around him. "It's a great business to get into, Brent. You can start at the bottom and work your way up fairly quickly."

Paul walked past, and Brent saw him signal Bill out of the corner of his eye.

Brent grinned. "That's great," he said before Bill could grasp Paul's warning. "I was hoping to get a job here for a few days a week after school."

Bill's eyebrows went up, and he cringed at Paul before facing Brent once more. "The problem is, that we are a little slow right now. As you can see, we only have the one Ford that needs to be balanced. Paul could take care of that alone. How about you leave your number and I'll reach out if we start getting busy."

Brent nodded and took the business card Bill offered. Flipping it over, he saw it was a jeweler's business card.

"I reuse them sometimes to save on paper. Just scribble it on the back there," Bill instructed, getting a pen from Paul.

Brent wrote down Mrs. Cornshaw's number. They were allowed to use her phone as long as she didn't need it. "If I'm not there, you can leave a message with my Mom or Mrs. Cornshaw."

"Good to know." Bill took the card.

"I'm out during the school day and have work most afternoons. But you can try back, can't you? I mean, if you can't get through."

"Don't worry I'll get through." Bill assured him.

Brent nodded, looking into the auto shop longingly.

"Well, I need to get this car balanced before the owner comes this afternoon," Bill said, trying to worm his way out of the conversation. "I'll be sure and give you a call if anything comes up."

Brent nodded, took one last look, and wandered away.

The door to the living room opened, and Brent lifted his head from his pillow, listening. Soft footsteps crossed the tile portion of their dining room area and came toward the bedroom. Relaxing, Brent waited. His mom moved around her side of the room, hidden by the curtain that separated them. Twice Brent heard her come to the curtain and pause, as if listening. He lay still, breathing softly.

Each time, her footsteps moved away again. She had something she wanted to talk to Brent about.

He considered getting up and going out to talk to her, but decided against it. Whatever it was, he was too tired to think about it tonight.

Chapter 9

"I will be out over lunch again today, Brent. I have to pick up some ironing once I have Ms. Cornshaw settled in for the afternoon." Violet stopped with her hand on the edge of the curtain that separated the single bedroom into two. "Brent?"

"Yes, Ma'am?" Brent stood and looked at her curiously.

She stood looking into his half of the room. His few belongings were strewn on the dresser, chair and floor, but the blanket on his bed was straight. "You made your bed."

"Yeah, I figured I should." It embarrassed him to see that the simple act had brought tears to his mom's eyes. "I'm not a kid anymore," he pointed out, slipping his homework into his backpack.

She covered her mouth with her hand, blinking back the tears. "You haven't made your bed since we moved from the apartment last year."

"I haven't made my bed since dad died," Brent corrected without meeting her eyes. He straightened the history and math books, adding them to his pack. "I'm sorry I haven't done it before now." Brent picked up his book bag and slid it over his shoulder.

"It's silly to cry about a bed," Violet laughed, wiping her eyes. He went to her and hugged her gently. "I'll get the ironing for you. The Perkin's place is just up from the school. I'll have time to bring it home over my lunch break."

"You don't have to do that," Violet protested. "I know

how embarrassing it is for you to carry the clothes past your friends. I don't mind getting it."

"I don't mind." Brent moved past her and into the second room which served as their kitchen, dining room, and living room. It was not much bigger than the apartment, but the rooms were nicer, and Ms. Cornshaw lived in a safer part of town. Brent no longer had to worry about his mother's safety while he was at school or work.

He opened the compact fridge and grabbed an apple.

"Do you have a few minutes? There's something I've been meaning to talk to you about," Violet asked from the bedroom.

Glancing at the clock on the wall, Brent slid his other arm through the second strap of his backpack. He would have to hurry. "Sorry, Mom. I've got to get to school. Maybe we can catch up later?"

"Sure. My news will keep."

He could not see her, but Brent could hear a hint of disappointment in her voice. "I'll see you later, Mom," he called, hurrying down the stairs and out the back door.

"Look who's in a hurry to get to school."

Brent heard Jimmy's comment but did not slow his pace. Make the bed and get to class on time. That was all Dr. Nee had asked.

"Your house catch on fire or something?" Jimmy pushed himself off the pillar of the shopping center where he had been loitering with Marvin and Henry.

Keeping his pace, Brent maneuvered around him. "Get lost, Jimmy."

"What's the hurry?" Jimmy cocked his head at the guys, and they eagerly fell in step behind him.

"Look, I'm just going to school," Brent informed them. "Get off my back."

"Didn't like the tardy slip you got yesterday?" Marvin asked, giving Brent's backpack a little shove from behind.

"Lay off, Marvin," Brent warned.

Marvin was big for his age. He had always been overweight as a kid, but somehow still muscular and active enough to knock down anyone who crossed him. Hoping to build up his self-discipline, Marvin's dad had put him in boxing classes over the summer. At school, this only made him more of a threat than ever. The other 9th graders already knew to give the big guy his space.

"Can't you take a joke?" Marvin jerked on Brent's bag, throwing him off step.

Brent spun to face him. "I said lay off, Marvin. You too, Jimmy. I'm serious."

"Serious, huh?" Jimmy stepped into Brent's space. "Are we not good enough for you after your little chat with Professor Nee yesterday?"

"Is that what all this is about?" Brent saw a clock through the window of the diner. His time was running out. "Let me ask you this, Jimmy. We tolerate each other now and then, but have we ever been friends?"

Jimmy sneered at the thought. "No."

"So, we still aren't friends," Brent pointed out. "Nothing has changed. If you are jealous because a teacher talked to me after school, then pick a teacher to talk to yourself."

Jimmy was glaring now, and Marvin's thick hands were in fists. Henry, bulky but awkward, was backing away, hoping no one would notice he was not involved. Brent grinned at him. At least one of them had enough sense to stay out of a fight right before school.

"What's so funny?" Marvin demanded.

"You two. All bent out of shape over me walking down

the street. It's the most ridiculous thing I've seen all day."

They moved toward him, but Brent only laughed and moved out of range. "You want to see something more ridiculous, Henry?" Brent tightened the straps of his backpack and shoved the sleeves of his long sleeve shirt up above his elbows.

Henry froze when the guys looked his way. "Not really."

"Watch this." Brent spun and bolted toward the school.

With an angry shout, Jimmy and Marvin ran after him.

Brent could hear Henry laughing behind them as he rounded the corner. Dodging the early morning pedestrians, Brent pushed himself to keep going.

After a few minutes, Brent could hear Marvin's panting fading. Glancing back, he saw Marvin stop and lean over to catch his breath.

Jimmy was still in pursuit. By the time he reached the school, Brent's breath was coming in gasps. Trying to take the cement steps two at a time, Brent misjudged the distance and fell hard. His right arm came up automatically, catching his weight and keeping him from smashing his head on the steps. Scrambling to his feet, he pushed his way into the school. Remembering Dr. Nee's comment about not having a class during the first period, Brent hurried to his classroom to catch his breath.

Closing the door, Brent stood against the wall where he would not be seen if Jimmy peered through the little window in the class door. While he stood there, breathing hard, his eyes found the clock on the back wall. The hands of the clock showed it was one minute before nine. Brent grinned and exhaled in relief. Still sucking in air, he leaned his pounding head against the wall. He had made it, but it would cost him. The bell rang and Brent pushed himself off the wall. His shin radiated pain and his arm tingled oddly as he reached for the door handle.

"I must say that was quite impressive."

Brent froze. Turning his head slowly, he groaned. Behind the desk sat Dr. Nee and beside him stood Principal Bond. How had he not seen them?

"I made it," Brent said lightly to buy himself time.

"So I see." Principal Bond's eyes moved to Brent's arm. "You do realize you are dripping blood on the floor."

Brent checked his arm and discovered he had taken off a layer of skin during his run in with the front steps. "How did that get there?" Brent shook his head as if at a naughty child. He spotted a roll of paper towels on the back table. "Don't worry, Principal Bond. I'll clean it right up."

"Brent."

Brent stopped and gave them his attention, expecting a lecture.

Principal Bond crossed the classroom and pulled several paper towels from the roll. "Put this on your arm so you don't leave a trail. Go straight to the school nurse and get that patched up. When she is done with you, I would like to have a word with you in my office."

Deflating slightly, Brent took the paper towels the principal offered. "Yes, Sir."

Gingerly pressing the paper towel to the abrasion on his arm, Brent moved toward the door. Glancing at Dr. Nee, he was surprised to see a pleased smile on the teacher's face.

"Thank you. Sorry about the interruption. And the blood on the floor." He was limping out of the room when Dr. Nee called to him.

"Yeah?" Brent asked, still holding the makeshift bandage in place.

Dr. Nee gestured to Brent's leg. "It might be good to have her check that leg too."

"I'm falling apart today, aren't I?" Not waiting for a response, Brent limped out to obey.

Taking the thick leather chair across from the principal, Brent tugged self-consciously at the sleeve of his shirt. He was grateful he had worn long sleeves that day because his right sleeve hid the new bandage on his arm. Brent looked around the room with interest. This was only his second day in high school, and already he had landed himself in the principal's office.

Some old, black and white pictures of football teams stood on the bookshelf, flanking a signed football on a stand. Some more pictures of Principal Bond shaking hands with people Brent didn't recognize were scattered around tastefully on the shelves and tables around the room. Though Principal Bond's desk was covered in stacks of papers, the rest of his office was neat and clean. The principal removed his reading glasses and leaned forward, resting his forearms on the desk. Brent guessed he was in his sixties. His gray suit was well fitted, and his matching gray hair was combed neatly to the side. Despite his age and professional air, there was something strong and imposing about the big man.

"What happened this morning, Brent?"

"I didn't intend to create such a grand entrance," Brent laughed nervously. "I was racing a couple of guys to school and tripped on the way up the front steps. Ever try to take them two at a time?" He crinkled his nose and shook his head in disapproval. "I don't think the architect got the spacing right."

"Who were you racing against?" Principal Bond was not easily distracted. He sat forward, his back straight, and did not fidget with his hands.

Brent shrugged. "Nobody special, just some guys."

"The way you entered Dr. Nee's classroom gave the appearance that you were hiding from someone."

"You know, you can't trust appearances, especially not these days." Brent saw the clock and frowned. "Oh, no. I'm late for my first class." Rising, he reached for his backpack. "I apologize, Mr. Bond. Could we pick this up another time?"

"Sit down, Brent." Principal Bond was firm but not unkind.

For a moment, Brent hesitated, looking longingly at the door. Then, with a defeated sigh, Brent let himself down gently and sank into the chair.

The principal studied the slouching fifteen-year-old before him. He was sloppily dressed and showed none of the potential Dr. Nee had spoken of. However, Principal Bond could see that beneath the surface, Brent was confident and a quick thinker."

"I looked over your grades from last year and have gotten some feedback from a few of your previous teachers."

Brent waited.

"Dr. Nee says you were bored in middle school. Is that true?"

"It wasn't too bad." Searching the older man's green eyes, Brent tried to read him.

Principal Bond cleared his throat. "We do our best to push our students to their full potential at this school, Brent. We have a wide range of experienced teachers and subjects that will help equip you for life after graduation. A few of our teachers even offer private tutoring sessions for students who are interested in furthering their education."

Brent was waiting for the punch line. The jab that the principal would use to try to cut him down to size.

"I think you are going to like it at this school, Brent." Principal Bond leaned back in his chair, easing the intensity of his next words. "You should know though, that one thing we don't tolerate here is fighting. If you have any trouble with any of the other guys, I expect you to come to me. Or at the very least go to Dr. Nee."

Brent nodded skeptically.

"Can you look me in the eye and tell me that what happened this morning was only a playful race and nothing more?"

The question caught Brent off guard. He scrambled mentally for the right words while still trying to soak in all that the Principal had said. "Dr. Nee asked me to be on time. So I was giving it a try," Brent finally answered. "I guess I cut it a little too close."

Principal Bond knew there was more to the story than what Brent was telling him. "If there is more trouble, you will come to me?"

"I'll let you know if I need help," Brent agreed vaguely, standing once more. He offered his hand to the principal. "It was nice to meet you, Mr. Bond."

Shaking his head, Principal Bond rose and shook Brent's hand.

"Here he is, boys, taking his laundry out for a walk," Jimmy laughed. A few other boys who had come along for some entertainment joined him.

Brent let his breath out in an exasperated sigh. "Hi, Guys," he greeted them unenthusiastically.

"I looked for you in our first class. You weren't there." Jimmy's tone was casual.

Brent glanced over at the well-built red head walking beside him. "I ate the steps on the way into the school and had to go to the nurse to get patched up." Brent twisted his arm to show Jimmy the bulge of the bandage beneath his shirt. "And then the principal wanted to have a little chat about it."

"Yeah?" Jimmy's voice said he didn't care, but his face

showed otherwise.

"Look, Jimmy," Brent adjusted the basket of clothes he carried. "I didn't say anything about you, if that's what you are asking."

"You expect me to believe that?" The red head was not sure if he should rile his supporters or dismiss them.

Brent kept walking, "Do you think Principal Bond would have let you stay in class all morning if I told him you were the reason I fell?"

Jimmy considered his words.

A few of the guys grumbled together and headed back to school. They could tell this would not be the lunch-time-show they had been hoping for.

"It wasn't my fault you were so clumsy," Jimmy challenged, moving around to stand in front of Brent.

"I know. No one said it was." The basket was awkward to carry without bumping his sore leg, and Brent was getting annoyed by the delay. He would not have time to grab lunch if Jimmy kept up the interrogation much longer.

"Disappointing," a tenth grader muttered. "Let's get out of here and let these two chums catch up."

The guys dispersed leaving only Jimmy and Marvin.

"So you didn't rat on us after all," Jimmy seemed confused.

"Why would I? You didn't do anything to me." Brent stepped around him and added over his shoulder. "Because you couldn't catch me."

Jimmy dug in his pocket and pulled out two five dollar bills. "Marvin, go get two burgers. I'll join you in a minute."

Because Jimmy was paying, Marvin made himself scarce without protesting.

"You didn't mention me, right?" Jimmy's tone was a little too urgent. "In your little talk with Bond."

Brent stopped and looked Jimmy in the eye. "Why would I tell him about you? Look, Jimmy, we are in this together.

We have to make this new school work and try to stay on our feet while we learn the ropes. So why don't we get off each other's backs and make it work."

Jimmy considered the proposition, glancing around to insure no one else was listening.

"Alright, you have a deal. You stay out of my way, and I'll stay out of yours."

Brent cocked his chin upward. "It's a deal."

CHAPTER 10

"Hey Paul, is the Civic ready? Thelma Heading just called, and she's on her way." Bill's voice echoed in the quiet auto shop garage.

Paul looked around the open hood of the Civic at his boss. "I thought you told her it would be ready tomorrow."

"You know Mrs. Heading. She's been a school teacher so long that she still expects everyone in town to hop when she says hop." Bill came over to look at the engine. "Can you get it back together in twenty minutes?"

"I'll have it ready." Glancing over at the open garage door as if expecting to see Mrs. Heading standing there, Paul's irritation faded. "Let me take care of the Civic, Bill. You have other things to worry about."

"What are you grinning about?" Bill asked skeptically.

Paul gestured toward the door. "That kid is out there hanging around again. If you aren't careful he'll get himself hired."

Bill looked and laughed, shaking his head in disbelief. "I'll deal with him. You just get this thing put back together before Thelma shows up."

"Roger that."

Bill strolled out to the front where Brent was leaning against the side of the shop. "Can I help you?"

"I'm Brent I came by last week." Brent pushed himself off the wall. "You don't need an extra hand around here, do you?"

"No, nothing has changed since last week." Bill smoothed his thick mustache to hide his smile.

Brent shoved his hands into his pockets and looked dejected. "If you ever do..."

"If I need you, I'll call your house. You gave me your number already."

"I thought maybe you had lost it."

"No, I have it inside," Bill assured him.

"Sometimes we miss calls," Brent pulled his hands out of his pockets and crossed his arms. "It's Mrs. Cornshaw's phone and sometimes we aren't home."

"Don't worry." Bill stepped back, hoping to end the conversation. "You haven't missed any calls from me."

"Good." The sound of a power tool came from inside the garage, and Brent's eyes lit up with interest. "What's Paul working on?"

Shaking his head, Bill sighed. "Look, Brent, we don't need an extra hand, and I don't have time to babysit you. There's dangerous tools in the shop, and if you get hurt, it could close me down."

"I know." Brent slouched against the wall again.

"Look, we are on a tight schedule today. Mrs. Heading wants her car back, and you know how she can be."

He was rewarded by a knowing smile.

"Anything I can help with?"

"Bill this new battery must be faulty," Paul called. "It's brand new, and the car still won't start. Any ideas?"

Excusing himself, Brent headed toward the car. Paul was sitting part way in the car with his right foot by the brake pedal and his left on the cement floor of the garage. He held the key out to Bill, who shook his head and walked around the front of the vehicle.

"Crank it again," Bill advised, resting his hand lightly on the open hood.

Reaching in, Paul turned the key. Brent sent a low surge of power to the battery of the Civic, and it started.

Jerking his hand away from the car, Bill rubbed his palm thoughtfully. "Did you feel that?" Bill asked as Paul came around to where he stood.

"Feel what?" Paul asked distractedly. He got the battery tester and hooked it up. "Everything reads normal. It is fully charged." Looking at his boss, Paul frowned. "You okay?"

"The weirdest thing happened when the car started," Bill confided, forgetting Brent was there. "I had my hand on the hood, and I got this electric shock just before the engine came to life. It was like there was a low grade power surge through the whole garage."

Brent frowned. What Bill said had triggered an old memory. After the bank robbery, Slinger had accused him of turning on the bank lights. He had never used his power before that night, though he knew he could feel electricity. In his desperate state of mind, Brent had only meant to power the streetlight, but maybe he had turned on the bank lights as well. Maybe, like today, when he panicked and used his power without thinking, he generated unstable electricity in all directions.

"Do you think it is safe?" Paul asked. "I didn't feel anything, but I wasn't touching anything metal."

"Turn it off and back on. If it happens again, we will keep it another day to be safe."

Paul grinned. "I'll let you be the one to tell her."

Bill gave him a friendly shove toward the driver's seat. "Go start the car."

The Civic came to life and ran smoothly when the key was turned. Paul looked out at Bill for direction.

"Looks good. I didn't feel anything that time." Bill shut the hood and used a rag to buff off a spot of grease. Take it around the block to make sure everything runs smoothly.

I'll get the paper work for Mrs. Heading." Bill turned and smiled at someone beyond where Brent stood. "Hi Dr. Nee, I didn't see you there. How's that clunker of yours holding up?"

Feeling out of place, Brent slipped away unnoticed.

Brent grinned as he looked down from the rooftop of the abandoned building. In one hand, he held a sandwich, in the other, a police scanner with the sound turned very low. He was watching the dark street below. Indistinct chatter came from the scanner. Brent carefully set the sandwich on his knee, leaning forward to get a clearer view in both directions.

"Having fun?" Dr. Nee's voice shattered the stillness of the night.

Brent started, and the sandwich that had been balanced on his knee fell to the dirty roof top under his feet.

"What was that for?" Brent retrieved his dinner, gingerly brushing off the bread before turning to face Dr. Nee who was walking toward him. "What are you doing up here?"

"I find it amusing to sneak around on the tops of abandoned old buildings and scare young men at night." Dr. Nee leaned against the low wall that surrounded the flat rooftop.

Brent's breath escaped in a silent laugh at the unexpected little speech. "Seriously, Dr. Nee. What are you doing up here?"

Dr. Nee looked around the dirty rooftop with interest. Silent air conditioning units were their only companions. Small debris and a few banged up crates littered the roof. "Henry told me you come up here sometimes. I was passing by and thought I would come up and see what made this place so attractive."

"Look, I'm not doing anything wrong." Satisfied that his sandwich was clean enough, Brent took a bite.

Dr. Nee looked out over the junkyard across the street.

"But you are doing something interesting."

"Says who?" Brent asked around the food he was chewing. He made a face and removed a tiny rock from his mouth. "I'm going to have to talk to the janitor. This rooftop is a mess." Flicking the rock away, Brent casually sat back as if he were simply there to enjoy the cool breeze.

"You have a nice view of the junkyard from up here." The knowing look in the professor's eyes made Brent uncomfortable.

"So do you," Brent responded. "Here to pick out your next ride?"

A genuine smile creased Dr. Nee's face. "What's wrong with my car?"

"Nothing. If you like that style. It was probably popular when you were a kid."

Dr. Nee shook his head in mock disappointment, "I see that your humor is as healthy outside the classroom as it is during class time."

"Now me? I would pick out that frame there. On the end by the fence. Anybody can see that piece of metal has a lot of potential. I bet it was a sleek ride when it was in its prime!"

"And you think my car is bad?" Dr. Nee asked with a laugh.

"Ha, ha," Brent's tone was dry, but his eyes betrayed his amusement. He enjoyed Dr. Nee's sense of humor.

"I didn't know you were involved in rebuilding cars." Dr. Nee cocked his head to observe the frame Brent had pointed out with new interest.

"I'm not. At least, not yet." Brent picked at something imaginary in his bread. "But I will. I've put in my application with Bill's Auto. I could get a call from him any day."

Some chatter came over the scanner, and Brent perked up. Holding the scanner, he listened, his face lighting up with excitement. When he glanced over at Dr. Nee, a slight frown clouded the eagerness in his eyes. "I bet you have somewhere to be about now, Dr. Nee."

Dr. Nee gave a negative shake of his head.

They could see the police lights on the buildings north of their position.

"Couldn't you think of somewhere else to go?" Brent chafed. "I was here first. So if you could find another rooftop that would be nice. I think there's a good one on the other side of town. I was hoping to be alone up here tonight."

The lights were getting closer. Another cruiser turned a corner to the south. They were closing in. Brent peered over the edge of the roof in time to see a dark figure slip through a hole in the junkyard fence.

"Seriously, Dr. Nee. I need you to go." Brent stood and put a hand on the shorter man's shoulder, guiding him toward the stairs.

Dr. Nee did not protest or resist.

"Quickly, if you don't mind." Brent looked over his shoulder. The police lights were getting closer to his position.

"I already know what you can do." His tone made Brent stop.

Dr. Nee met his eyes, and Brent frowned slightly. "What are you talking about?"

"You control electricity," Dr. Nee responded calmly.

"Whoa!" Brent stepped away from his teacher, his eyes darted to the edge of the rooftop and back to Dr. Nee. "I don't know what gave you that idea, but it is pretty far-fetched."

"I've seen you do it."

Brent shifted, glancing back toward the edge of the roof.

"I'll let you get back to what you are doing," Dr. Nee was studying Brent. "But we need to talk about this. I can help you. You have my card. You can call or drop by any time."

"Sure." Brent gave Dr. Nee a little more room than necessary as he moved around the teacher to open the door to the stairs. "Maybe you can find Jimmy and scare him next."

Dr. Nee's eyes twinkled with amusement. He bowed slightly before disappearing down the stairs. Brent shut the door behind him and ran to the edge of the roof. He picked up the scanner that he had set aside and took in the scene below him.

Several police were lacing their way through the cars in the junkyard. They had not caught their man. Moving to his backpack, Brent took out the binoculars he had borrowed from Henry. He scanned the junk yard carefully with his eyes until he spotted something dark in the bed of a banged up Junker. Using the binoculars, he confirmed it was the man they were searching for.

Brent turned on the junkyard light above the Junker. The dark clothed man scrambled out of the truck bed. Crouching out of sight, he wove his way through the cars to the other side of the yard. A bubble of light followed him. Car headlights, security lights, and even interior lights on the cars lit up, tracking his progress.

The scanner came to life as the officers closed in on their prey.

Brent watched triumphantly as the officers drew in the circle.

Brent tried to narrow it to show his exact location, but the ring of powered things stayed the same. Wondering, Brent leaned out over the edge of the roof and saw the room below him had a light on. Somehow he knew it was not Dr. Nee. In his excitement, Brent realized that he had been creating a radius of power that not only revealed the criminal across the street, but also lit his own position.

Keeping his head low, Brent clicked off the scanner and threw it, and Henry's binoculars, into his bag. He waited until the police had their man in cuffs before he backed out.

Brent had almost reached the bottom of the stairs when he heard someone coming up from the bottom. Panicking,

Brent slipped out of the stairwell into the second floor. Running lightly down the long hall of the closed factory, Brent found the fire escape on the opposite side of the building. Scrambling down it, he barely had enough time to jump into the dumpster before an officer came by. Brent heard the word sandwich come across the radio of the man guarding the alley. Brent scolded himself for abandoning a perfectly good sandwich. Not daring to move, he waited as they radioed and double checked for nearly half an hour.

Finally, the search was abandoned. Brent made himself wait ten extra minutes. When he didn't hear anything, he stood stiffly and peered out of the dumpster. No one was in sight. Climbing out, Brent shouldered his backpack and hurried home.

"Yo, Jimmy. You have a minute?" Brent strolled over casually and leaned against the pole of the streetlight a few feet from where Jimmy sat.

Jimmy was lounging at one of the patio tables outside the old fashioned diner. The place was run down, and the food was greasy, but it was cheap and made for a good place for the older kids to hang out after school.

"Do you mind if we have a private conversation?" Brent looked meaningfully at Marvin and Henry.

Jimmy looked amused. "Not up to facing us all, huh?"

Henry shook his head. Bopping Marvin's shoulder with the back of his hand, he peeled himself out of his chair and stood to go.

"What? Are you two friends now?" Marvin rose, looking from Jimmy to Brent. "You know, Brent, I miss getting to pound you."

"I wish I could say the same, Marvin," Brent answered

casually.

Marvin frowned, trying to sort out Brent's meaning.

Shaking his head again, Henry shot Brent a grin. He purposefully walked between Marvin and Brent as he left, breaking the tension between them.

"I'll be looking for a good excuse to knock you off your high horse, Macintyre," Marvin threatened, following reluctantly as Henry moseyed over to join another group.

"What's up?" Jimmy asked.

Brent could tell his guard was up.

Plopping into the chair Marvin had occupied, Brent propped his feet up on the third chair and looked across the table at the slouching red-head.

"I've got a challenge for you," Brent shook his head at the waiter who came toward him.

"I'm all ears." Jimmy adjusted himself in the chair, lacing his fingers behind his head so his elbows stuck out on either side.

"You make your bed every day for a month, and I'll give you twenty bucks."

Jimmy was not impressed. "I know where you live, and your job doesn't pay that well. Either you are involved in some crime, or you are bluffing."

"You got a problem with earning twenty bucks?" Brent asked. "Or maybe the requirements are too much for you."

"Doing it will be easy." Jimmy wasn't looking at Brent. He had to keep up appearances with the other guys. "I just don't believe you have the cash."

"Oh, I have it, but I don't think I'll actually need it," Brent answered casually.

Jimmy's arms came down, and his eyes lit up with interest. "All I do is make my bed every day?"

"Every morning," Brent corrected.

His eyes narrowed. "Why?"

Brent shrugged. “Dr. Nee has me doing it, and I got tired of suffering alone. So I thought you might be interested in a little bet.”

“How do you know I won’t just say I did it?” Jimmy was hooked but didn’t want to show it.

Smiling, Brent rose. “Because you aren’t that low.”

The rough complement sobered Jimmy.

He looked thoughtful for a moment before meeting Brent’s dark eyes once more. “Alright, I’ll do it,” Jimmy agreed. “Say goodbye to your twenty bucks.”

CHAPTER 11

Thirty more minutes and Brent would be done for the night. He was ready. Retrieving another box from the back room, Brent carried it up front to refill the shelf of knick-knacks that were on sale.

The chime sounded, and Brent looked up from the shelf he was stocking to see the man who had burst through the front door.

"Someone call an ambulance! My stepdaughter is having a seizure, and my phone just died." There was a hardness in the man's face that made his plea for help seem cold and hollow.

"I have a phone here," Noah Ornstein, Brent's boss and the owner of the shop, pulled out his cell phone. The man hurried over to him.

Curious, Brent put down the box he had been emptying and pushed open the door. There was a rusty, old truck parked at an angle partway in the street. Brent could see a blonde girl who looked close to his age jerking strangely in the passenger seat.

Allowing the door to close behind him, Brent walked out to the edge of the sidewalk.

"The streetcar is coming!" Someone across the street shouted, "That truck is on the tracks!"

There wasn't time to move the truck. Brent knew it instantly. The electric wires that powered the streetcar ran above where the truck was. If it didn't stop, the girl's door would be the first thing struck by the streetcar.

A man in blue coveralls ran forward to try to move the truck off the tracks. Several others joined him.

"There's no key!" the would-be-hero in coveralls shouted. He jerked at the driver's door handle and looked around for something to try to smash the window.

The streetcar's horn blasted a warning as an oblivious delivery driver zipped his van around the parked truck and across the tracks. The van blocked the engineer's view of the truck until it was too late.

Focusing on the streetcar, Brent pulled its power. Removing electricity was something he still struggled with. He had found in the past that in a crisis he did not have time to wonder if he could do something or not. He only had time to act. Each time, he found he could do more than he realized was possible. Brent's head ached with the strain, but he did not waver.

The scream of the streetcar's breaks mingled with the screams of the onlookers as it slid to a stop with the unmistakable crunch of metal against metal.

Brent felt like he was going to be sick.

"My truck!" The step-father bumped into Brent as he went racing from the shop to the site of the accident. Jamming the key into the lock, he flung open the door.

"Don't move her. The ambulance is on the way," a deep voice instructed.

The crowd stepped back to allow the confident stranger a path to the truck. "I'm a paramedic. I'll do my best to stabilize her until they come."

The flustered step-father moved out of the way. Everyone paused at the sound of a siren in the distance.

"She's okay!" The man in coveralls called to the crowd, relaying the paramedic's message. "No visible injuries," he shouted after a pause.

The deep voiced paramedic said something to the herald. The man nodded seriously and stopped shouting.

"I've never seen that streetcar stop so fast," an elderly man told Brent as the crowd parted to let the ambulance through. "You just witnessed a miracle, son."

"Just a few seconds more and it would have crushed her," the lady on the other side of Brent agreed.

"Those things aren't built to stop like that," a nerdy teen with thick glasses informed them. "If the power had not failed, she would be dead."

Brent frowned at him, "What do you mean?"

"Look around." The teen gestured at the shops around them. All of the store signs were dark. All of the shops were dark inside. Even the streetlight that had been flickering on and off, triggered by the fading light, now showed no signs of coming on. "I have to get home. This could affect my research that I left up on my computer." He scurried off down the street apparently having completely forgotten about the accident.

The crowd was pushed back to give the ambulance workers room to do their job. Brent watched as they carefully extracted the unconscious girl from the truck and secured her on the stretcher. He guessed she was sixteen or seventeen. Her long, straight blonde hair was brushed aside out of the way, and her face was hidden by the oxygen mask she wore.

"Not much older than you," the older man observed.

"Yeah." Brent couldn't take his eyes off her. Had he saved her? Or had he merely prolonged her suffering.

"God used you, Brent."

Brent jumped at Dr. Nee's comment. "Dr. Nee? No way! What are you doing here? This is getting creepy."

Dr. Nee appeared to enjoy startling Brent. "I shop at the Asian market up the street." Dr. Nee held up two plastic grocery bags. One had several types of greens sticking out of the top of it. "They have a lot of good sales today. I was on my way to my car." He craned to see around the people milling around them. "There's my beautiful vehicle by the curb."

Grinning, Brent shook his head. "We have very different versions of beautiful, Dr. Nee."

Shifting the bags he held, Dr. Nee looked up at Brent. "What are you doing downtown?"

Cocking his thumb over his shoulder, Brent said, "I work at Ornstein's, at least until Bill Trever has an opening at his auto shop."

"That was impressive that the streetcar stopped in time."

Brent shifted uneasily at the abrupt subject change. "Yeah, pretty cool how that happened."

"Do you want to talk about it?" Dr. Nee asked, cocking his head toward his car.

"About what?" Brent asked warily, remembering the professor's comments on the rooftop.

Again, Dr. Nee adjusted the grocery bag he was holding. "I think it would be better to speak privately."

Until that moment, Brent had been so focused on what was happening with the injured girl that he did not realize how many people had gathered on the street to watch. They were standing in little groups, talking excitedly about their version of what had happened or the cause of the sudden power outage.

Brent considered the professor's invitation. A second ambulance pulled in, blocking Brent's view of the truck. Firemen and rescue workers were scrambling over the scene like ants while the police tried to enforce a safe perimeter around the area. EMT's questioned the streetcar engineer and the few passengers who had been on board. They were checking vitals and offering each a ride to the hospital for further screening.

"Brent?"

Pulling his attention away from the action, Brent followed Dr. Nee to his car. He was drained from the exertion of stopping the streetcar and not in the mood to argue. Sliding inside, Brent closed the passenger door behind him. "What do you want to talk about?" He tipped his head back against the headrest, knowing the answer.

"The energy that stopped that streetcar."

"And killed the power in the shops around it," Brent added, turning his head to look at Dr. Nee.

"That was a lot of energy," the older man observed.

Brent had to find a way to wriggle out before the phenomenon was pinned on him. "Maybe there is a God after all."

"Of course there is," Dr. Nee answered without hesitation. "That is not in question. It is a well-known fact that God often gives special gifts to specific people to help them do His will. A gift like yours is especially rare."

"You think I have some kind of gift of electricity? Isn't that a little far-fetched?" Brent was still trying to shake him off the trail. He didn't dare meet his professor's eyes. "All this time I thought you were reading educational books at your desk. Now I know that they are science fiction novels instead."

Dr. Nee chuckled. "You are a talented young man, Brent. Wildly creative and especially gifted. You will not evade the topic so easily. I know you were a part of the energy deficiency that stopped that streetcar."

"Me?" Brent sat up and tried to laugh, but it sounded hollow. "That's crazy." He looked over at Dr. Nee, hoping his protest was believable.

"Crazy does not always mean untrue." Dr. Nee met Brent's eyes. "I can help train you to use your gift so that you can become even more effective."

"Because you have the same gift, so you know how?" Brent pressed, hoping to move the focus from himself to Dr. Nee.

"Have you not been paying attention in my classes?" Dr.

Nee tipped his face downward and raised his eyebrows at Brent as if he were about to scold him. When Brent did not respond, Dr. Nee went on. "As you should remember from my class, I know quite a bit about electricity. When the car at Bill's wouldn't start, you created an energy wave. Today, you pulled energy to stop the streetcar."

"You can't prove that," Brent objected, sitting up. "You are just making stuff up."

Dr. Nee pulled an EMF Meter from his coat pocket, and Brent fell silent. "This device measures electricity. Both times the electricity source was you."

Brent dropped his eyes to the meter in Dr. Nee's hand.

"Both times it was scattered, which reduced its impact," Dr. Nee went on. "As I said before, I have studied electricity extensively. I think I can train you to target your energy. To be more intentional and effective with your power."

"Why are you so convinced it was my power?" Brent pointed at the thinning crowd. "It could have been that lady, or the man with the coveralls who was by the truck."

"But it was not." Dr. Nee seemed to be looking at something deep inside him.

Brent shifted uncomfortably, putting his hand on the handle of the door beside him.

"I will keep your gift to myself, Brent. And I advise you to do the same. You have been given a great skill. I want to help you learn to use it well." Dr. Nee could see Brent was not ready to open up. "I will not force you to accept my help. You may come to me when you are ready."

"Yeah, sure." Brent pushed his door open. "I'll see you in class."

"It's been a couple of weeks now. Don't I get another

assignment?" Brent asked from the doorway of the classroom. It was halfway through the lunch hour, and the halls had cleared.

Dr. Nee looked up with his chopsticks poised over his bowl. "You were late yesterday," he observed without emotion. Putting a bite into his mouth, Dr. Nee laid the chopsticks neatly across the top of his bowl before turning back to the textbook that was open on his desk.

Brent remained where he was, leaning casually against the door frame.

The clock at the back of the classroom ticked loudly in the stillness.

Dr. Nee picked up the chopsticks and glanced up. "Oh, you are still here."

"Yes, I am." Brent watched his teacher select a piece of a green vegetable from the bowl and pop it into his mouth.

"My lunch is not usually a show for others." Dr. Nee laid the chopsticks on the bowl again without looking up at Brent.

"It makes for a very interesting show."

Dr. Nee glanced up at Brent, his eyes betraying his amusement. "You are a stubborn young man."

Brent kept a straight face. "Only when I want something."

"And what is it you want?" The professor gave Brent his full attention. Brent knew Dr. Nee was hoping he would agree to the electricity training he had offered.

"All I want is my next assignment. I've made my bed and been on time every day for two weeks, including to work and on weekends."

Dr. Nee started to protest, but Brent spoke first.

"Except for yesterday, and I was only five minutes late."

"Late is late." Dr. Nee's eyes crinkled at the edges.

"What's next?"

"Posture."

Brent pushed himself off the door and stood tall before

his professor. "And?"

"And your words. You are not to insult or tear others down with your words."

"And?" Brent prompted.

"Nothing else." Dr. Nee smiled, "You might be surprised how hard these two will be."

"When you say posture, what do you mean?" Brent asked suspiciously.

"Sitting up straight, standing up straight, walking tall, and holding your head up like a man who is going somewhere." He picked up his chopsticks and dipped them into his bowl. "You think 'easy peasy,' but you have many weak muscles to build in your back, and a very strong one to tame in your mouth."

"What?" Brent's face was a mixture of confusion and disgust.

Dr. Nee chuckled. "Your tongue, Brent. It is a muscle, you know."

"That one won't be so hard."

Dr. Nee's eyebrows went up together. "You may find that insults flow off your tongue more easily than you realize. I will give you my advice. Practice over the weekend. No slouching, and no insults starting on Monday."

Brent looked thoughtful and let himself lean against the door frame to consider the new information.

Dr. Nee cleared his throat.

Brent laughed and left him to finish his meal in peace.

CHAPTER 12

"What's with you? Did you break your back over the weekend?" Henry asked sliding into the desk beside Brent's. "My sister's friend married this guy who broke his back, and they had to put in a metal bar to help hold up his spine. He sat like you. All upright and stiff."

Brent eyed him with annoyance. The day was only half over and already his back was killing him.

"I'm only asking because it's not normal. You know, people sometimes get injured but are afraid to tell people. I told the guys you probably broke your back." Henry had started gravitating to be where Brent was more and more often. They weren't exactly friends, but Brent enjoyed having someone to hang out with now and then.

"I didn't break my back, Henry. I'm having good posture."

"You are an odd duck," Henry responded with a laugh.

More of their classmates straggled into the room. The English teacher had not appeared yet. She was usually late.

"Hey, guys," Henry announced. "He didn't break his back. He's having good posture."

Laughs and taunts erupted.

"It's easy to laugh it off," Brent responded loudly, drawing the class's attention. "I dare you to try it. Anyone who sits up straight through this whole class period gets a dollar. Anyone who slouches, gives me a dollar."

The room buzzed with challenges, dares, and laughter,

but when Mrs. Gram bustled into her classroom, the whole class was sitting up with impeccable posture.

"Well, this is a nice change." She looked them over skeptically. "Nice to see you actually have spines. I was beginning to wonder."

The murmur was less enthusiastic than normal. Some of them were already feeling the burn and regretted taking Brent up on his challenge.

Mrs. Gram's 9th grade class got very little out of her lesson that day. One by one they dropped out, slouching with pained groans and eyeing Brent with new respect.

Brent, on the other hand, was sweating now. The effort of the day was taking its toll. He was holding on, counting the ticks of the clock, keeping Clive, the big 9th grader from Sweden in sight. He was the last one who was still sitting straight. Clive was new to the school, and it was easy to see that this bulky, blond guy had an incredible level of determination.

Mrs. Gram tried every way she could think of to engage her students, but nothing seemed to help. They were eagerly focused on whether or not Clive would outlast Brent. Finally, after what felt like an eternity, the class was over. Brent slipped out of his seat and lay in the floor with a groan.

"Brent?" Mrs. Gram asked standing up with a concerned expression. "Are you okay?"

"Yes, Ma'am. I just need a few minutes."

"If you aren't hurt, get up off the floor." Mrs. Gram was collecting her things. She only taught one class period at this school and was headed on to her other position. "The floor is disgusting. Seriously, Brent, you would think you were in kindergarten the way you are acting." Not wanting to be late, but already being in that position, Mrs. Gram left Brent laying in the floor and hurried out.

The other guys and girls grudgingly dropped their dollars onto Brent as they left the class. The last one to leave was Clive. He looked down at the dollar bills Brent had not bothered to collect and carefully chose one. "Thank you, Brent," he said with a wide smile.

"Wait, Clive." Brent propped himself up on his left elbow. "How'd you do it?"

Clive smiled. "You know that metal bar Henry was telling us about?"

"Like in people's backs?"

Clive nodded.

"Sure, what of it?"

"I have one." Clive was grinning now. "It is nice to be paid for something I cannot stop doing."

"Well, you earned it." Brent put up his hand, and Clive helped him to his feet.

"You got a lot of money from them. What will you do with it?"

"Pay off Jimmy if he kept his end of our bet." Brent could see Clive didn't understand, but he made no effort to explain things. Folding the money and the two IOU notes, Brent shoved the twenty-two dollars he had earned into his pocket. Posture was a productive skill to have.

———

"Brent? Are you in there?" Violet Macintyre called from her side of the curtain.

"Yeah," Brent did not invite her to come into his side of the room.

"Are you okay?"

"Yeah." He was laying on his bed, giving his sore back muscles a chance to relax.

"I'm sorry I am so late. Did you get dinner?"

"No."

"I could make you something," she offered hopefully.

"That's okay I wasn't hungry."

There was a long pause.

"Brent?"

"Yeah, Mom?"

"I haven't seen much of you this week." She paused, then added, "I feel like I haven't seen you since school started."

With a heavy sigh, Brent got up and slid the curtain back. "Tada! Now you have." He gave her a tired smile before flopping on his back on the bed again. "Welcome to my world." Brent could see she was concerned about him.

She glanced around his little space, and her mouth opened slightly.

"It's so clean!" She laughed a little. "Brent, your room is cleaner than mine."

He couldn't help smiling. It was true. He had found that having a made bed caused everything else in the room to look out of place. So now, he did a quick two minute clean up each morning before he left for school. His eyes moved to her side of the room. Things were strewn about. Neither of them spent much time at home. Besides that, his mom's side of the room had the rope across it which also doubled as a hanging rack for the clothes she had ironed for her customers.

Violet came toward him, thought better of it, and chose to sit in the chair near the foot of his bed.

"Brent."

"Is something bothering you, Mom?" Brent asked. Swinging his legs over the side of the bed, he sat up straight, searching her face for a clue.

"I have something I need to tell you." She hesitated again, unconsciously turning a ring on her finger.

"That's a classic start." Brent's tongue moved around the inside of his teeth as he prepared himself for what he knew was coming.

Violet bit her lip, still trying to work out how to tell her son her news.

Laying back on the bed, Brent laced his fingers behind his head and stared up at the ceiling. "So you met a nice guy and think you want to marry him?"

Her eyes grew wide with surprise. "Brent, I'm sorry. I meant to tell you before it got this far, but I haven't seen you long enough to get it out." She came over to the side of the bed. "It's my fault, not yours. I was afraid of hurting you. I should have made time to tell you."

Reaching up, Brent took her hand in one of his. His thumb turned the ring slightly, causing it to sparkle in the lamplight. "It's pretty, Mom. I'm happy for you."

She looked like she was going to cry but was fighting valiantly to hold it in.

Dragging himself from the bed again, Brent hugged her.

"Sorry, Brent. I didn't want to tell you like this." Violet slipped around the curtain to her room, and Brent heard her blow her nose.

"Why are you crying, Mom? You like him, don't you?" Brent sat on the edge of his mattress to wait.

"Of course I do." She reappeared, armed with a tissue box, and came to sit beside him.

She was right. It had been a long time since they had talked.

"But I want you to like him, too." Violet pulled out a tissue and fiddled with it in her lap. "I wanted you to meet him before, but you were so busy with your job and school. You hardly have time to breathe."

"I would have made time for you, Mom. You should know that. The school and work is all for you anyway."

She looked up at him. "You have changed a lot since school started, Brent. Sometimes I'm afraid you…" She stopped and turned away. "I've seen some of your dad's..." She stopped to rethink her words and then started again. "Some of the men who used to work with your dad have been seen around town. I saw one of them yesterday." When she looked up, her face was concerned. "They haven't talked to you, have they?"

Brent patted her hand gently. "Let's not worry about that, Mom. Tell me what the lucky guy is like."

"Brent, you promised me you would tell me the truth. You said not to ask if you are involved, and I'm not. I'm only asking if any of them have talked to you."

He shook his head. "No, no one from Dad's gang has approached me."

"Have they talked to you?" Violet pressed.

"Mom, seriously." Brent laughed nervously at her probing look.

"You don't have to be approached to be talked to, Brent," Violet pointed out. "Everyone has phones and gadgets these days."

He laughed, shaking his head. "Alright, you win. As far as I know, no one from Dad's gang has talked to me. Now can we move on?"

She nodded. "I needed to know."

"So I could tell." Brent was still smiling, "Now it's my turn to know. What's he like, Mom, this guy of yours?"

Eagerly, she turned so that she could face him. "He's the kindest, most considerate man I've ever met. And he's a Christian. Not one of those fake ones who are always preaching but doesn't live anything they say. He's real. Real Christians are different. The ones that follow Jesus care about other people even if they don't get anything back."

Dr. Nee came to mind, and Brent frowned. Was that why Dr. Nee was going out of his way to help Brent? "Was that a requirement?" he asked, cocking an eyebrow. "Him being a real Christian?"

She looked shy, "Yes, it was."

"That's new," he observed, not sure what to think.

"I've known about Jesus a long time. Even before you were born, Brent. When your dad was killed, well, I started thinking about things differently. I wanted to be sure I knew where I would go if something happened to me."

"So you found religion?"

"No, Brent. I found Jesus. All that time I only knew about Him." She saw him disengage mentally and put her hand on his arm. "Please hear me out, Brent." Her tone begged him to care.

Sighing, Brent met her eyes. "Sorry, Mom. Go on."

"I met this lady at Perkin's Cleaners," Violet told him. "She was so radiant and confident that I finally asked her about it. She said it was because she knew Jesus. We talked a long time that day. She actually knew Him, Brent. Not just about Him like me. I didn't see her for several days. And that whole time I couldn't stop thinking about what she had said. When we ran into each other again, we decided to start having lunch together on Tuesdays." Violet looked embarrassed. "You were packing a lunch anyway, so I didn't think you would mind."

"Just because dad died doesn't mean you can't have a life, Mom," Brent told her. "I'm glad you found something that makes you happy."

"It's more than that, Brent."

"I know, but this is a pretty big change." Pausing, Brent rephrased his thoughts. "Well, I'm not really interested. No offense."

Violet nodded and fell silent. "You have changed, too," she ventured after a moment. "You carry yourself differently and keep your room clean. You leave early to get places on time. What's going on?"

Brent shrugged. "I've got a teacher at school who thinks

I can be more than a bum of a teenager."

"He's right," Violet agreed.

Brent didn't answer. He thought of the night his dad was killed. A night that was etched vividly in his memory. That night he had used what Dr. Nee called his 'gift' to get his dad killed and land his mom in a cramped upstairs room that belonged to a cranky old lady.

"He's not pushy about religion," Violet added, seeing his frown. "I think you will like him."

"Who?"

"John," Violet laughed. "Brent Macintyre, are you paying attention to anything I'm saying?"

Grinning, Brent put his arm around her. "I'm sure I will like John." Brent tried to sound confident. His mind was sorting through the things that would need to be done. He would need to find another place to live, and wondered if apartment managers would rent to minors. "When is the big day?"

"Brent, look at me."

He obeyed, and she saw the lost look in her son's face.

"I'm not asking you to move out. I'm not in a rush to marry John and leave you. You are mine first. If you don't like him, or even if you have any cautions, I won't marry him. Not until you are sure it is what you want too. He's not replacing your dad. If we do get married, you don't have to take his name unless you want to."

"Thanks, Mom." Brent had not expected the emotions that tightened his throat and burned his eyes.

"Do you want to meet him?" she asked gently.

"He's been in the other room all this time, hasn't he?" Brent rose hotly.

"I would never do that to you, Brent." Violet smiled up at him.

He was almost a foot taller than her now. His recent

change in posture accented the difference.

"You forget what a kind mother I am," she told him with a laugh. Before he could protest, she hugged him around the middle.

Embarrassed, Brent slipped from her grasp and walked the length of the tiny room, rubbing his face.

"Alright, I've decided." He came to a stop in front of her.

"And?"

"And the answer is yes. I would like to meet this John of yours."

"How about Friday after school?" Violet asked, excitement shining in her eyes.

"This Friday? As in tomorrow?" Somehow Brent had expected a little more time to prepare. "Sure, we could do a late dinner so it won't interfere with your work at Ornstein's."

Turning away, Brent pretended to consult the calendar hanging on the wall. "I'm not going in tomorrow. Ornstein has decided to update the store's electric system since the power failure. He's closing tomorrow to have that put in." He steadied himself and turned to his mom with a smile. "Tomorrow would be perfect."

Violet smiled up at him. "You are a good man, Brent Macintyre."

CHAPTER 13

Glancing around, Brent knocked on the door of the modest little house. The address matched the one on the card Dr. Nee had given him. He stood tall and straight, glancing up and down the street for any sign of Dr. Nee.

Everything in him shouted that this was a bad idea, but still he waited.

The doorknob rattled, and Dr. Nee peered out. "Brent? Is everything okay?"

"Yeah, you said to come any time. Did you mean it?"

Dr. Nee chuckled and pushed open the door. The professor was wearing a neatly pressed pajama set beneath his robe. "Come in. Excuse me for not being company ready at 3 a.m."

Brent didn't even smile at his joke. Closing the door behind himself, Brent followed Dr. Nee through the brief entryway into a large, scarcely furnished main room. The house gave him the strange feeling that this was some kind of temporary residence for Dr. Nee.

"You approve?" Dr. Nee had a way of pointing out what people were thinking.

Brent shrugged. "What did you mean about training me in this supposed power you think I have?"

"Just that. Come here." Dr. Nee was untying the tie of his robe as he crossed to the far side of the main room.

Brent obeyed hesitantly.

There was a couch, a coffee table and an arm chair across

from the couch. An end table with a lamp stood beside the arm chair, and Brent guessed this was the professor's preferred seat.

"Put the tie from my robe over your eyes so you cannot see," Dr. Nee instructed once Brent joined him.

Now Brent was even more hesitant. "What for?"

"I want to show you what I meant," Dr. Nee assured him. "Don't worry. I won't hurt you, Brent. You are bigger than me. If I make you nervous, just push me away like a little, annoying dog."

Brent was surprised to find Dr. Nee so lively in the middle of the night. Especially since his face betrayed the fact that he had been awakened by Brent's knocking. Fighting his instincts, Brent put the tie over his eyes and knotted it behind his head.

"You cannot see?" Dr. Nee asked.

"Not a thing," Brent agreed.

"Cross the room back to the door and turn on the light switch that is on the left," Dr. Nee instructed.

Brent could hear by his voice that the professor was moving aside out of his way. Moving forward hesitantly, Brent started to feel his way across the room.

"The couch is right in front of you." Dr. Nee warned.

Brent changed course, feeling with his hands to avoid hitting his shin on the coffee table he knew was in front of the couch. Brent located the entryway wall. Now his hands ranged all over the wall, groping for the light switch. After a few seconds of searching, Brent clicked it on.

"Very good." Dr. Nee congratulated. "Now take the blindfold off."

Brent freed himself from the cloth strap and returned it to Dr. Nee.

"Now, go turn the light off and on without the blindfold." The professor was tying the strap back around his robe.

Brent looked amused as he walked across the little room to the switch and flipped it off then on.

"Which was a better use of your energy?" Dr. Nee asked.

"The second one, when I could see."

"Very good. Sit down there on the couch."

A frown flitted across Brent's face, but he moved to obey.

"You are using energy like you found the light switch with the blindfold," Dr. Nee went on once Brent was seated on the couch across from him. "Broad wide sweeps of it, instead of focused movements. I have read about another man, years ago, who had a power like yours. This is not a mystic power or a mind trick. He described it as having an extra arm you can reach out or withdraw."

"An electric arm?" Brent was smiling at the thought.

"It is 3 a.m., Brent," Dr. Nee informed him. "Stay focused."

Brent nodded, but the smile didn't fade.

"Your brain tells your arm to reach out and turn on the light. Am I correct?"

"You are the teacher," Brent agreed.

"Unlike others, Brent, your brain has the unique ability to tell electricity to reach out or pull in depending on how you want to use it."

It made sense so far.

"With the streetcar incident, you not only removed power from the streetcar, but you also removed it from the whole block of stores. That is incredible power."

"That's your theory," Brent interjected.

"We are way past that point, Brent. You are the only one who is pretending to be unsure." Dr. Nee waited, looking at his student steadily until Brent nodded his agreement. "Now, turn on this lamp here by me."

Brent started to rise, but Dr. Nee held up a hand to stop him.

"Do it with your electric arm," he clarified with a slight

smile.

Brent did not move.

Dr. Nee laid the EMF meter on the chair beside himself and waited.

"And if I don't have the power?" Brent asked after a long, awkward silence.

"Brent, I understand that trusting me enough to share your secret is a scary thing. However, if you are still pretending you don't have it, then why did you come tonight?" Dr. Nee leaned forward with his forearms on his knees.

Brent shifted in his seat. "I don't know." He fell silent, and Dr. Nee waited.

The clock softly ticked on the mantel, and an early bird tested out its song hesitantly outside.

"I didn't know where else to go," Brent finally blurted. "My mom is planning on getting married again. I've never even met the man. I want her to be happy because," he ran his fingers into his hair. Two and a half years had passed, and he had never told anyone what he was about to tell Dr. Nee. Taking a deep breath, he looked across at Dr. Nee. "Because it is my fault my dad was killed. It is my fault she has to live in poverty, alone."

"Not alone, she still has you."

Brent frowned. The professor seemed to have missed the point. "That's different. She lost the man she loved because of me."

"Would you like some tea?"

"What?" Brent blinked at the random question. "Um, sure. I guess so."

Dr. Nee rose and went into the adjoining kitchen. "Tell me about your dad," Dr. Nee prompted after he had filled the teapot with water.

Brent heard the professor set it onto the burner to heat. "He was a mastermind criminal." It was easier for Brent to talk about his dad with Dr. Nee busy in the other room. "As a kid, all I knew was that Dad was pretty high up at his job. That's why he was gone a lot. When he was home, if the job had gone well, he would be happy. He would promise me the world, and we would go and get special treats as a family. Mom would get a new dress. Sometimes, when he gave it to her, she would cry. That made my dad mad, and they would argue about where it came from." Brent paused, remembering. "Now I know why she cried." There was another long pause.

From the kitchen, Dr. Nee asked, "And if the job went badly?"

"When the jobs went bad, he was moody and not to be bothered. Sometimes men would come home with him who had been shot or stabbed. He always said that he found them by the road. I was dumb enough to believe him. I should have seen that it was just a lie to cover the truth. He was a criminal, and the men we were helping were wanted by the police."

"Would you say, near the end, that there were more good days or moody days with your dad?"

"Moody," Brent answered without hesitation.

"Would it be safe to say then," Dr. Nee offered. "that your mom lost the man she loved before the police killed him?"

Brent sat silently, considering the possibility.

"I do not think your mother blames you for what happened."

"You don't understand," Brent stood. He felt restless, but did not know what to do with himself.

"Would you like green tea or black?" Dr. Nee's question caught Brent off guard, pulling his focus from his restless thoughts.

"Whatever you are having is fine." Brent made his way into the kitchen where he leaned his shoulder against the door frame. "Mom doesn't blame me because she doesn't know what I did."

"Can you tell me what you did?" The water had started to steam. Dr. Nee poured it through a little mesh basket of dried leaves into a small metal tea pot waiting on the counter. He closed the lid and faced Brent.

"I turned on the power." It was the first time Brent had ever admitted having his power to anyone.

Instead of gasping or acting shocked, Dr. Nee merely nodded as he set out two cups on the counter. "And that led the police to your dad?"

"Yes, there was a police car passing right after…" Without wanting to, Brent saw the face of the man his father killed go from pleading, to horror, to death. Brent ran his hand over his face to erase the memory. "I had never used electricity like that before. I wanted it so bad, and it happened. My dad killed someone, Dr. Nee. In cold blood. I saw Dad kill him." The steam curled up silently from the spout of the tea pot as Brent struggled with the memory. "I don't think I will ever forget his face."

"There are some experiences that hurt so badly that they leave a scar inside. You did the right thing, Brent. You saved the life of the second bank clerk who was working that night." Dr. Nee carried the tray with the tea things back into the living room, and Brent followed him. "As painful as it is to say it, Roland Macintyre was a ruthless killer. Your stopping him saved more innocent people from being killed. And it saved your mom from being hurt in one of his rages at home."

"I never said he raged at home," Brent interjected with a frown.

"Did he?" Dr. Nee appeared to know the answer. Setting the tray down, he poured the tea into one of the cups and held it out to Brent.

Brent took a cup of the strong smelling tea and sat down in his place on the couch again. "Sometimes," he finally admitted.

Dr. Nee nodded sadly, "That kind of man often does. When do you meet your mother's friend?"

Brent welcomed the change in subject. "Tomorrow after school. Mr. Ornstein doesn't need me. He's getting the electric wiring replaced in his store. That was my fault too," Brent slouched back into the couch.

"You saved a young lady's life, Brent. I would think the electrical stability of a few buildings downtown is a good trade for a life, wouldn't you?"

Brent considered the new information in silence as he stared into his cup of tea.

"Is there anything else weighing on you?" Dr. Nee's voice was gentle.

Brent thought for a moment before shaking his head no.

"Good. Turn on that light, so I can see my tea."

Brent focused, and all three of the lamps around the room flickered to life.

"Not quite."

Brent tried again with the same result.

"You are still throwing power out, hoping it will hit your target."

"How else am I supposed to do it?" frustration surged through Brent.

Dr. Nee looked at him, his expression softening. "You don't want to be like him, do you?"

Clinching his teeth, Brent raised his chin defiantly.

"You feel the surge of emotions, and see your father in them."

"What do you know about it?"

Dr. Nee could tell that the teen was on the verge of leaving. If he was not careful, his influence on Brent would end tonight. "You are fighting valiantly, Brent. You have lived through hard times, and still you are choosing to be different.

You are not like him because you are choosing to respond differently. Don't give up." Dr. Nee saw him relax slightly. "And remember, you don't have to do it on your own. God can help you."

Looking amused, Brent sipped the hot tea. "Noted. I'm not here to talk about religion. Back to controlling my power. How do you suggest I go about honing it?"

Dr. Nee acknowledged his subject change with a slight bowing of his head. "First, take a deep breath. You are carrying a lot emotionally. For tonight, you are not using your power to impress someone or save someone's life. You are simply trying something new. Give it a try like a kid would kicking a ball for the first time, or trying to do a cartwheel. If it's not perfect tonight, no one will get hurt."

Brent took a slow breath and nodded.

"My advice would be to look at the lamp and turn it on."

The edge of Brent's mouth went up in an amused half smile. "Just like that, huh?"

Dr. Nee smiled back. "It seems reasonable to me."

Brent looked at the light. His eyes darted to Dr. Nee for a split second.

"You are focusing too hard." Dr. Nee rose. "Relax and take your time. While you do that, my tea is lonely and needs a friend. I will be right back."

"Your tea is lonely?" Brent turned in his seat to watch his teacher go back into the kitchen. Shaking his head, Brent looked at the light again. "Just turn it on," he told himself casually. Nothing happened. He could hear Dr. Nee in the kitchen rattling a package of some kind.

When he worked for Leno, Brent could power the generator alone. The heavy depression he had felt after finding out he was part of a counterfeit ring settled on him again. Brent glanced back toward the kitchen. Dr. Nee was not in sight. This man believed he could be great. His mom believed he could make something of himself. Why was it so hard for Brent to believe?

Maybe his strange power was the only out. Brent felt his breathing increase as the pressure of his future weighed on him.

The room lit up, including the lamp. Embarrassed, Brent pulled the power, and everything went dark.

"If you don't mind, I could use a little light in here," Dr. Nee's voice called.

"Sorry." Brent lit the house once more.

"Try putting your finger in the air between you and the lamp like you are going to turn on a light switch, and flip it on," Dr. Nee instructed.

"Just like a light switch, huh? You may not know this, but it takes energy to make energy," Brent informed him. Glancing back to make sure Dr. Nee wasn't watching, Brent put his index finger over the lamp and turned out the room.

"Not quite," came the voice from the kitchen.

"I used to be able to do this." Brent flopped back on the couch, letting the room go back to its normal state. "I could have done it in my sleep. I just…" He looked miserably up at the lamp. The light bulb lit up, illuminating the lampshade, and Brent stared in amazement. Looking toward the kitchen Brent saw Dr. Nee standing in the doorway with a pleased smile.

"I did it! Did you see that?"

"It was done very well."

The small complement sank deep, and Brent wished he could hang onto that feeling. He could remember very few times when his dad had been pleased with him, or with something he had done.

Dr. Nee brought a bowl of shortbread cookies to the coffee table and set it down. "Your tea might be lonely too."

Brent grinned. He took a cookie and turned on another

lamp. A lamp near his target had flickered, but only the one stayed on. Sitting back in the couch, Brent popped the cookie into his mouth and turned the lights on around the room in a clockwise circle and then off again the same way. His eyes were shining with excitement when he looked back at Dr. Nee.

"You are doing very well," the older man observed. He sipped his tea. "Now I think it is time to try to get a little sleep before tomorrow is upon us."

Brent helped carry the dishes to the sink, turning on and off lights all around the room.

"Thank you, Dr. Nee. I thought I had lost my gift." Embarrassed, Brent quickly added, "That's what you call it, anyway. Now I've got it again."

Instead of congratulating him, Dr. Nee looked him in the eyes, his face serious. "You must remember, Brent. Your gift is precious. Guard it carefully, and only use it for good."

"I will," Brent promised. The light stayed on and steady.

"I will drive you home."

Brent looked at the clock. It was 4:30. "That's okay, I don't mind walking."

"No, Brent, let me drive you. It is dangerous here at night. I will only be a minute." He crossed the room, passing one of the two closed doors, and disappeared inside what Brent assumed was the man's bedroom.

While he was changing, Brent slipped from the house into the night.

CHAPTER 14

The moon was low enough now for the buildings to block its light, and there was no sign yet of the sun. Brent walked with his head up, scanning the street as he went. Dr. Nee was right. It was not the safest part of town, but it was the quickest way home. Cutting across the parking lot of a shopping center, Brent glanced into the shops of the closed businesses as he passed. There was an eerie glow inside each from random security lights or technology that had been left on. Brent was wondering how the massage place stayed in business when a movement caught his eye. Thick square pillars were spaced evenly along the storefronts to hold up the roof of the covered walkway. The movement he had seen was down by the last pillar. There, the black shadow of the pillar stretched out to merge with the thick darkness cast by the edge of the building.

For an instant, Brent considered trying to light the burnt out security light he knew was right around the corner of the building. He knew he could do it now. The time with Dr. Nee had shown Brent that he had not lost his power. He had allowed fear to disable him and keep him from really trying.

The silhouette of a man was visible in the shadows for an instant. Stopping, Brent considered his options. He could go around, but it would take much longer. Deciding to press through, he moved forward again. Unconsciously, Brent's path veered out away from the pillars and the shadows they cast.

"Macintyre."

Brent froze. His eyes were on the last pillar where he had seen the shadow of a man.

Remembering His mom's warning about having seen Roland Macintyre's men in town, Brent stepped away before calling back. "What do you want?"

"I've got something that's important to you." It was hissed from the dark shadows.

"Who are you?" Brent looked around. There was no sign of anyone else, but then, he couldn't see this guy either. The dim lights from the storefronts would give Brent enough light to see if anyone came at him.

"Who I am doesn't matter," the stranger said mysteriously. "Your dad hid something at Second Trust Bank that he doesn't want anyone to know about."

Brent frowned, keeping his distance. "If he doesn't want anyone to know, why are you telling me?"

"Get over here before someone sees you." The speaker sounded annoyed.

"Nothing doing. If you want to have a creepy whisper talk in the middle of the night, you will have to come out to me," Brent challenged.

"You are a foolish kid. You don't know what you are messing with."

Brent thought of a good return insult, but swallowed it when he remembered Dr. Nee's challenge not to insult or tear down.

"Well?" The stranger was growing impatient.

"Well, what?" Throughout the conversation, Brent had been slowly moving to his right lining himself up with the side of the building. He could see the dim outline of the man now. He was standing in the shadow cast by the pillar and looked around often as if he were afraid. Brent located the powerless security light up on the wall and faced the man.

Here he could turn on the light if needed. "Why do I care if you have a secret about my dad? He's dead."

"He was adamant that no one knew about this."

Brent crossed his arms. "So don't tell me."

"Look, I need money." The voice sounded older than Brent, yet still young and desperate. "Your dad paid me to keep quiet about this for ten years. Now, the bank is going to open the box if no one claims it."

Curiosity peaked, Brent asked, "What's in it?"

"I told you. He doesn't want anyone to know."

"Right, I forgot." Brent dropped his arms, hooking his thumbs into his pockets. "Let me get this straight. You want me to pay you to keep my dad's box a secret?"

"Yes."

"No, thanks." Brent started walking.

"Wait. If you don't pay me, I'll go to the other side," he threatened.

"Go ahead." Brent could imagine the man's shocked expression. "I don't have money to pay you. The police already liquidated his assets. Besides, my dad was a criminal, and everyone already knows it. So one more box of evidence against him isn't going to change anything."

"You are making a really dumb choice."

"Dumb choices are my specialty," Brent responded. "My answer is 'no.'"

Brent saw the man's shadow moving. The man was pulling something from his pocket. Fear surged through Brent. Pivoting, he ran across the parking lot away from the stranger. With a quick glance in both directions, Brent sprinted across the street.

Brent had been running regularly since his flight from Jimmy on the first day of school. That day, he had been lucky to get away, but Brent knew that luck didn't last.

Alternating lefts and rights, Brent zigzagged a few more

blocks before slowing down to check his surroundings. There was no evidence he had been followed. Relief washed over him, and he walked on, glancing around as he went to ensure he was not being followed.

When he reached Main Street, Brent looked up and down the well-lit road. He was trying to decide if it was safe to go home when a car pulled up to the curb.

Brent stepped away instinctively and then relaxed. It was Dr. Nee.

"That was unwise, Brent. You should have waited for me," Dr. Nee scolded through the open window. He cocked his head to the passenger seat. "I'm glad you are okay. Get in."

Brent obeyed without a word.

"You got the shirt?" Brent asked, glancing around the empty stair well. His late night had made paying attention in class very difficult.

Jimmy smiled, enjoying seeing Brent in need. "I said I would, didn't I? Let's see the cash."

Brent dug into his pocket and pulled out the crumpled bill. "Here's five. Let me see what you have."

"Sorry, Brent, the prices went up last night. These are quality shirts we are talking about."

For an instant, a deadly glare crossed Brent's features. It was gone as quickly as it came, but Jimmy had seen the wave of anger on his classmate's face, and it scared him.

"I'm kidding, Brent." He backtracked quickly to save his honor. "Don't take life so seriously."

Brent relaxed a little, his attention moving to the backpack Jimmy was sliding from his back.

"I brought you three options: blue, gray, and green." Jimmy pulled three polos out of his bag. Unceremoniously flopping each onto the rail of the stair to the basement, Jimmy crossed his arms and waited. They were not supposed to be down there, but Brent had no desire to let the other kids know he was buying shirts off Jimmy to meet his potential step dad.

"I'll take the green. You wear the others too often. Everyone will know I got them from you." Brent eyed his classmate suspiciously. "Although, I have the feeling that news of this sale will be all over the school by tomorrow morning."

"The shirt is five bucks. The privacy? That will cost you more." Tossing the green polo to Brent, Jimmy shoved the others back into his bag.

Brent held out the five, "Thanks, man."

Plucking the bill from Brent's hand, he shoved it into his pocket. "Still not friends, got it?" Jimmy told Brent seriously. "This is purely business." He would have enjoyed a friendship with Brent, but he had too much built up to wreck it now.

"You got it." Brent held the shirt up and looked it over. "This will have to do."

"Chill, it will fit great. You and I don't have much in common, but we are roughly the same size."

"If you say so." Brent folded the shirt and slid it into his backpack.

"One more thing."

Brent waited, expecting the worst.

"You are doing more than making your bed now. What else did he put you up to?" Jimmy smirked, "Besides the sissy posture."

"Who? Dr. Nee?" Brent was having trouble reading Jimmy.

"Who else?"

"You haven't finished your month of making your bed." Brent pointed out.

Jimmy looked annoyed. "Neither have you, Hot Shot. And you never mentioned the bed thing came with cleaning your room."

Brent smiled, enjoying the common ground. "You, too, huh?"

"So the stiff back was Monday's gig. What else are you doing with him? Henry said he's seen you leave Nee's class late a couple of times. What are you doing there?"

"You just now heard about that?" Brent shook his head. "You gotta get yourself a better source of information. We've been meeting every other Monday since the start of school."

"Yeah?"

"He's tutoring me in electronics." Brent grinned at Jimmy's disappointed expression.

"You need it."

"Yeah, and you," Brent caught himself. No insults. "You probably don't need extra help," he finished lamely.

Jimmy eyed him suspiciously. "You're pretty weird. You know that, right?"

"That's one thing I'm not forgetting any time soon." Brent shouldered his backpack. "You have always been gracious enough to keep that in my face."

"So what else is there?" Jimmy was nonchalantly blocking the stair door that led out of the restricted zone.

"Good posture and keeping my words in check." Brent saw Jimmy's confused look. "Dr. Nee said, no insults on purpose. Period."

"That's for losers." Jimmy slung his backpack onto his back, pulled the door open, and headed to class without looking back.

CHAPTER 15

When Brent came home from school that afternoon, their little table had been moved to the center of their living room so three chairs could fit comfortably around it. Brent wondered briefly where the third chair had come from. A man stood beside his mom in the kitchen area holding a plate for her as she transferred the grilled chicken from the griddle. He was as tall as Brent, with short, wavy, strawberry-blonde hair. He turned to see who had entered and seemed genuinely happy to see Brent. John was dressed professionally, button up shirt, slacks, and a tie. Brent was tempted to look around for the sports coat he knew John must have shed to help with lunch. Despite his polished appearance, John had kind eyes and a ready smile.

"Hi Brent!" He looked for a place to put down the plate and settled on the table. Once that was done, he offered his hand. "I'm John Starclish."

Brent shook his hand, not missing the happy smile on his mom's face. Because John's back was now to Violet, Brent was the only one who saw her tug on the shoulder of her day dress, point at the neat polo Brent was wearing, and give him a thumbs up. Acknowledging her pleasure with his eyes, Brent turned his attention back to John. John glanced from Brent to Violet, aware he had missed something. When Violet turned back to the stove, John let it go without pushing to be included.

"I am really glad to get to meet you, Brent," John told him, moving a bowl from the counter to the table. "I feel like I know you a little from all the stories your mom tells," John caught himself with an embarrassed laugh. "That was an awkward thing to say, wasn't it? 'Hi, Brent, your mom tells me stories about you, but you don't know me at all.'" He smiled at Brent. "Sorry. Let me try again."

"It's okay. I know what you were trying to say." Brent appreciated John's effort to reach out. "So, what do you do for work, Mr. Starclish?"

"Please, call me John."

Brent nodded, not bothering to re-ask the question.

"I'm a contractor. I do work for the city." John took the bag of chips Violet handed him and filled the bowl on the table. "I have worked as an architect as well as an engineer, so that gives me a little more job security to have experience in multiple fields. My current assignment is to work on the upgrades for the new street car downtown." He laughed, "Actually, we need to get it running again before we can upgrade it. I'm sure you heard about the accident." He stopped and looked at Brent, "Wait, your mom told me you work at Ornstein's after school. Were you there when the accident happened?"

"What accident?" Violet asked, coming over to the table with a bowl of steamed vegetables. "I hadn't heard about any accident."

Brent did not miss the meaningful look his mom gave him. He had not told her about the incident with the streetcar and the truck. In fact, he had not told her about last night's strange meeting either.

"A truck stopped on the track of the streetcar," John had picked up on the tension he had caused and was working fast to clear it up. "It was a miracle no one got hurt." He made an apologetic face at Brent across the table. Brent shrugged and used the tongs to take a piece of chicken from the plate in the middle of the table. His mom cleared her throat and discreetly folded her hands.

Without looking at John, Brent returned the empty tongs to the serving plate and dropped his hands into his lap.

"Do you mind if I thank God for His provision?" John asked, looking from Violet to Brent.

Shaking his head no, Brent kept his eyes on his plate until John was done praying.

"Amen," Violet echoed softly, glancing at Brent who sat waiting in case there were other rituals that had been added to the mealtime routine. "Brent, why didn't you tell me?" his mom asked, putting a hand on his arm. "Was anyone hurt?"

Brent and John looked at each other. She had not been listening well.

"No, Mom. No one was hurt in the accident," Brent answered quickly. "It happened a couple of days ago. That's why I have today off. The power went out in that area, so Ornstein's had to close to get some things repaired."

"Well, tell me what happened." Violet was passing the serving plates around so everyone got some of each dish.

"A girl about my age, maybe a little older, was in a truck on the streetcar's track. There was this weird power outage surge thing, and the streetcar came screeching to a halt."

"Did it hit her?" Violet's attention was on the bowl of rice she was serving from.

"It bumped the girl's door, but she wasn't hurt by it." Brent received the bowl of veggies that John offered him without stopping his account. "The ambulance team took her to the hospital just to be safe. It was weird to see a girl so close to my age going through something like that. Made life seem delicate somehow." Brent caught himself, remembering their guest. "The TV at Ornstein's has been out, so I didn't get to see what happened to her."

"John has a television. Did you see what happened to the teen in the truck?" Violet asked him eagerly, grateful for a flowing conversation.

John looked up, searching his memory. "If I remember right, she was released. There was something about a seizure, but I don't remember if it was before or after the accident."

"Before," Brent inserted, around his mouthful of food. He swallowed before adding, "That's why the guy stopped in such a crazy spot. He was trying to get help."

"Did you see it all happen?" John asked with interest. He put a piece of chicken on his plate before passing the dish on to Violet.

"Yeah, I went out after the girl's dad came into Ornstein's to ask for help."

"How dreadful!" Shaking her head, Violet returned the plate to the middle of the table. "I'm so glad the driver got it to stop in time."

"The driver said in an interview afterwards that if the power hadn't gone out, he wouldn't have been able to stop it in time." John was enjoying relaying the story. "That power outage caused the emergency breaks to engage."

"Well, couldn't he see the truck on the track?" Violet asked.

"He had just come around the corner and the traffic was heavy that day. By the time he realized that no one was inside, he didn't have time to stop. Some people said it was a miracle." John paused and looked at Brent. "You were there. What's your opinion?"

"I don't know what to think," Brent answered honestly. He was grateful John did not press the question.

The meal went on, and conversation turned to something they had obviously discussed before. Brent phased out. His mind went to Dr. Nee. He was different from all the other teachers Brent had before. He was puzzling about this when John's voice broke through his thoughts.

"The pie is not ready. Do you want to go on a quick walk while we wait?"

Brent looked up to see them both looking at him. "Wouldn't you rather walk with Mom?" he asked dumbly.

John's ready smile appeared again. "I do love walking with her, but I'd like a chance to get to talk to you some, too."

Brent shot a pleading look at his mom, but her only response was a slight head tilt toward the door.

"You guys go ahead," Violet told them. "I'll put the food away." She raised a hand when Brent started to offer to help. "I'll save the dishes for when you get back."

Defeated, Brent got his jacket and followed John Starclish to the door.

Out of habit, Brent checked for Mrs. Cornshaw before hurrying out the back door.

"What do you know that I don't know?" John asked once they were clear of the house.

Brent couldn't help smiling. He was pleased by John's ability to adapt. The successful, well-dressed man had ducked and darted along with Brent, without needing to know why before he followed Brent's lead.

"Mrs. Cornshaw likes to talk." Glancing back at the house, Brent turned on the sidewalk to go up the road in the opposite direction of his school and his more traveled routes. He didn't want to be pestered about John at school. "If she catches you, there's always an errand to be run."

John laughed, "My sister was like that. As soon as you got up, you were free game. I used to plan my escape and try to get out of the room before she caught me."

"Was? Did something happen to her?" Brent was expecting a good sob story about the tragic death of John's sister.

"Marriage happened to her." John was enjoying himself, looking around with interest at the scenic neighborhood. "She's mellowed out some over the years," he continued. "Now, she's got herself a husband. He's a good guy, and they get along well."

A man stepped out from behind a parked van, and Brent recoiled without thinking. Adrenaline surged through him.

"Excuse me," the man said politely and continued on to his mailbox.

Taking a second to steady himself, Brent attempted to laugh it off. "Didn't see him coming."

John was quiet as they resumed their walk.

It was a short walk to the bridge that went over the train tracks. Out of habit, Brent stopped at the top to look out over the scenery.

"You okay?" John asked. "You kind of froze up back there."

"I'm fine. He just surprised me."

John was still looking at him quizzically.

"What did you want to talk about?" Brent asked without taking his eyes from the place where the train tracks disappeared around a bend. "Probably not your sister and Mrs. Cornshaw." Brent shot him a quick grin, deftly changing the subject.

John shook his head. "No." He paused, looking out over the scenery as he searched for the right words. "Brent, I love your Mom. I have for as long as I have known her."

"Not very long then," Brent couldn't help adding.

"Longer than you might think. We met casually at Perkin's Cleaners last year. We have talked off and on since then. I knew I loved her, but I also knew your family had been through a lot, and I didn't want to push her into a relationship she was not ready for. I want her to be happy and well cared for. As a fifteen-year-old, you have done a great job of taking care of her. Violet, I mean, your mom, told me about you getting the extra job and how she would be back at the other apartment if it weren't for you sharing your salary. I want you to know that I'm not trying to replace you. No one can. But I have enjoyed getting to know your mom, and I would be honored if you would let me get to know you too."

Brent nodded. "You are right. My mom has been through a lot. I don't want her to get hurt again."

Turning to face Brent, John leaned his arm on the rail of the bridge. "You have my word that I will never purposefully hurt her."

"What do you do when you get mad?" Brent's gaze was direct and searching.

John hesitated, caught off guard by the intensity of the young man beside him. His eyes searched upward as if sorting through memories. "I usually get quiet. I like to get away and pray. Kind of cool off before I say something I'll regret."

"Have you always done that?" Brent was rewarded with a half-smile.

"No." John's eyes got a far-away look. "Before I met Jesus, I struggled a lot with anger. My mom died when I was young, and my dad remarried." He glanced over at Brent. "That's where I got my sister." John's gaze drifted out to the horizon. "The new lady, my dad's second wife, she didn't care for me. I couldn't do anything right. I let it get under my skin and said a lot of things I regretted. I don't know if you have hit this yet, Brent, but there's a place where trying isn't enough. All your efforts get you nowhere. You need someone to give you a hand up and take you to the next level or you will lose hope and slip all the way back into the man you never wanted to become."

Brent remembered his dad's cruel expression and shuddered.

John noticed and clapped Brent on the shoulder. "Sorry, Brent. It's chilly up here, and I'm just jabbering away. Should we head back?"

Brent nodded.

They had walked for several minutes when Brent ventured his question. "So, who gave you a hand up?"

John's eyes shone with gratitude. "Jesus."

Brent waited, but John did not go on. Instead, he walked on, looking pleased.

"How'd He do it?" Brent finally asked.

"I was a little older than you are. By then, it had been about five years since my dad remarried. I was a good-looking teen with good grades, nice clothes, and the works. Everything looked good on the outside, but inside I was so empty and hopeless. I was fed up with the trying and failing. One day, a guy at school gave me this little folded paper that told about the Ten Commandments and Jesus. I checked in at home and found a quiet place where I could be alone. I must have read that paper a dozen or so times. I knew I had broken God's commands and deserved to be separated from Him. The thing that gave me trouble was the fact that God would send Jesus as payment for my sins when I didn't want anything to do with Him. I struggled to think of what to say to Someone so incredible.

I mulled it over for the rest of the day. That night, I couldn't sleep. I knew I was separated from God. And, I knew that if I wasn't forgiven, I'd be separated from God forever. God, the source of everything good and loving. Because I couldn't sleep, I finally I rolled out of bed, knelt on the floor, and I told Jesus how I'd failed. I asked Him to forgive me, and I gave Him permission to call the shots. He filled me from the inside, Brent." John was smiling now. "I had hope. I had tried to conquer my anger more times than I could count. When I gave it to Jesus that night, that anger totally lost its power. Was I tempted still? Of course, but Jesus gave me the power and desire to say no. The more I did it, the easier it became to choose to obey God instead of my emotions. I started meeting with some guys who already knew Him, and they helped me stay on track with what Jesus was doing in me. I can't ever thank Him enough."

Brent didn't respond.

"Anything else you want to know?" John asked cheerily as they approached the house.

"Not that I can think of." The conversation about Jesus had made Brent uncomfortable. He was like John had been. On the outside everything was going well, but no matter how hard Brent tried, he always slipped back. Even though he wasn't sure what all ten of God's commandments were, Brent knew in his heart that he, too, was separated from God. He knew he needed help, but he was determined to try harder and make it work.

"Alright then," John turned up Mrs. Cornshaw's driveway, unaware of Brent's inner struggle. "Let's go have some pie!"

CHAPTER 16

"Hey Mom, do you need any help?"

Violet looked up at her son with a concerned frown. "It is Saturday, Brent. What are you up to?"

"Sometimes I help you on Saturdays," Brent pointed out. Coming over to where she sat by the window, Brent lay flat on his back near her chair like he used to do when he was a little boy.

Laughing, Violet set down the shirt she was mending and looked down at him. "What do you need, Brent?"

He tried to look hurt, but could tell by Violet's face that she was not buying it. "I had a question about Dad."

The amusement faded from her face, and she waited.

"Did he have any kind of safety deposit box here from maybe ten years ago?"

"Ten years ago?" She shook her head, going back to her mending. "No, Brent. Back then we lived five or six hours from here. Your dad wouldn't have had any reason to put anything in a bank so far away."

"Why do you ask?" Violet probed when he did not respond. Even though Brent was staring up at the ceiling, he could feel her eyes on him.

Brent shrugged, his fingers toying with the smooth wood leg of her chair. "Just wondering."

She tried unsuccessfully to read his thoughtful expression. "Do you remember the house on Cherry Street?" Tying off her thread, she snipped it with the tiny scissors she kept in her pocket. "It had a big tree out front. You and I hung a swing out there one summer."

"I remember bits and pieces." Brent put his hands behind his head. "Like the piano, and the broken shovel that always leaned against the wall outside the back door."

She smiled as she folded the shirt she had mended and placed it into her finished basket. Taking up the next shirt, she spread it on her lap before reaching down for her jar of buttons. "We lived there for almost five years. You were just learning to walk when we moved in, and that was where you had your sixth birthday." A memory clouded her face, and Brent waited, wondering what she was thinking. A moment later, she caught herself and smiled down at Brent. "It is hard to imagine that almost ten years has passed since you turned six." She selected a white button from her jar and compared it to the original shirt button.

"Mom, you thought of something just a minute ago. Something sad. What was it?"

She looked uncomfortable, "I don't know if I have the right button for this shirt."

"That's not what you thought about, Mom," Brent countered. "It was something you thought of right after you mentioned me turning six."

"Something happened soon after that." The haunted look was back in her eyes. "Trust me, Brent. It is a memory you do not want to have."

"You will tell me if I need to know?" he asked seriously.

She smiled gratefully and nodded. "Yes. And here's the button I needed." She replaced the jar lid and set it on the floor again. "Speaking of birthdays, you turn sixteen soon? What do you want for your birthday? We could do a cake and maybe have a few friends over."

"Friends like John?" Brent grinned. Pushing himself up

onto his elbow, he exaggerated a wink at her.

She tried to suppress her smile. "I won't lie John did come to mind."

"Naturally." He enjoyed seeing his mom so happy. "I think that would be fun."

This time, Violet made no effort to hide her pleasure. "We could invite a few of your friends too."

"That's okay. I'm not really wild about big parties. Just you and John is good with me."

She paused her sewing to look at him. "How is it at school, Brent?"

Brent flopped onto his back again, so he would not have to meet her searching gaze.

Her needle moved again with swift, careful movements. "You don't talk about anyone at school, so sometimes I wonder."

"Mom, you found a guy you wanted to marry this year without me knowing about it." His mouth smiled, but his eyes did not. "We haven't really hung out much this year. Besides, there's nothing to talk about. The work is harder, and the classmates are trying to figure out life. Pretty boring. But," he looked up at her with anticipation. "I did think of something I want for my birthday."

"And?"

"I want a used car frame, so I can build my own car."

Violet glanced at him to see if he was joking. "Wouldn't you like a running car instead?"

"No, I'm happy with a frame. I have a custom design in mind." Brent's dream of having a car he could control with electricity was never far from his mind. What he was learning about electricity with Dr. Nee only solidified the fact that it was a possibility. He had even toyed with the idea of designing some kind of remote, so he could drive it without being inside.

Violet saw the dreamy look in her son's eyes and smiled

to herself. The counterfeit scandal had taken away Brent's will to succeed. This was the first time she had seen him dream of the future in years. "I'm not making any promises, but I'll see what I can do."

"What do you think of this battery, Brent?" Dr. Nee set it on the work table beside Brent.

It was Monday night, and Brent was scanning an electronics textbook for the answer to a question on the page before him. Grateful for a distraction, Brent slid the book out of the way and picked up the battery.

"I've made three, each with a different feature," Dr. Nee informed him.

"Looks okay on the outside," Brent responded, turning the square battery over in his hands. It was about the size of a loaf of bread "What's it for?"

"There are countries that do not have power that will find this battery quite useful."

"What are they going to do with them?" Brent tried to hide his skepticism, but his voice betrayed him. Even though they had been spending an evening a week together for some time, Brent was just now learning about Dr. Nee's inventions.

"You still do not trust me." Dr. Nee shook his head sadly when Brent could not think of a fitting response. "There is a line of wheelchairs that I am developing for people in poor countries who are disabled. They cannot get to school or work without a wheelchair. The chair must be able to cross uneven terrain for it to be of any use to them, but, as you know, this consumes more power. I would like to test these new batteries and see which would power the chair the longest."

Chewing his lip thoughtfully, Brent considered the information.

"I feel that when I win your trust, I will have won a great thing," he told Brent seriously.

Crossing the small spare room that had been converted into a workroom, Dr. Nee stooped and pulled a three ring binder from the book case. He opened it and flipped through the pages until he found what he was looking for.

"There you are, my doubting friend." Returning to Brent, he laid the binder open on the worktable. Brent leaned over to see a slew of 4x6 pictures that had been taped to a paper and slid inside a page protector. The pictures were of wheelchairs of all shapes and sizes. Some were only partially assembled.

Eyeing his professor with new respect, Brent turned the page to reveal more designs. "You designed all these?"

"Those were my earlier models, and though they will be helpful for specific needs, they do not function well for this particular project." Turning the page back, Dr. Nee tapped a picture. "These are more fitted for the terrain."

Smiling, Brent added power to the battery he still held. "There you go!" He handed it to Dr. Nee. "I'm excited to see you drive to school in one of those all-terrain wheel chairs for the next couple of months to test it out."

Laughing, Dr. Nee set the other batteries on the table. Each was labeled clearly. "I am sorry to say you will be disappointed, Brent. I will not be changing my mode of transportation. However, we may still have some fun with them. I'm planning a wheelchair derby for fall break. A bunch of teenagers will give the batteries a thorough test."

Brent watched Dr. Nee return the binder to its place, wondering what other projects his teacher was involved in. Whatever they were, Brent was sure he wanted to be involved.

———

Brent was on his way home, lost in thought, when someone grabbed him. He was jerked off balance, and before he could react, Brent found himself being shoved face first against the rough brick wall of the alley he'd been passing. Strong hands gripped Brent's wrists, twisting them up against his back. "I've been looking for you, Macintyre," a rasping male voice informed Brent.

Cold fear swept over Brent. The sunlight streaming into the dim alley seemed out of place as he struggled against his captor. He squirmed, his cheek scraping against the rough wall, but could not free himself from the vice-like grip of his captor. Brent stood tense, biding his time. "Look, I'm a different Macintyre. You got me mixed up with my dad."

"I don't think so. I know who you are, Brent Macintyre."

Another chill went down Brent's spine. He had heard the rasping voice before.

"Your dad quit suddenly, and it seems he was holding out on me."

"He was killed by the cops. He didn't quit on you," Brent blurted desperately.

"I just encountered a snitch who said your dad had something that belongs to me." He pushed harder against Brent. "I paid a pretty penny for the information, and I want it back."

"The penny?" Brent was struggling to keep up.

The force against him increased. "Your Dad hid something that belongs to me, and I want it back." His captor repeated angrily.

Brent turned slightly to relieve the pressure. Sweat ran into his eyes, and his mom came to mind. Was this man what she had thought of when they were talking about the past? Did he have something to do with the bad memory that she did not want to share? Something about him tugged at a lost memory in Brent's mind.

"Listen, and listen well," the voice continued. "Your dad

has a deposit box in the bank. Get it and bring it to me."

"Oh, so that guy sold it to you?" The pieces were coming together. This rasping stranger had gotten his information from the skittish man Brent had seen slinking in the shadows.

"So you know about it?" The pressure released slightly.

"No. I have no idea what he was talking about. Only that he had some information he wanted to sell. I don't know anything about a deposit box. The police took all the money dad had after he was killed."

"You think you can get out of this that easily?" The man pressed against him, pushing the right side of Brent's face into the rough surface of the bricks. The stranger was on Brent's right, but the wall made it impossible for Brent to turn his head to see who it was.

"That's all I know. I promise. We didn't even live here ten years ago," Brent's fear was increasing, releasing a flow of information that confirmed his story.

"No need to panic. Yet," the stranger rasped ominously. "The deposit box is at the bank. That's why I need you, Little Macintyre. You go in, prove to the bank that you have a right to that box, and bring it to me. It's a quick job. And if you do it well, it will take care of the money problems you have been having. If you squeal, your dear mother will take the hit."

"Look, I don't know anything about the box. Mom didn't know about it either. I asked her after the guy stopped me. She didn't think Dad had anything here. Leave her out of this." Brent winced against the pressure on his arms which had been steadily increasing. "What if the box doesn't exist? Someone could be leading you on. You know, sending you off on a wild chase to get you out of their hair."

His suggestion was met by a rasping laugh. The stranger loosened his grip again, giving Brent room to catch his breath.

"Desperate people do desperate things, Little Macintyre. Seems you weren't willing to pay. Now it will cost you. Besides, what would Roland say if he knew his wife was living in a rundown apartment instead of the neat little house he bought you? It's a quick job, Brent. There's nothing illegal about getting a bank box that belongs to your father. What do you say?"

"No." Brent struggled against the stranger, managing to move enough to determine there were two men holding him. He gasped in pain as they shoved him into the wall again.

"You are making a big mistake. You have ten days to get that box, Brent. After that, we will pay a little visit to your mom. Keep in mind, if the police learn about the box before I get it, your mom will be the first to pay."

Brent heard the unmistakable metallic click of a gun being cocked.

"Keep up against that wall and count to ten real slow," a second voice instructed. "Understand?"

"Yeah." Brent waited. This time, the gun was only for show. If they had intended to hurt him, they would have had a bullet in the chamber before they jumped him. He wondered how long they had been waiting. Five days had passed since his strange night meeting with the snitch.

Whoever was holding his wrists let go, and Brent started counting softly. He could hear their swift footsteps. Increasing the speed of his counting, Brent reached ten in half the time needed. Turning, he caught a glimpse of someone disappearing around the corner. He would not be able to give a description from what he had seen, but Brent had no desire to follow and get a better look. He was clearly outnumbered. The only thing he wanted was to get away from them.

Jogging through the streets toward home, Brent stopped suddenly. If he went home, he would be leading them straight to his mom. The raspy one had mentioned an apartment which meant that there was a slim chance that they didn't actually know where to find his mom.

Brent would keep it that way as long as he could.

CHAPTER 17

Mrs. Gram rapped on her desk, calling the class to order. "Brent Macintyre, your test time is gone, and you have wasted it completely." She strode to his desk and snatched his blank test paper. Holding it up for the class to see, she stared at him sternly. "This type of behavior will not be tolerated."

Brent blinked up at her in surprise. "I'm sorry, Mrs. Gram."

She had expected a quip or a joke, but not the soft apology she received. It left her unsure of how to proceed.

"Brent, what happened to your face? Have you been fighting?"

Brent's hand moved to cover the right side of his face, and he leaned on it casually. He had hoped the scrapes from his encounter would fade overnight, but they had not. "No, Ma'am." Brent was keenly aware of the other students who were watching.

"I think you had better go and see Principal Bond. I don't know what is going on, but you are not yourself today, and it is affecting your class work."

"I let my mind wander. I'll do better if you give me another chance."

She studied him for a moment. "You will return to my class after school and retake this test."

"Yes, Ma'am."

Again, Mrs. Gram was puzzled by his quiet response.

"I hear we are going to have a big celebration for your birthday." John slid into the booth across from Brent.

"Yeah, that's what mom said," Brent agreed halfheartedly. He wished he had not agreed to meet with John over lunch. He had one hour and could have gone to the bank to ask about the deposit box.

Frowning thoughtfully, John considered the somber, straight backed teen across from him. The scratches on Brent's face had turned red over the course of the day, making them stand out even more.

The elderly waitress came to their table, and John ordered first. "Get whatever you want, Brent. My treat."

Brent stared at the table top, chewing his lip pensively.

"He'll have what I'm having," John told the waitress.

She left to deliver their order to the cook.

Several minutes passed before Brent seemed to remember where he was. "Sorry." He looked around. "Did the waitress already come?" Shifting in his seat, Brent looked at the clock on the wall above the cash register. Time seemed to have stopped. "I have class at one and can't be late."

"She already took our orders. And your school is across the street. I think forty-five minutes is plenty of time to cross."

"Oh, yeah. Right. Sorry." Frowning, Brent looked at John for the first time. "Did I order?"

"Sort of," John grinned. "You were kind of out of it."

"Yeah, I have a lot on my mind. School and stuff," Brent added quickly.

"I could be wrong, but I'm guessing the "and stuff" is more of the problem today."

"Yeah."

John leaned back in the booth, looking at Brent with an amused expression.

"What?" Brent asked, checking his shirt to see if he had something on it.

"I was just thinking what a nice conversation we are going to have over lunch. I'll ask questions, and you'll say, 'yeah,' to everything."

"Maybe we should reschedule this I'm not really in a talkative mood."

"You would leave me to eat two of these heart stopping, greasy cheese burgers alone?" John tried to look hurt. "I thought you didn't mind me being around."

A silent laugh eased Brent's tense face. "Greasy? People travel miles to eat here. Isn't that right, Dina?" Brent smiled up at the waitress as she set his food in front of him. She placed the other greasy plate in front of John with an annoyed thump.

John's face reminded Brent of a naughty child who had been caught. Once Dina had left them, Brent leaned forward and said in a low voice. "You probably shouldn't have said that with Dina right there. Her dad started this restaurant."

"Ouch. I'm striking out on this one." John picked up the burger. The bun was damp. He pointed at it with an "I told you so" look.

Brent shook his head, amused. "Maybe you had better pray before you eat it."

It was John's turn to laugh. Setting down the burger, he wiped his hands on the napkin and bowed his head.

Brent watched him pray, not really listening to what he said. Brent wondered if John's God would be interested in his problem.

"So?" John popped a French fry in his mouth. "About that "stuff" that's bothering you. Do you want to talk about it?"

"Not really." Brent took a big bite of his burger so he could not say more.

Downing a few more French fries dipped in ketchup,

John looked over at Brent. "Do you need to talk about it?"

He was rewarded with a half-smile from Brent. "I'll handle it for now. But thanks."

"Okay, if you need to talk, you have my number, and you know where I work." John took a deep breath as if steeling himself before taking another bite of his burger.

Brent thought of Dr. Nee. Why did the people who knew God care about him? Why was it they could see him for more than the son of a criminal when no one else could? Did God see him as more?

Glancing behind himself to insure Dina was out of range, John set the burger back on his plate. "Brent, do people really travel for miles to come here?"

Brent grinned. "Yeah, Henry lives two miles from here."

"Hi, I'm Brent Macintyre. Someone said my dad had a safety deposit box here. I need to get it."

"One moment." The bank teller pinned the papers before him with a paperclip and carried them away.

Brent waited. The day had crawled by, and Brent was ready for some closure. He had not been able to focus in any of his classes, and retaking Mrs. Gram's test had been a waste of time.

"Are you a signer on the account?" The teller was a chubby middle-aged man with glasses and thinning hair. Whenever he was not occupied, his hand traveled a gold watch chain that disappeared into a little pocket on his vest.

"No, I'm not." Brent leaned his arm casually on the counter between himself and the teller's counter cubical. "See, my dad passed away about four years ago, and I just now found out about the deposit box. I honestly didn't know the box existed. We never found his will, so I'm hoping it is inside.

Do you mind doing a quick search on the computer for Roland Macintyre? Once I know for sure that the deposit box is here, I can work on the next steps."

The man's fingers moved over the keys again, and he paused to read the screen. Brent waited, glancing at the back of the monitor as if by some chance he could see the information through it.

"Hmm. Spell the last name for me."

"M-a-c-i-n-t-y-r-e," Brent spelled slowly as the man's fingers clicked on the keys.

"No, I'm sorry. I don't see a deposit box registered to that name. There's not even a checking account. Macintyre isn't in the system."

Brent frowned. "Are you sure? Someone told me my dad had a box here."

"Maybe he put it under a business name. Sometimes people do that."

"Wouldn't a business account still have the individual's name on it?" Brent asked.

"Oh, yes. That's right." The watch came out of his pocked and slid back in with a soft clink. "I'm sorry. There's nothing else I can do. His name is not in the system. He adjusted his glasses and looked up at Brent. "At this point, your only option is to bring the deposit box key your dad has and let us match it to the box."

"What if I don't have the key?"

"You would have to ask your dad for it," the bank teller responded. Brent could tell he was ready to move to the next customer. "I can't give you access without knowing which box is his." He was fingering the gold chain again.

Brent cleared his throat. Maybe the man had not heard him before. "Sir, my dad is dead. That makes it kind of hard for him to tell me where the key is. Is there any other way? Any documentation I can get? Any other records you can search?"

"You would need to start with a death certificate, but without the key, there's nothing I can do. He would have to give you the key."

"How is he supposed to give it to me?" Brent's frustration was rising. "He's dead, Curtis," Brent informed him, using the name on the teller's nametag to get his full attention. My dad was killed and buried four years ago. He's not able to give the key to anyone because he's dead."

Other customers were starting to stare, but Brent ignored them.

Letting his breath out hard, Brent leaned toward the man. "I'm kind of in a hurry. Extenuating circumstances and all that. If my dad didn't share the location of the key before he died, do we have any other options?" Brent glared at the man who fiddled anxiously with his precious watch chain.

"I'm afraid not." The teller shifted uncomfortably, but did not waver in his response. "I can't help you without the key."

"Okay. Let me think." Brent rubbed his hand over the left side of his face, avoiding the scratches on the right side. His attention drifted to the door to the hall behind the teller. There was an electronic keypad beside it.

"Is there anything else I can help you with?" The teller pulled out his watch to check the time as if there was somewhere else he needed to be.

Shaking his head no, Brent removed power from the keypad for an instant. An alarm above the door sounded, and Brent silenced it. "Whoa! What was that?" he asked, eyes wide.

"I don't know. That was highly irregular. We recently installed a new, more secure system, and it is very sensitive."

Frowning, Brent studied the alarm above the door. "But the security boxes are locked with keys right? They aren't controlled by electricity. I mean, my dad's things are safe."

The teller was quick to reassure Brent that the deposit boxes were keyed and secure.

As the man droned on, Brent mentally traced the faint electrical current through the wall between the keypad and the alarm above. That was his wire. As long as he kept the power steady in that wire going up to the alarm, it should not sound.

He shook his head. What was he thinking? His dad was killed robbing the bank across town. Brent wasn't a thief. But, he reasoned, was it actually stealing to take something that already belonged to your family?

The bank president came out of his office. He was talking on the phone. His eyes questioned the teller Brent was with, and the man pointed to the offending alarm above the hall door.

"I'll let you get this sorted out," Brent told him, turning from the counter.

"Have a good day," the man responded absently.

Strolling out of the bank, Brent headed for the street car stop. He had just enough time to get to work.

———

"Where's the box? You were at the bank today. Where is it?"

"You said I had ten days on Monday. This is Wednesday. It has only been two days." Brent was doing his best to stand tall before the man who had confronted him on his way home from work. He was a gaunt man with thin wispy hair that was mostly hidden under an old fashioned cloth cap. Roland had called him Cincher. The moment Brent had seen Cincher's face, the vivid memory of their first meeting had returned. He knew his earlier suspicions were right. Cincher was the memory his mom had not wanted to share. The man had come to the Macintyre house the night of Brent's sixth birthday, after Brent and his mom had gone to bed. Brent had gotten a new puppy for his birthday. In the middle of the night, the puppy had started crying. Brent could vividly remember the moment the puppy's cry had changed abruptly into a whimper. In the silence that followed, Brent had run down to check on his dog. He had found Cincher, gaunt and cruel, standing over the puppy. It was dead. The man's hard face and his rasping voice embedded Cincher in Brent's childhood memory as a foul and evil man.

"I don't have it," Brent told him, feeling the same rush of angry emotions he had felt as a boy. "There's nothing there under my dad's name. The bank says they can't find it without the key or a name. If they do somehow find it, I can't get clearance to access it without going to the police."

"You go to the police, and you are a dead man." Cincher growled.

"Do you see my problem?" Brent glanced around, hoping to draw the attention of someone who would stop and help. He knew in his heart that it was futile. Not helping the Macintyres was something that had sunk into a subtle culture of their town. "Look, Cincher, everything Dad owned was turned over to the police. Dad never told us about the deposit box. If it had been under his name, the police would already have it. I don't have any way to find out if it even exists."

"You will have to find the key then, won't you?" Cincher rasped with a sneer.

"I don't know where else to look," Brent told him. "I've looked through everything we own. It's not there. If dad had it on him when he died, the police would have it."

Cincher pulled out what looked like a length of paracord from his pocket. He toyed with it in a way that made Brent uneasy. "It's your mom, or your dad's deposit box. I'll let you choose. But remember, your time is running out, Little Macintyre." He turned and walked away without looking back.

CHAPTER 18

Dr. Nee sat behind his desk looking with concern at Brent. The boy's head was bent over his studies, but he was anxious. He moved around in his seat, and glanced often toward the door. On the first day of school, Brent had been sloppy and without direction. Over the course of the first month and a half, he had learned the skill of self-discipline and grown in confidence. Now, he sat straight. His clothes, though still from the local thrift shop, were neat and well-fitted. On the outside, he looked like a successful teen on his way to greatness. On the inside, something was wrong. Brent had come to Dr. Nee's house every Monday to study electronics and hone his gift. What he could do was incredible. The amount of potential packed inside this one student was baffling.

The class was supposed to be reading silently over the material they had just covered. Dr. Nee cleared his throat, catching the guilty looks of the students who were whispering to each other instead of reading. They were silenced by their teacher's firm look and slight shake of the head. Brent had not turned the page once, while other students were already finishing the two page assignment. Something in Brent had shifted since their meeting on Monday. Had Dr. Nee shared his invention too early? Was that what this was about?

Something had happened on Monday night. Brent had been restless since Tuesday morning, and the humor that had been his trademark had faded away almost completely.

Dr. Nee's eyes drifted to Jimmy, sitting straight at his desk. He too had undergone a drastic transformation. Dr. Nee had not asked, but he knew Brent was somehow behind it. Instead of sticking to his original plan of bumming around and living off of his mom, Jimmy was now going to trade school in the evenings and working part time at the city office as a clerk.

Brent twitched, bringing the teacher's attention back to him. If Dr. Nee did not find out what was weighing on Brent soon, he feared the weight of it would crush him, leaving only the cold hard shell his father had been.

"Hey, long time no see," Jimmy sat uninvited on the school picnic table where Brent sat alone. "The month's up, and I haven't seen any cash. It feels a little bit like you have been avoiding me, so I'm here to collect." Jimmy held out his hand, palm up. "Pay up."

Brent looked up at him, confused. "What are you talking about, Jimmy?"

Jimmy's face darkened. "Don't you pull that with me, Brent. If you turn out to be a swindler like your dad, I'll…"

"What? Bust my nose." Brent glared up at him. "I have no idea what you are talking about. Why don't you go ahead and knock my head off and be done with it."

Eyeing him curiously, Jimmy backed off. "Cool off, Hot Shot. Its twenty bucks, so I'll spell it out. You told me that if I made my bed…"

"Ohhh!" Brent exclaimed. His anger disappeared. "See what happens when you communicate? I have a lot on my mind right now, so I forgot about our little bet. You're sure you made your bed every morning?"

"Every morning," Jimmy confirmed without looking away.

Brent eyed him skeptically, but Jimmy merely returned the skeptical look.

"I have a new respect for you, Jimmy." Brent dug in his pocket and pulled out a five. "Here's my down payment. I'll bring the rest tomorrow."

Jimmy took the cash and inspected it carefully. "This is the real deal, right?"

Brent did not respond. He was staring at his uneaten sandwich like he had been when Jimmy approached.

"Yo." Jimmy bumped him, and Brent flinched like a dog that is kicked often. "Whoa, you okay, man?" Jimmy put both palms up to show he meant no harm.

"I'm fine. Just give me some space. Okay?" Brent gathered his things and, without a word, walked back to the school, dumping his food in the trash as he passed.

John saw Brent waiting at the corner and waved to him. Brent waved back half-heartedly. When John was almost to him, Brent turned and started for home, making no comment when John hurried to catch up with him.

"It was nice of you to invite me tonight." John could tell there was more to Brent's invitation than dinner.

"It's been almost a week since I met you. If you are going to marry Mom, we should all get to know each other."

"Good thought." John waited, giving Brent time to choose the topic.

Out of the corner of his eye, Brent saw someone slip around the corner across the street. "Let's keep walking a little longer. Mom may not be ready. You know how ladies can stress over things like food." Sweat had sprung up on his forehead, and Brent wiped it away, hoping John had not noticed the fear that gripped him.

John glanced at Ms. Cornshaw's door. "Um, okay. If you want to."

"Don't look at the house," Brent instructed keeping his own eyes on the houses across the street.

John glanced around but didn't see anything unusual. "Brent, are you sure you are okay? The other day..."

"Just keep walking," Brent interrupted trying to look casual.

"Are you in some kind of danger?" John had noticed the change in Brent's breathing.

Brent's look was intense. "You have to protect my mom. You have to take her away from here."

John stopped in surprise, but Brent walked on. "I'm serious, John. Take her on some kind of trip. To meet your sister or something. People do that before they get married, right?"

"I guess they do, but Brent, your mom and I both have jobs. We can't just skip town like that."

"Ask off now and see what they say."

"Brent, are you in some kind of trouble? If you are, we need to contact the police."

Brent shook his head. "You don't really understand my family, Mr. Starclish. My dad was a criminal and a killer. I don't care what happens to me..." Brent turned to scan the street behind them. No one was in sight. "We can cut across here." He led the way through an unfenced yard. Traveling along the backs of the houses, they made their way back to Mrs. Cornshaw's house. Brent paused outside the back door.

After he checked their surroundings, he locked eyes with John Starclish. "I don't care what happens to me, got it? I need you to take my mom somewhere safe."

John nodded slowly. "Okay."

"Don't say anything to mom about this." Brent saw a flicker of fear in John's face and knew he had seen the face of Roland Macintyre in his son. "I want you to marry her. This whole Jesus thing is working for you both. The next step is to go visit your sister and make sure the rest of the family approves. Got it?"

John nodded with a concerned frown.

Brent took a breath, brought up his chin confidently, and pushed open the back door to the house. "Let's go have some dinner to celebrate your surprise trip."

"There he is! I've been looking for you," Bill called as Brent passed the auto shop. "Your dream has come true. Business is picking up, and I'm going to need another hand. I can't promise it will be long term, but you can see if this line of work is for you."

"Thanks." Brent stood politely, waiting for a chance to leave.

"I'll start you right after school tomorrow. I already talked to your Mom. She said she's going on a surprise trip with that special someone." Laughing, Bill slapped Brent on the shoulder. "Don't look so down. John's a good guy." Picking up his tool caddy, Bill carried it around the white Buick parked inside the garage. "The trick with marriage is to view it as a forever commitment right from the start," he said to Brent over his shoulder. "It seems like people are hopping in and out of marriage like it's a game of jump rope. That's no way to build trust." Bill put the caddie on the shelf. "You have to treat the other person with kindness and give them the benefit of the doubt." He looked over at Brent and laughed. "You didn't come here for marriage advice, did you?"

"No, Sir." Brent did not feel the thrill that the idea of working at the auto shop had given him before.

"You might be sorry you wanted to work for an opinionated person like me." When Brent did not respond, Bill went on, "Your mom said she's happy for you to work here.

Mentioned something about you wanting to learn to rebuild a car from scratch. If that's true, this is the place for you. She also mentioned you work for Ornstein in the afternoons. You can work for an hour or so here right after school and still have time to catch the bus over to Ornstein's for your evening shift."

"Okay." Brent stood looking into the garage. He had always dreamed of working there and learning the ins and outs of each car. He would need to know it in order to make his electric car. Before his run-in with Cincher, Brent used to stop at the old factory on the way home from work to practice using his gift. Each time, he found he could be more and more precise with what he controlled. Dr. Nee had been right. It was not some kind of mental power. It was more like a muscle he had to learn to use properly. Some things took more energy than others, but Brent was extending his endurance each time he practiced.

Now, Brent was faced with the opportunity of his dreams, and he felt no excitement. Only deep fearful despair. He could not find the key, and he only had one week left.

"This trip is so sudden, Brent. I hardly know what to think." Violet Macintyre stood with her hands on her hips by the front door of their apartment. "I thought maybe you would want to get to know John a little more before you agreed. I only told you about him a week ago."

"A week and a day," Brent corrected, trying to sound cheery as he carried in the suitcase they had borrowed from Mrs. Cornshaw.

Violet put a hand on his arm to stop him as he passed her. She searched her son's eyes. "What is going on, Brent?"

Allowing his grip on the suitcase to slip, Brent caught it,

avoiding eye contact. "It's normal to go meet the rest of the family," Brent told her, carrying the suitcase to his mom's room. Violet followed him, watching as he laid the bag on the bed. "You will have a good time," he reassured her. "John said his sister has mellowed out and is more pleasant to be with now."

"It's just so sudden." Violet said again.

"John got the time off, and Mrs. Cornshaw said her niece is coming for a visit anyway. You haven't gotten to travel in ages, Mom. Take the opportunity!"

"I feel awful leaving you. Do you need anything before I go?"

"There is one thing," Brent busied himself with the latch on the suitcase, so he would not have to look at her while he spoke. "I was wondering if Dad had any documents or anything like that we should go through."

"It's been four years, Brent. Why are you so interested in this now?"

"With you getting married and all, I thought it would be good to have all that closed up," Brent answered vaguely. "What if we are paying for a deposit box or something at the bank and don't even know it? We could deal with the papers and have that much more to work with each month."

"If the police let us keep it." Violet put her hand on Brent's arm. "Brent, you asked me about the deposit box last Saturday. Why all this sudden curiosity?"

"Please don't ask me, Mom. I'm not doing anything illegal. You mentioned people dad knew are hanging around town. Wouldn't it be better to get the rest of the documents to the police before one of them tries something?"

She nodded, not fully convinced.

"When I asked you about the deposit box before, you made a sad face, and I could tell you were remembering something. Did Dad have a deposit box?"

"If there is this much fuss about it, I would assume that there is a deposit box." She pulled a stack of folded clothes from her dresser and arranged them in the suitcase.

Brent felt a queasy feeling building in the pit of his stomach. "Do you have the key?"

She went to the hanging line and took her other work dress and her nicer dress from their hangers. "No, I don't have it."

His shoulders drooped. "Who does?"

"I don't know, Brent. I've never seen it. Your dad never mentioned having a box at this bank." Violet stopped with the dresses draped over her arms and looked at him again, her eyes sad. "I don't want to leave you if you are in some kind of trouble, Brent."

"There won't be any trouble if I can find the key."

Chapter 19

As the bus pulled away from the curb, Brent sighed with relief. His Mom and John were off to meet his sister. They would be out of town and hopefully out of Cincher's reach. Now he had five days to search their belongings for that key or try to convince the bank to give him that box.

"Brent, do you have a minute?"

Brent turned to see Officer Cane strolling toward him.

"Hi, Officer Cane." Brent glanced around for any sign of Cincher.

"Was that your mom and John you were seeing off?"

"Yeah." He was trying hard to conceal his nervousness.

Following the retreating bus with his eyes, Cane frowned. "I thought John had a car."

"It's in the shop. It was leaking something, so he left it with Bill."

"Are they taking the bus to the airport or all the way to his sister's?" Cane noticed that Brent had crossed his arms and turned away slightly.

"How do you know that is where they are going?"

"John told me." Cane frowned. "Brent, are you okay?"

Dropping his arms to his sides, Brent shifted away from him. "Why do you ask?"

"Because I want to know if you are okay." Officer Cane watched with concern as Brent mentally scrambled for an answer. "You've been keeping to yourself a lot lately, Brent.

I haven't seen you around, and some of your classmates are concerned."

"Jimmy's got a big mouth." Crossing his arms, Brent shot a quick look up the street. The bus was out of sight.

Officer Cane smiled, "I'm not dropping any names, Brent. I'm just checking in."

"You know, I've been hoping our paths would cross," Brent told him. "Mom and I were talking yesterday, and she mentioned that she had not seen a key she thought my dad might have had when he died. Do you remember if they found a key on him?

"What kind of key?" Officer Cane took out his notebook and scribbled something down.

"I guess it was some kind of keepsake box." Brent's words were halting as he tried to formulate something that would be true without giving any information about the deposit box.

Officer Cane frowned thoughtfully, "I don't remember. I wasn't on duty that night. I can look at the report and get back to you. Was it small like for a jewelry box? Or more like a home safe?"

"I'm not sure what size it was." Brent was grateful he had never seen the size of a bank box key. "No problem, I'll look into it." Cane put his notebook back into his pocket. "In the meantime, can I ask you a question?"

"If it's quick, I've got to get to work. Ornstein is expecting me. " Checking the area again, Brent tried to quiet the panic that welled up inside. If Cincher saw him talking to the police, Brent would be dead. Or worse, his mom would suffer.

"It will only take a minute." Officer Cane reassured him. He had not missed Brent's constant uncomfortable movement and the way he checked his surroundings from time to time. "Have you seen the man known as Cincher? I don't know if you know him by sight. He worked with your dad some. He's five foot three, wears a..."

"No, I haven't seen anything." Brent answered too quickly. His face had gone pale.

"Brent, Cincher is a dangerous man. If you have seen him, I need to know."

"I know I spend a lot of time at work, and someone like that hasn't ever come in. Oh, look, that's my bus, I gotta go. I hope you find him." Brent turned and hurried onto the bus. He never took the bus to work, but he needed to get away from Officer Cane.

A quick glance out the window as they pulled away from the curb told Brent he would not get away so easily. Officer Cane was staring after him with a concerned frown.

His hand went to his radio "Headquarters, this is Officer Cane. I have reason to believe that Brent Macintyre has been approached by Earnest Centuro, aka Cincher. I'm requesting a detail to keep tabs on him for the next forty-two hours. This young man could be the key to putting Cincher back where he belongs."

Sunday was a restless day for Brent. He had searched every inch of their two rooms without finding the key to the deposit box. The bank was closed, so there was nothing he could do about the deposit box even if he did find the key. Besides, the clerk had been adamant about bringing the proper paperwork. Brent flopped on his bed. It was lame. Everyone knew Roland Macintyre was dead. Why did he have to prove it?

Brent's stomach growled, and he pulled himself out of bed. Passing through his mom's room, he made his way to the kitchen. Opening the refrigerator, Brent looked in. His job at Bill's Auto had helped give them a little extra cash to work with. His mom had stocked the fridge for the week before she left, but nothing looked good to him. In four days, Cincher would move in. With his mom safely out of town, Brent should have been at ease, but fear kept gnawing at him. What was in the deposit box that Cincher wanted so badly? Was his mom really safe with John?

Brent shut the refrigerator and made another aimless circuit around the apartment. Standing by the window, Brent twisted the rod to open the blinds. A man below turned his head away from the window where Brent stood and back to the newspaper he was holding open.

Brent frowned. Why was the stranger watching their window?

Stepping back from the window, Brent studied him. The daylight outside would make it hard to see into the room where Brent stood. There was something familiar about the straight shouldered man. He was wearing a sports coat and slacks which was not unusual for the well-to-do residents of Ms. Cornshaw's neighborhood. Brent shook his head. The man across the street was sitting in a relaxed position, but nothing about his body language was relaxed. He was on duty. This guy was a cop.

Pulling the blinds up in one quick motion, Brent allowed the undercover officer to see him at the window again. Their eyes met for an instant, and the officer was the first to look away. The man's mouth moved, and he folded the paper he had been pretending to read.

"You cops think you are clever, don't you?" Brent muttered to himself. He watched as the man stood, brushed himself off, and walked purposefully off down the street.

"They are tailing me," Brent said to the empty room. He let the blinds drop and moved back again, watching the street. Several minutes passed before Brent's patience was rewarded. A non-descript gray Toyota pulled up to the curb a few houses down, but the driver didn't get out.

Brent focused, removing power from the Toyota. He watched with an amused smile as the second undercover cop got out and popped his hood to check the engine.

This was his chance.

"Hi, Dr. Nee, I thought maybe you needed some company."

The professor smiled knowingly and stepped aside to allow Brent to enter. "You are welcome to keep me company any time. In fact, you can help me. The new shipment of batteries came in yesterday, and I need to charge them before I send them on to the manufacturer."

"And you need me to charge them?" Brent followed Dr. Nee to the work room.

"If you don't mind, it would be a big help to me." Dr. Nee pushed open the door. Several large open boxes lined one wall of the room.

Brent walked casually over to the first box and looked inside. "These aren't the wheel chair batteries you showed me before," Brent pointed out. For a moment, the weight of the threat to his mom lifted as Brent examined the four rectangle batteries seated neatly in the box.

"No, I told you, those are still in the testing stage." Dr. Nee retrieved a clipboard from on top of another box. "These are generator batteries." As he spoke, Dr. Nee's eyes lit up with excitement. "I have perfected a design where one of these batteries, if charged properly, can harness enough power to run a small generator for nearly six months. This saves the cost of gasoline and produces a much more stable power source." Dr. Nee touched Brent's shoulder, "The power must be added very evenly. Take your time."

Brent nodded, adjusting his method slightly to match the professor's instructions. "Let me guess, these are for people in other countries who don't have power in their houses?" Brent didn't wait for him to answer. "How long have you been supplying power to other countries?"

Dr. Nee gave him a patient smile. "The question is not how long, Brent. The question is how many people can be helped. There are places where the hospitals and medical clinics can open only a few times a month because the cost of gasoline is so high. In other locations, it is nearly impossible to get the gasoline to the mission because of the dangers of transportation. I make the batteries so that the missionaries can focus on their mission. Medical help brings people to the mission stations and allows the people to both see and feel God's love before they meet Him."

"You are pretty passionate about that, aren't you," Brent observed with a half-smile. As soon as he said it, he was sorry he had. Every time he met with Dr. Nee, Brent learned a little more about how important honoring God was to his teacher. Brent quickly changed the subject. "Don't your batteries get stolen during transportation, just like the gas?"

"No they do not."

Brent glanced up in time to catch the cunning look on his teacher's face. He had never seen this side of Dr. Nee.

"Transportation details are left to an elite team of men and women I employ for this purpose. They have never lost a battery, or a member of their team," Dr. Nee informed Brent with a hint of pride.

"I guess you make a lot of money off of these." Brent moved to the second box. It took less energy to send power a shorter distance.

"I don't keep any money from my inventions."

Brent blinked at him in surprise, totally forgetting about the battery he had been charging. "What? How do you fund all this?"

For a moment, Dr. Nee considered the wisdom of sharing this part of his life with Brent. "Nothing is hurt by your knowing the truth." Dr. Nee finally told him. "People donate to my work, and I put one hundred percent of their donations into the research, production, and transportation of the end products."

"But if you don't make money, then why do you do it? Do you get some kind of recognition for your lofty contribution?" Again, Brent was immediately sorry he had said it. "What I mean is, why do you do it?" Brent corrected lamely. The batteries could hold a lot of power, and carrying on a conversation while filling them was proving to be a little more than Brent could handle.

"I have trusted you with something very few people know about, Brent. It may not make sense to you yet, but many lives depend on these batteries being properly charged and making it to the missions safely."

"But why do you go through all this trouble?" Brent wiped away a bead of sweat that trickled down the side of his face. He had only done one and a half boxes, and there were four more to go.

"People were made to bring honor to God. He's so incredible that He deserves it. I have found the best way that I can bring glory to God is by helping the other people He created." Dr. Nee glanced up from the number he was logging on his clipboard. "Including you Brent Macintyre."

Brent shifted uncomfortably. Dr. Nee would not think so highly of him if he knew that Brent had recently considered robbing the bank. That thought brought all of the weight of the impending deadline down on him once more. He had to get that deposit box.

"Are you okay?" Dr. Nee was looking at him with a concerned frown. "Why don't you take a break. You have already saved me so much time."

Sitting back against the leg of the workbench, Brent

looked at the other boxes. "If you have been doing this for years, how have you been charging them?"

"Have you ever seen a cellular phone, Brent?" Dr. Nee pulled his from his pocket.

"Cellular phone," Brent repeated, suppressing a laugh. "They are called cell phones now."

As he often did in class, Dr. Nee dismissed Brent's humor with a shake of his head and an amused twinkle in his eye. "Terms are irrelevant for this illustration."

"I beg your pardon, Sir. Yes, I have seen a cellular phone." Brent was still grinning. He moved to the partially finished box and worked on charging the battery he had only partially filled.

"And how are cell phones, as you call them, powered?" Dr. Nee asked, sliding his phone back into his pocket.

"You charge them with an electric cord by hooking them up to an existing power source," Brent answered, turning his attention to the last battery in the box he was working on.

Dr. Nee nodded. "Many things can be charged in the same way."

"Makes sense." Brent looked thoughtfully at the remaining boxes.

"But I must say, your method is much faster and more efficient than a cord."

A soft beep sounded, and Dr. Nee laid aside his clipboard. "The rice is done cooking. Come, we will get some lunch and return to our task after we have eaten."

"You think a lot about other people, don't you?" Brent asked, getting to his feet.

"I do. The love I was shown makes me want to give back."

"To God," Brent finished, following him out into the hall.

Dr. Nee smiled. "Yes."

They reached the kitchen before Brent spoke again. "What you do is really neat, Dr. Nee. I want to help people too."

"I'm glad to hear it." He was busying himself getting out plates and silverware for their meal.

"There's some stuff I've got going on the next week or so," Brent took the plates from him and set them on the little table. "After that's over, I want to help you."

The searching way Dr. Nee looked at him made Brent wonder if he could somehow read what was going on in Brent's mind.

Finally, the older man nodded. "I would be grateful for your help."

CHAPTER 20

"For someone who is supposed to love cars, you sure are far away," Bill observed. "Did you have a rough weekend?"

When Brent didn't respond, Bill cleared his throat loudly.

"I'm sorry. What did you need?" Brent picked up the first tool he saw and held it down to Bill.

"Just put the tool box down here by me, and I'll finish up. Sorry, Brent. You were a little distracted last week, but this is the third time you have zoned out today. You only work for me for an hour. Until you get your head in the game, I'm going to have to let you go. I can't afford to pay you to stand around and think."

"I'll do better. I promise," Brent begged.

Bill was shaking his head no before Brent had finished. "Nothing doing. You go take some time to deal with whatever is on your mind. Come back next week, and we will talk."

"Next week?"

"That's right. I was trying to hire that eager young guy who used to hang around here after school. Not some moody teen who can't keep his mind on the job."

Brent knew the mechanic was right. He moved the tool box down to where Bill could reach it from where he lay. Bill used a grease covered hand to select the ratchet he needed before sliding back under the car. "The good news is, the car lift should be back up and running by then. My cousin is sending me the part I need." Bill saw Brent's feet had not moved and slid out to where he could see the distracted teen. "Is it anything I can help with, Brent?"

"No, I can work it out," Brent answered too quickly, shoving his hands into his pockets.

"You sure?" Bill was good at fixing cars, but people problems were a different league.

"Thanks for being willing to give me another chance." Brent turned away and left the garage.

Brent walked aimlessly. He had an hour and a half before he had to be at Ornstein's. Someone approached from behind, and Brent stepped aside to allow the short, stubby man to hurry past. He was traveling in the same direction Brent was going, but made no effort to respond to Brent's half hearted greeting. Brent smiled, momentarily distracted by the man. His head was ducked forward which, from behind, gave him the appearance of a rectangular block. Brent sighed. Bill had been right, Brent had let finding the deposit box and his fear of Cincher consume him.

He was considering this when he heard a young boy's call for help. Brent looked around to locate the boy. The sound was coming from behind the donut shop up ahead. It stood alone, separated from the other little businesses on the street. A new, bright blue coat of paint had been added to try to hide the places where the walls were cracking. The whole area between the mechanic and downtown had the sad feel of something that was dying slowly.

"Help, I'm stuck," the boy called. "Someone help!"

The street was deserted. Shaking his head, Brent went to investigate. The shop's sign said it was open from 5 a.m. until 10 a.m. and again from 3 p.m. to 4:30 p.m. Brent guessed the boy had been trying to get a donut after hours and fell in the dumpster.

"Someone help me!" the voice shouted desperately.

"I'm coming," Brent called back. "Where are you?"

"By the dumpster," came the response.

Brent rounded the corner and spotted the boy crouching beside the dumpster. Brent stopped short. Something wasn't right.

The smirking boy deftly finished tying his shoe before he stood to face his would be rescuer. He was nine or ten years old and wore his baseball cap backwards over his uncombed hair.

"Gotcha!" the boy crowed. He snagged a five dollar bill from someone behind the dumpster and ran off.

Frowning, Brent stepped back, putting more room between himself and whoever had paid the boy off. He paid no attention to the laughing boy who disappeared around the front of the donut shop.

"Kid's these days." The rasping voice behind him sent chills through Brent.

Whipping around, Brent found himself face to face with Cincher. The gaunt man had emerged from the back door of the empty shop.

"He didn't want to chat, but I do." Cincher moved toward Brent.

Brent glanced back in time to see another man step out from around the dumpster a few feet behind him.

"I'm here for the box," Cincher informed him coldly.

"Look, Mr. Cincher, I don't have the key yet." Brent tried to back away. He had already forgotten about the other man. Cincher's side-kick moved in, and Brent felt the dull jab of metal against his back. He froze. Fear tightened his throat. This time the gun would be loaded and ready for use. Swallowing his fear, Brent went on. "Dad never brought the key home, or we would have found it when we moved. Neither of us even knew the box existed. Dad must have kept the key on him. I asked an officer, and he's going to check the list of belongings to see if they found a key on him when he died."

"He was killed," the gun man behind Brent corrected.

Moving away from the gun barrel in his back meant moving closer to Cincher. Brent could not decide which was worse. "Yeah, he was killed, and he died at the same time. That's what I meant." Brent was talking fast.

"You weren't supposed to go to the police." Cincher reminded him with a scowl. Once more, he pulled the two foot long cord from his pocket. His long fingers toyed with it ominously.

"I didn't go to him," Brent protested, trying to hide the fear that gripped him. "He just walked up. There's a cop around here who does that. Kind of a teen relations officer, I guess. I didn't tell him about the box." Brent tried to edge sideways to relieve the pressure of the gun.

"You were supposed to give the key to me today," Cincher pointed out.

"No, you said ten days," Brent corrected. "Today is the eighth day." Irritation swelled up inside him, and he did nothing to stop it. "Why don't you set an alarm on your phone? Or maybe you should have your sidekick buy you a little pocket calendar to carry."

Cincher's eyes narrowed, and he moved a step closer. Now there was less than three feet between them. The cord was still moving fluidly through his hands.

Brent's belligerence faded. "Look, I'm sorry. I guess the pressure is getting to me. I don't have the key. I looked through everything we own and couldn't find it anywhere. I asked at the bank, and they said they don't have a box under Dad's name. Without the key, there's no way to find the box."

The gunman was crowding Brent from behind, pushing him toward Cincher.

"That's not good enough, Macintyre."

The gang had always maintained control through fear, and Brent felt its debilitating power. "I don't know how to find the key. I've tried everything I can think of." Brent's hands were trembling.

"You tried all the legal ways," Cincher pointed out. His eyes said more than his words. "You look like a smart kid. Maybe you take after your dad in that way. It might be time to start thinking outside the safety box of rules your mom wants you to live in. If you don't, she may not live to care."

"What do you mean?" Brent demanded.

"You will know soon enough."

Brent felt a new surge of anger. "Stop threatening me, and just tell me what you want me to do. Better yet, why don't you stop hiding behind kids and go get the box yourself?"

Cincher's face darkened, and he lashed out at Brent. It was a predictable swing which Brent dodged easily. Brent heard the man's fist connect, but felt no pain. In the same instant, the pressure of the gun barrel was removed from his back. Stepping out and away from between the two men, Brent turned to locate the gunman.

For an instant, Brent looked with confusion at the man. The gunman was holding his left eye, and glaring with his right at Cincher.

Brent's face lit up and a short, surprised laugh escaped him. "You totally just punched your own guy in the face!"

"Quiet!" Cincher snapped at Brent.

The fear had been broken, and the tragic memory from Brent's childhood had been joined by the comical scene he had just witnessed.

"What was that for?" the gunman asked angrily, making no effort to keep Brent covered.

"It was an accident, Ace. Let it go." Cincher was glaring at Brent. He could see that the teen was no longer in his power.

"I could accidently shoot you," Ace threatened.

Brent's laugh escaped through his nose.

Cincher made a grab for Ace's gun, but the other man had seen it coming.

Distancing himself, Ace stood ready. "Don't try that again, Cincher," he threatened darkly. "The boy doesn't have the key. This is a dead end. If Macintyre had the key on him, the cops would have gotten the deposit box years ago. You might as well give this up and skip town. Find yourself some new turf where you aren't as well known."

"I'm not paying you for advice," Cincher sneered. "I want the box. And I'll get it."

"If my hunch is right, you will know if they ever find it."

The gaunt man's face darkened. "No one asked you."

"I did a little research," Ace informed him. "The big news almost exactly ten years ago was a shooting."

"That has nothing to do with me."

"You are missing the point." Ace was getting annoyed. "You don't carry a gun, Cincher. Everyone knows that. They have nothing to pin on you. You kill the kid, and you are going to be hunted by every cop within fifty miles of here. Let the kid go, and we'll move on."

Brent's attention was on Ace, causing him to react too slowly when Cincher closed the gap between them. Cincher's gaunt face became even uglier as it contorted in anger. In his attempt to get away, Brent stumbled backwards, landing hard in the sand.

Cincher's hand snapped forward, and the rope lashed out like a venomous snake. Before Brent could move, he felt the cord encircle his neck. Grabbing desperately for the rope, Brent's fingers hit his own throat leaving a short vertical scratch just to the right of his windpipe. He froze, realizing that the cord still hung limp and loose around his neck. The fact that the ends of the rope were in Cincher's hands was enough to subdue Brent.

Keeping his fingers curled slightly around the loose cord, Brent tried to steady his breathing. He could taste the sickening feeling of fear that welled up inside him.

Cincher hung over him, the stale sickly smell of his breath caused Brent's stomach to churn.

"Do you know why they call me Cincher, Brent?" he tugged the cord a little, causing Brent to close his fist around it. It was not tight, but the thought of what Cincher could do produced the result the cruel man desired.

Despite the terror that gripped him, Brent refused to beg. He clinched his jaw, keeping his grip on the thin rope. His eyes met Ace's, pleading silently for help.

"Let him go, Cincher," Ace's tone was firm.

Cincher's hard gaze moved to Ace, and then to the gun Ace was pointing at him.

"You never could take a good, slow kill." Cincher let the rope slip a little.

Brent remained where he was on the ground, making no effort to get up.

"You have two days to get that key for me," Cincher breathed.

Brent nodded. He would agree to anything to be rid of the strangling fear that gripped him.

"Take it off. And do it easy," Ace commanded. "You leave a mark, and I might leave a more permanent one on you."

"You don't scare me, Ace," Cincher retorted. "He's the one who scratched up his neck, not me." Cincher flicked his wrist, and the rope left Brent's throat. "I'll be back in two days," he said, his sickening breath enveloping Brent. "And remember, Ace won't always be around to babysit you. Breathe one word about this to anyone, and I'll find you and finish what I started," he warned darkly before stalking away.

Brent lay where he was. His mind raced through what

could have happened. He felt weak and vulnerable, knowing his encounter with Cincher could have ended very differently.

A shadow fell across him, and Brent scrambled to his feet, stumbling in his haste. Brent couldn't stop trembling. Breathing deeply, Brent tried to steady his nerves. Though Cincher had not hurt him, it was as if his body could not shake the trauma of the possibility so quickly.

The shadow did not move as Ace waited for Brent to right himself.

Looking up, Brent found Ace watching him, gun in hand. Brent wanted to run, but he forced himself to stay, knowing the distance would make very little difference if Ace used the gun he still held.

"Why did you help me?" Brent searched the man's face. "Aren't you working for him?" he added when Ace did not respond.

"We have different methods of getting what we want." Ace answered. His gun disappeared into a concealed holster in his waistline. "Cincher is not playing games, Macintyre. He is already several steps ahead of you." Ace's expression was void of compassion.

"What does that mean? Ace, what do I do?" Brent shoved his hands in his pockets to hide their trembling.

"I've done all I can for you without getting myself killed. After this, you are on your own." Putting his hand into his pocket, Ace pulled a three inch pouch from inside. "Take this."

Brent automatically caught the object Ace threw. When he opened it, he found two narrow, oddly shaped metal pieces. One was narrow at one end, and the other had a bent end like a long L. He looked across at Ace, his eyes conveying his confusion.

"That's your kit to get in any door, anywhere," Ace explained. "I would learn to use them tonight if I were you. That may be your only chance."

Brent felt the color drain from his face.

"Now get lost. I owed your dad a favor, and now I'm paid up. Next time you see Cincher, you'd better have that box."

Brent did not wait for Ace to tell him a second time.

CHAPTER 21

"Brent," Dr. Nee's face betrayed his concern. "Won't you tell me what is going on?"

Staring at the carpet without actually seeing it, Brent made no answer.

"Brent?"

Looking at Dr. Nee as if seeing him for the first time, Brent's forehead creased, and the light on the side table came on.

"You weren't yourself in class today, Brent. Or last week for that matter. Are you okay?"

"Sorry." Brent touched the Band-Aid on his neck unconsciously. "Would you mind if we cancelled today? Something came up this afternoon, and you are right, it is making it hard to focus. I don't know why I didn't think to call."

Dr. Nee seemed concerned by the suggestion. "And you are sure you scratched your neck at the auto shop?"

Brent could tell that his teacher did not believe his story.

"That's my story, and I'm sticking to it." Brent's attempt to be light-hearted and humorous fell flat. And Dr. Nee was not buying it.

"I saw Bill earlier this evening, and he said he gave you a break from work."

"After I got hurt," Brent agreed, knowing it was a lie.

"He did not mention you getting injured." It was a statement, not an accusation. "He said you have been distracted, and it is affecting your work."

Brent shrugged and got up. "Glad to know it was a private dismissal." There was a hint of annoyance in his tone. "Bill probably didn't want it spreading around that I got hurt there. Bad for business, you know. It's best if I go." Struggling in his haste to get his jacket on, Brent moved toward the door, hoping to get out before too many questions were asked.

"You aren't very good at lying, Brent," Dr. Nee observed.

"Who says it's a lie?" He kept his attention on the zipper of his jacket.

"How is your mom?"

Brent paused, thrown off by the random question. He remembered Ace's comment earlier that day, and could feel the little lock picking kit in his pocket. "Mom? She's good. I don't remember if I told you, but Mom's got a nice guy to take care of her. She's out of town right now. Meeting his family and stuff. It's good for her to get away."

"Not so."

Brent stopped zipping his jacket midway up. "What do you mean?"

Dr. Nee pulled a folded piece of copy paper from his suit pocket. Unfolding it deliberately, Dr. Nee held it out to Brent. On the paper was a copy of both sides of a note that appeared to have been slightly crumpled. The original note had a hole torn in it on one end.

"It was hooked on the gate by the school entrance this morning. Because it had your name on it, I took the liberty to remove it before it was seen by your schoolmates. I was going to talk to you about it after I got the copy, but I couldn't find you during lunch. You left right after school so I didn't get a chance. That's why I was at Bill's."

Brent felt a wave of dread wash over him. "What does it say?" He made no move to take the paper Dr. Nee held out.

The professor adjusted his glasses and read the note. "We have your mother. Will trade her for the box. Come alone."

Dr. Nee looked up at Brent, his gaze sympathetic.

Brent took it slowly, his eyes on Dr. Nee. Forcing himself to look at the note he held, Brent read it for himself.

"You didn't get the scratch on your neck from Bill's, did you?" Dr. Nee asked.

"Come alone," Brent read aloud, frowning. "Come where? It doesn't have a meeting place."

Dr. Nee shook his head. "Brent, Officer Cane spoke to the school today at the morning assembly. Do you remember?"

Brent was silent.

"Officer Cane talked about some dangerous men who have been spotted a couple of times around town. One of the men goes by the alias, Cincher." Dr. Nee did not miss the slight shiver that went through Brent at the mention of the name.

"Okay, I'll be careful."

The police were already tailing him, but not doing a very good job of it. Cincher had to be paying someone to watch him as well. It was Cincher who knew about Brent getting off work early, not the police. And that was why Cincher was able to jump him. The police were probably planning on showing up again just before Brent got off work at Bill's. He was on his own and running out of time very quickly. "I'll see you around."

"Are you taking that note to the police?" Dr. Nee asked.

Brent stopped with his hand on the handle of the door. "I'll deal with it," he answered vaguely, keeping his back to Dr. Nee.

"Whatever is in that box is very important to them," Dr. Nee observed. "Any idea what is in it?"

"No."

"How long did Cincher give you to find it?"

"What are you, the police?" Brent didn't move or meet his teacher's eyes.

"Do you know why they call him Cincher, Brent?" Dr. Nee watched as Brent's hand moved up toward his neck.

Brent caught himself and lowered his hand quickly. "Yes. I remember him from when I was a kid."

"And from today." When Brent didn't respond, Dr. Nee went on "Cincher kills people by choking them. Your neck is bandaged, Brent. It doesn't take a lot of brains to figure this one out. You cannot fix this alone. Cincher is too dangerous. If you tell me we can go to the police, they can help you."

"Help us die faster," Brent muttered, looking down at the note in his hand.

"How long did he give you?" the professor asked again.

Turning to face Dr. Nee, Brent frowned, "You already told the police, didn't you?"

"Yes."

Brent would have protested, but Dr. Nee went on before he could.

"The note was in a public place," Dr. Nee pointed out. "Any potentially threatening notes are taken to Principal Bond, and then on to the police as needed. If he told you not to tell, it doesn't make sense that he would leave a note in a public place like that." Dr. Nee took a thoughtful sip of his tea. "Unless it was not Cincher who left it."

Brent frowned thoughtfully. If Ace was sabotaging Cincher's plan, whatever was in the box was not important to him, only to Cincher. Was that what Ace had meant about not helping him any more? Had he left the note to let Brent know his mom was already in danger?

Dr. Nee rose. "There's something else you should know." He retrieved a newspaper from the table by the door.

"This came today."

"Doesn't it come every week?" Brent asked.

"Read this article, on page three."

"Mayor is honoring wife's plea to further investigation.

Police detectives have been hired to further investigate the ten year old case involving James Nelson and the murder of Randy…" Brent looked over at Dr. Nee with a confused frown. "James Nelson, as in, Jimmy Nelson?"

Dr. Nee shook his head no. "James Nelson is Jimmy's dad. But that's not the part I was referring to if you read…"

"Jimmy said his dad was dead," Brent blurted.

Dr. Nee looked confused. "According to the article, his dad is in prison. Brent, you are missing the point."

"Thank you, Dr. Nee." Brent slipped out the door without waiting for a response.

"Hey Brent, I stopped by the auto shop last week, and you weren't there. Did you give up on your dream to…" Jimmy stopped short, his mouth dropping open at the sight of Brent's bruised face and fat lip. "What happened to you?"

Brent had no desire to talk about the beating he had taken the night before. He passed Jimmy in the hall without a word. This was the new Jimmy, tall, smartly-dressed, confident. Everything Brent should have been. Brent wanted to hate him for it. He wanted to rage and shout at the unfairness of life. He wanted to shout to the whole school the truth about Jimmy's murdering dad. With the desire, came a memory of his dad's rages, and Brent simply sighed in defeat.

Marvin pushed himself off the wall he had been leaning against and sauntered over. Stepping in Brent's path, Marvin crossed his arms. "He asked you what happened."

"Lay off, Marvin," Jimmy cut in. "I'll ask for help when I need it. I got to him first."

"You don't have the right to boss me around, Jimmy," Marvin shot back. "You used to be someone people respected, because you demanded their respect. You were worth knowing until you started tagging along with this no good crook's kid. Now you are a nobody, just like him." Marvin was moving into position, just out of range and ready to fight. "People used to get out of your way when they saw you coming. Now, look at you. So stiff and squeaky clean, they ought to use your empty head to clean the school floors instead of the mops. You're worthless."

Jimmy's chin went up defiantly, his eyes blazing. He moved in, only to be stopped short by the Principal's commanding voice.

"Jimmy, Marvin, that's enough. You boys better cool off, do you hear me?" Principal Bond had come from his office and was moving toward them. He was a force to be reckoned with, and neither boy wanted to face the restrictions that came with crossing him.

They glared at one another. Brent stayed where he was, knowing that one wrong move could set them off.

"Marvin, one more write-up for you, and you are suspended," Principal Bond reminded him. "Is he worth it?"

"This garbage pile?" Marvin shook his head, his lip curling in disgust. "He's not worth a dirty sock to me. You think you're better than me now, Jimmy? Well, you aren't. I'll show you." Stalking away, Marvin headed for class.

The hall was clearing out. Several girls saw Brent's bruised face and buzzed together excitedly about it, looking back often as they hurried down the corridor.

Jimmy ignored them. "So, Brent, now that Marvin has blown over, what happened to you?"

"I don't want to talk about it." Looking at Principal Bond for permission, Brent hurried after the other students. He knew it was far from over. He had expected a stir from his classmates, but not a clash between Jimmy and Marvin.

"Mr. Bond, what happened to him?" Jimmy asked, watching Brent go. Most of the students didn't even bother looking at Brent's face as he passed.

"I advised him to go home and rest," Principal Bond informed Jimmy. "However, Brent insists on attending today. Give him some space today." Principal Bond held his gaze, his face serious. "I don't want you making things any harder for him. Do you understand?"

Jimmy nodded, looking after Brent.

"Thanks. Now get to class. And keep away from Marvin today if possible."

CHAPTER 22

At lunch, Jimmy found Brent in Dr. Nee's empty classroom. He was sitting in a back desk that could not be seen from the door.

"I thought students weren't supposed to be in the classrooms during lunch," Jimmy observed casually, breaking the ice. He slid into the desk beside Brent's.

Brent didn't move or look at him. Everything hurt. He sat with his arms crossed tightly and both of his hands tucked under his arms. For a moment, Brent considered confronting Jimmy about his dad being in jail. The thought passed as quickly as it had come. The beating from Cincher's thugs had numbed the fiery passion Brent had felt before. Now, he didn't have the energy to confront anyone.

"Brent, you look like you got pounded." Jimmy's concern was real. "What happened to you?"

"Nothing. Just give me some space," Brent muttered.

Jimmy made no effort to leave. "Nothing? Brent, you didn't look like that yesterday." He paused. Tilting his head, he looked at Brent's knuckles. "It wasn't a fight. Someone roughed you up, didn't they?"

Brent did not answer.

"Where did it happen?"

Brent was not about to admit that he managed to dodge the police shadow and get back to Cornshaw's only to be pummeled by a couple of thugs Cincher hired. Apparently, it was Cincher's way of punishing Brent for letting the police find out about his mom's kidnapping.

The silence stretched on, and Jimmy made no move to go.

"Look, why do you care?" Brent finally asked trying not to move his mouth.

"We already agreed not to be friends, so I can't say I care because you are my friend." Jimmy was rewarded by a momentary upward twitch at the edge of Brent's swollen lip. "Maybe I'm not as keen on fighting as I used to be. Brent it isn't right for someone to knock you around without giving you a chance to defend yourself."

"Maybe I picked a fight with someone," Brent murmured sullenly.

"If you had been in a real fist fight, your knuckles would show it," Jimmy pointed out. "I used to fight a lot, remember?"

Brent pulled his fists in under his elbows and crossed his arms tighter.

"Look, I don't like admitting it, but you have helped me a lot. I don't know where I would be if it weren't for your dumb make the bed challenge." Jimmy smiled, but Brent did not. "I've got something to live for and a future because of you." When Jimmy went on, his voice was gentler. "And somehow you ended up with the short end of the deal. I want to help you."

"Stay away from me, Jimmy," Brent warned. "You have a nice set up and a nice job. Getting close to me will just mess all that up."

"That's not true."

For the first time, Brent met Jimmy's eyes. "You don't know how things are. You were right. I'm a crook's kid. I always will be. So I don't get a chance to have a normal life like everyone else. Who cares? Or maybe you forgot that you told me that for years? Now I know you were just hiding behind me."

"What?" Jimmy's exclamation was sincere, but a worried look flitted across his freckled face. Brent could tell that his red-headed classmate understood what he was talking about.

The buzzer echoed through the halls, signaling the end of their lunch hour. The class would be coming back in soon.

"Brent, come on," Jimmy urged. There was something unsure about the way he said it, as if he were afraid of what would happen if he pushed Brent too hard. "You gotta tell somebody what happened to you."

"Just keep your distance, okay?" Brent fell silent. For now, he would leave Jimmy to worry about how much Brent knew about his dad, and if he had told anyone else at school.

Jimmy shook his head. "Look, I don't know what happened last week, but you haven't been the same. I want to help you, Brent."

"Why?" Brent demanded, searching his face. "Why is it you are suddenly so interested in my life?"

"Maybe because I really do care." Jimmy shot back.

A few students trickled into the room.

Standing, Jimmy moved to his usual seat, letting the intensity of the moment dissipate. Leaning toward Brent, he added, "and maybe because I made my bed for a month, and you still owe me fifteen bucks."

"What happened to you, Brent?" Officer Brandon asked when Brent entered the room. "You look like you lost a street fight. Your face is a mess."

Officer Brandon had a full sized legal pad laying on his crossed leg and was leaning back casually in his chair. Beside him sat Officer Cane.

"Sit down, Brent," Principal Bond instructed kindly. He waited until Brent had lowered himself gingerly into the only remaining chair. "These officers are here to ask you some questions about what happened to you last night. What can you tell them?"

A shrug was his only response.

"Do you think it is connected with your mom's disappearance?" Officer Brandon asked, jotting down notes before Brent could answer. Brent didn't respond.

Brandon glanced over at Cane.

"Do you have any idea where your mom could be, Brent?" Officer Cane asked, leaning forward.

Brent shook his head. "If I knew that, I would go help her."

"That's what we are trying to do, Brent. We want to help you."

Fighting to control his temper, Brent clinched his teeth and looked away. He had told Principal Bond he didn't want the police involved. Now, not even an hour later, Brent was seated in the principal's office again. And his request had been totally disregarded.

"Look, I'm missing class. If you guys keep pulling me out, I might as well stop coming to school."

"Brent," Officer Cane waited until Brent looked at him. "Who did this to you?"

"Stairs can do a number on someone who is a bit clumsy." Brent's bruised face still reflected the annoyance he felt.

Officer Cane's gaze dropped to Brent's knuckles, and Brent shoved his hands into the pockets of his jacket. He looked at Brent's bruised face and bandaged neck for a long minute, taking in the damage.

"We can't help you unless you are willing to give me some information," Officer Cane told him.

"Why don't you ask the cops who have been tailing me?" Brent's look was accusing. "They should have seen the whole thing. Only they didn't, did they?"

"Brent, you can't blame the police force when you were the

one who purposefully snuck out on them and went walking into whatever it was alone," Officer Brandon pointed out hotly.

"Is that why they knocked you around, because the police were trailing you?" Cane asked. Officer Brandon sat with his pen poised over his pad.

Brent kept his eyes on the worn carpet. "I didn't stop to ask."

Officer Cane was disappointed. "You are not going to work with us at all then?"

"No." Brent met his eyes defiantly as he said it.

"Brent, your mom is missing, and we are doing everything we can to find out where she is being held. Any information you have could be the key to finding her."

"Tough luck." Although his face was hard, Brent's heart was breaking. The masked men who knocked him around last night had been very clear about the fact that any information given to the police would directly affect his mother's situation. They warned Brent to shake the police and get that deposit box before it was too late.

"You weren't supposed to be out wandering the streets at night," Officer Brandon pointed out, flipping his legal pad closed. "The city paid for an apartment for you and it is safer for you to stay there under police surveillance. At least until we can catch these guys."

"Can I go now?" Brent asked, his attention on Principal Bond.

Bond looked at the officers. It was Officer Cane who nodded.

Brent rose and left the room without looking at any of them.

"Jimmy, someone is here to see you." The clerk glanced

apologetically at the city commissioner.

"For me?" Jimmy shook his head. "Must be a mistake, I'm not expecting anyone. Could you tell them I'm at work?"

"I did, and he said it was important enough to interrupt. I think he might be in trouble."

"What do you mean, Mrs. Pane?" The commissioner looked up from the paper he had been reviewing.

"It looks like he's been in a fight or something," she answered.

Jimmy looked to the commissioner, "Do you mind if I take my break a little early and check this out?"

"Not at all. Do you have the blueprints for the renovations of the buildings on the south side?"

"Yes, Sir." Jimmy rose and brought the papers to him.

"I don't think I need anything else for the moment. Go ahead and see what your visitor wants Take the rest of the evening off if you need to."

"Thank you, Sir." Jimmy hurried to the front desk, stopping short at the sight of Brent's swollen, angry face. His eyes were hard.

"You said your dad was dead," Brent stated hotly.

"He is." Jimmy slipped around the counter with a 'this is awkward' smile to the clerk as he guided Brent out the front door.

"If he's dead, why are they talking about him in the paper?" Brent held up the newspaper Dr. Nee had given him. "James Nelson shot a man down ten years ago and was put in prison for life."

"Look, Brent, my dad is dead. End of story. Don't believe everything you read." Taking the paper, Jimmy looked it over. "This is from some backward town several hours north of here. Why do you even have this?" Jimmy's eyes were scanning the text.

"Dr. Nee gave it to me." Brent cocked his head slightly.

Had he seen fear in Jimmy's eyes? Brent knew his tirade was accomplishing nothing, but he was angry and wanted to blow some steam. Jimmy made a perfect target.

Jimmy frowned. "Newspaper guys just want to sell a story. Nelson is a pretty common name."

"Or," Brent jabbed his finger on the article. "This is your dad, and you made up the story about him dying to save yourself some embarrassment at a new school."

Jimmy met Brent's eyes, but his bold, challenging look was gone.

"The murder happened over ten years ago," Brent went on hotly. "Just before you moved here. That's when you started pushing me around, so you could make me the center of your jokes and keep people from asking about your family's past."

"Brent, listen,"

"No, you listen," Brent interrupted. "Your dad is a killer, and he's in prison for it." Digging in his pocket, Brent pulled out fifteen dollars and shoved it into Jimmy's hand. "I'm paid up, but you owe me more than you can ever pay. You labeled me a killer's kid, and I took the heat for it. After all these years, maybe you were right. Maybe that really is all I'm good for. I guess we're going to find out." Brent turned and stalked away before Jimmy could respond.

"Doing something stupid won't prove anything, Brent." Jimmy called after him.

Brent did not bother to answer him.

CHAPTER 23

"Can you help me, Sir? The power in my apartment keeps going out." She was a slim, pretty young lady with a thick blanket wrapped around her. The legs of her light pink pajama pants dragged on the floor around her bare feet. "I don't know how to fix it."

Brent smiled from behind the thin door of the apartment the police had rented for him. His story about being tired had been true enough that the officers had believed that Brent was going to bed early. Now, he stood dressed and ready for his chance to escape.

"Ma'am, I can't leave my post. I've got my orders." the officer responded. Brent could tell he was wavering. "Have you checked with the building's janitor?"

"He doesn't come in until nine tomorrow morning," she pouted. "It will only take a minute."

"Okay, but only for a minute," he agreed. "His light is out, and I haven't heard anyone moving around. He's probably asleep by now."

Brent leaned back, away from the door as the officer softly tried the doorknob to his room. It was locked.

The officer looked up and down the quiet hall. "It should be okay."

"I'm sure you can fix it," she chattered on. "It has never done this before."

Brent could hear the flattering smile in her voice.

Listening, Brent counted the steps the officer took down to the next landing. When he was sure the coast was clear, Brent slipped out onto the stairs. His room was on the third floor.

As quickly and silently as he could, Brent navigated the stairs down past the lady's door. He made her lights flicker again to keep the officer inside. The stair turned, and Brent paused to look down at the first floor. Another officer was standing in the lobby below. They would be changing sifts soon. Crouching just out of sight, Brent waited. He sent another quick wave of energy into the lady's apartment, knowing his time was running out.

The front door opened, and a young, fresh officer walked into the lobby. Watching them through the rails, Brent felt the hope draining out of him. Then, as if on cue, both men strolled over to the front door. The incoming officer pushed it open and pointed something out to the man he was replacing.

Three quick steps took Brent around the curve and part of the way down the final flight of stairs. In one swift movement, he gripped the side rail and jumped, pulling his legs up and over it. Using his arms, Brent lowered himself quickly and quietly, leaving only a short drop to the floor below. Glancing over at the officers, Brent was relieved to find them still discussing whatever it was they were looking at outside. Ducking under the staircase, Brent waited for the shouts of discovery he expected at any moment. They never came. He heard the front door close and their voices grew louder as they neared the center of the small lobby.

Steadying his breathing, Brent listened as the younger officer chatted about the events of the day. He perked up when the officer being relieved asked if there were any new leads on the case.

"The Chief called in some kind of expert to find the Macintyre dame." The rookie informed his companion. "It's all pretty hush hush. I think the department is throwing everything it's got into catching this Cincher character."

"Honestly, Burk, you sound like you are from one of those cheesy gangster shows. You have been on the force long enough to know that police don't talk like that."

Burk muttered something Brent could not make out.

"Well, it's your life, but if the Chief hears your gangster slang you will get an earful. The city puts in a lot of money to educate its police force. Yeah, the kid's upstairs. Rocko is up on the landing. "He doesn't get relieved for another hour, so stay out of his way. He doesn't like to be bothered when he's on the job."

"Thanks for the tips, Richardson." Burk was still sore about the officer's comments about his slang.

Richardson laughed and slapped him on the back. "Have a good one."

As the officer walked to the front door, Brent chanced a quick peek to locate Burk. The rookie was standing with his back to Brent. Moving along the wall, matching his footsteps to the steady confident ones of the retreating officer, Brent slipped into the maintenance room. He waited for a few seconds to ensure he had not been spotted. Unlocking the door to the alley, Brent cracked it open just enough to peer through.

Richardson had stopped to chat with the officer on guard in the alley on his way out. Brent slipped out and crouched in the shadows. He could see them from where he waited. He could tell their conversation was coming to an end, but Richardson was still facing up the alley in Brent's direction. Brent was about to make run for it, when something drew both men's attention away from him. Jumping to his feet, Brent sprinted out of the alley.

———

"Why did you give him this paper?" Jimmy demanded, holding up the creased newspaper. "What do you have against Brent? Or is it me you were trying to knock down?"

Dr. Nee blinked up at Jimmy in surprise. "Hello to you as well, Mr. Nelson. Would you like to come in and discuss this issue?"

"I told you the first day of school, I don't want to be called Mr. Nelson. And no, I would not like to come in and discuss this issue." There was a hint of mockery in Jimmy's tone. "You can tell me right here on the porch. You had no right pulling up some obscure newspaper and convincing Brent that some random guy is my dad. We had a chance to be friends, you know. A slim one, but a chance just the same."

"A friendship built on lies will not last."

"Oh, the wisdom is killing me." Jimmy twisted the paper in both his fists. "You got him all worked up, and he went storming away to commit a crime and prove he's a Macintyre. Was that the plan? Are you working with the guys who roughed him up?"

"Jimmy, you aren't thinking straight. You know I am not working with them."

"Oh, now you are a psychologist?" Jimmy tapped his temple. "Now you know what I'm thinking? Is that why we all call you doctor? What kind of doctor are you, anyway?"

"A knee doctor," Dr. Nee answered with a straight face.

For an instant, Jimmy stared at him without comprehending. And then, without meaning too, Jimmy laughed softly. Catching himself, he frowned. "Okay, Knee Doctor, I'll give you one for humor, but this is serious."

"I know it is. I'll do everything in my power to help Brent avoid becoming like his dad." Dr. Nee looked Jimmy in the eyes, "And for you Jimmy Nelson."

Jimmy's brow creased slightly. "You really think there's a chance?"

"I do."

Jimmy looked away. For an instant, the tall, successful teen seemed childlike and vulnerable. "I wish you were right." He stood quietly for a moment more, and Dr. Nee did not interrupt. As if remembering where he was, Jimmy looked down at the crumpled paper in his hand. "It's getting dark. I'm going to go look for Brent."

"Where are you headed?" Dr. Nee asked. "I'll call Officer Cane and then come help you look."

"I'll check the factory roof where he likes to hang out."

Dr. Nee nodded. "Good idea. Meet me at Second Trust Bank if you don't find him. I'll check the school and drive through downtown. Noah Ornstein told me this afternoon that Brent hasn't shown up for work the last two days. The police are supposed to be keeping an eye on him, but I imagine a clever, active boy like Brent could easily give them the slip if they aren't on their toes."

"Brent's a good guy, Dr. Nee." He kept his eyes on the paper he was twisting again.

The professor nodded. "I know. And I'm sorry about the article, Jimmy. I was not aware you had told your classmates that your father was dead. I showed Brent because it mentioned Earnest Centuro."

"Who?"

"He goes by the name 'Cincher.'"

Jimmy's eyes widened. "That's the man Officer Cane mentioned in the school assembly, isn't it?" Jimmy looked out into the dark night. "Do you think Brent is working with Cincher?"

"No, but I do know that we need to find Brent before Cincher does."

Jimmy hesitated. "If Brent gets himself killed tonight, this," Jimmy held up the paper, "won't matter." Allowing his arm to drop to his side, Jimmy turned and walked away.

Once he was out of sight, Brent put on speed, distancing himself from the apartment. He was heading to Mrs. Cornshaw's again and wasted no time disguising his route. After several blocks, he slowed to a fast jog that he could maintain. He was exhausted, but forced himself not to think about it.

That morning, Brent had slipped away before the sun rose to do one more fruitless search at Mrs. Cornshaw's. That was where Cincher's thugs had found him. Brent was no match for the two experienced fighters. They had seemed to enjoy pounding into Brent the fact that Cincher was serious about his threats. Demanding the key, and his silence, they knocked him around a few times to prove their point.

Brent's lungs were burning, and his anger rose with the memory. The last thing he remembered about the fight early that morning was himself shouting in a burst of passion that they could not prove they had his mom. The next thing he knew, he was picking himself up off the floor, and the sun was already shining through the blinds into the empty room.

Now, Brent was grasping at one last hope. He knew he would be seen running through the streets, and if he had played them right, he would get to talk to his mom tonight.

Jimmy scanned the rooftop clutter for any sign of Brent. "Come on, Brent. Where are you?" Moving to the edge, Jimmy scanned the street below. Nothing. Moving to the other side, Jimmy checked the street. He was about to turn away, when a movement below stopped him. A short, stubby little man trotted along the sidewalk in the direction of Second Trust Bank.

Wishing his parents would buy him a cell phone, Jimmy hurried down the stairs to try to catch up with the strange man.

A police car was parked across the street from Mrs. Cornshaw's house.

Brent saw it soon enough to change course and cut in between the houses. The house beside Cornshaw's belonged to a kind old man named George, who enjoyed chatting with Brent when he came back from work in the evenings. Beside George's house was an extension ladder which was always left leaning up against the house. Brent had offered to put it away for him, but George said his daughter visited more often when it was left out.

Brent climbed the ladder and moved across George's rooftop. There were only about three feet between the edges of the two roofs. Gauging the distance, Brent sprinted toward the gap and leapt lightly onto Mrs. Cornshaw's roof. He crouched for a moment before moving to the attic window where he used his pocket knife to pry open the flimsy latch.

Swinging the window open, Brent slipped inside. Almost as soon as his shoes hit the rough boards of the attic floor, Brent heard the phone ring in the room below. Dashing through the attic, Brent slammed into the door to their rooms. The phone was still ringing as he fumbled with his key. Shoving the door open, Brent raced across the room without bothering to check if it was empty. Snatching up the phone, Brent held it to his ear.

"Hello?" he asked breathlessly.

"Brent? What are you doing there?" Violet's voice came through the speaker.

Unable to stand, Brent sank to the carpet, holding the

phone in one hand and his head in the other. "Mom, are you okay? Where are you?" Brent asked into the phone. Maybe they had been bluffing. Maybe she was still safe with John.

"I'm okay," she hesitated. "The trip didn't go as planned."

He could hear both fear and tension in her voice.

"Where are you?" Brent asked again.

"I can't tell you, Brent." Violet's voice was sad.

"Is John okay?"

"Yes, he's okay. They let him go."

"And he left you?" Brent frowned darkly.

"He had no choice, Brent. It's not his fault. I'm so sorry. I should have stayed home with you."

Brent choked back his emotions. "I was the one who suggested you go. I made you go. I thought you would be safer away from me."

"Oh, Brent. It isn't your fault." She paused, and Brent heard an indistinct male voice in the background. "I have to go. They want me to tell you that they have me. You are to get them the bank box by tomorrow morning."

"How do I get it?" he asked, clutching the phone to his ear.

The phone went silent, leaving Brent alone.

He stood resolutely. If he wanted to save his mom he knew what he had to do. Tomorrow his time was up. It had to be tonight.

"Anything at the house?" Officer Brandon asked over the radio. He was stationed on the opposite street where he could observe the back of Mrs. Cornshaw's house.

"Nothing." Officer Cane responded, his eyes drifting over the picturesque two story white house across from where he was parked. "I thought I saw something earlier, but I walked the perimeter of the house, and there was no evidence anyone had approached. Any sign of him on your end?"

"I don't know how he did it, Cane. Maybe the lady was in on it. Either way, that was a clever scheme to get Rocko away from the door so he could escape."

"He's a bright young man," Officer Cane agreed.

"A lot like Roland."

"Brandon, don't," Cane cautioned firmly.

"It's what we were both thinking. Admit it."

"Cane, Brandon, do you have eyes on the Macintye boy?"

"No, Sir. The house is dark, and I haven't seen anyone coming or going."

"One of you go up and check their rooms. Last time he was seen, he was heading your way."

Climbing out the attic window, Brent moved stealthily across the rooftop once more. A thick cloud moved across the sky toward the moon, and Brent waited, crouched low against the shingles.

"Come on," Brent muttered softly. The wind continued to move the cloud until the moon was covered and the sky went dark

Three running steps gave him the momentum needed to leap across onto George's rooftop. After a quick check over the edge, Brent slipped down the ladder. Again he waited, glancing up at the dark sky. The dim orb of the moon seemed to be sliding towards the edge of the cloud. He would have to hurry. Brent felt his pocket for the lock picking kit Ace had given him. It was still there. Creeping to the side of the house, Brent flickered the lights in the upper room of Ms. Corshaw's. Three times they flickered on and then off again. He did not have to wait long before he saw a tense officer approaching the back door. Brent caused one more blink of the lights for the sake of the officer out front before sprinting off into the darkness. He only had a few more hours before the sun would come up.

CHAPTER 24

Jimmy pushed open the fire escape door at the base of the abandoned factory and stood looking down the street in the direction the stubby man had gone. He squinted in the darkness, wondering if he were seeing movement, or only imaging it.

Just then, the moon came out from behind the cloud, washing the street with its pale light. Jimmy grinned, letting the door close behind him. The little man was turning the corner two blocks away. Running along the sidewalk, Jimmy closed the gap between them. When he reached the place he had lost sight of the man, Jimmy slowed. Making a wide turn, he checked the empty street. Nothing. Jimmy understood why Brent enjoyed viewing the world from the top of the building. He wished he were up there and could see which way the man had turned. Here on the street, it was hopeless. All Jimmy knew was that the short, rectangular person had been traveling in the general direction of the bank.

Officer Cane felt the vibration of his phone and pulled it from his shirt pocket. "Yeah?" His attention moved back to the house across the street.

"Cane? This is Rocko."

"I'm driving home from my shift, and I'm pretty sure

I just saw the Macintyre boy on 10th and Glen. If I'm not mistaken, he's heading for the bank."

"That kid." Cane muttered to himself, putting his cruiser in gear. "We just had a false positive at the Cornshaw place. Some lights flickering upstairs. Brandon and Mike went in but didn't find anything out of place."

"I know how you feel." Rocko's tone betrayed his embarrassment at being lured away from his post at the apartment by a damsel in distress.

"Brent's a clever kid, Rock. He must have rigged the lights somehow to throw us off his trail."

"That's what I don't get." Rocko sounded distracted. "That kid had been running since three or four this morning and got a major workover from Cincher's thugs before school started at nine. How is he still alert enough to be outsmarting us? Hang on."

Cane waited, listening. He heard Rocko's car radio and knew he was still trailing Brent.

"Yeah, it's him. He's about a block away from the bank. You'd better get over here. He's moving toward the bank like a man on a mission. "You're good with kids, Cane. I think he's going to be too shook up and tired to listen to anyone else."

"Roger that, I'm in route."

As he sped through the streets, Officer Cane radioed Brandon and updated him. Brandon would stay at the house in case anyone showed up.

Flipping his lights on as he approached the intersection, Cane checked for oncoming traffic. Rocko was right. If he wasn't able to talk Brent down from whatever he was planning, it might be the tipping point for the teen. Cane reached for his phone. Unlocking the screen, he expertly tapped twice with his thumb without taking his eyes from the road. He was almost to the bank.

The police chief answered on the second ring.

"Chief, Rocko spotted Brent Macintyre near the bank. I need to get in and talk to him without adding pressure."

"Tell me what you need," the Chief instructed.

"I need you to pull the officers from that area. Give me a wide perimeter. I don't want him to see any police cars besides mine."

"You sure about this?" The Chief did not sound convinced. "It would be a lot simpler to pick him up now."

"I know." Cane shut off his lights and turned onto 10th Street several blocks from the bank. "Give me a chance to try."

"You're the best youth officer I've got, Cane. Consider it done. Anything else?"

"It wouldn't hurt to try to contact his teacher, Dr. Nee. He's the one who tipped us off tonight about Brent's escape from the apartment."

"I'll get someone on it."

Cane slowed, pulling up to the curb as the all-units announcement came over the radio.

"Be careful," the Chief warned. "He's a live wire, and unless we handle him carefully, people will get hurt. I'll have backup on standby. You give the signal if the kid's not cooperating, and we'll move in."

"Roger that." Cane hung up the phone and let the darkness settle around him. He would only have one chance at this, and he could not afford to fail.

Stepping into the shadows, Brent waited silently. He had been intentional in his route walking home from school since he had run into Cincher and Ace. Brent knew the placement of every outside camera in the bank. He could not do a full power outage or the alarms inside would go off like they had when he disabled the keypad behind the teller. He could, however, disable the outside cameras to give himself a little more cover to work. Once those were powered down, it would be a quick sprint to the back door of the bank. The security light above the back entrance made the keypad visible.

"Brent, are you okay?" Cane's voice was low and soft.

Brent whipped around, his eyes locking on Officer Cane as he moved toward Brent.

"What are you doing here? Get lost," Brent hissed angrily.

"I'm here to stop you, Brent," Cane had stopped, giving the high strung teen space to think. "You don't want to do this."

"I don't have a choice." Brent's attention moved to the bank. "In six hours she dies if I don't pay up."

"Your mom?"

"Who else?" Brent demanded a little louder than he had intended. "You traced leads and asked questions, but you don't know where she is any more than I do."

"This won't help."

"You don't even know why I'm here," Brent countered. He put up his hand. "I don't want to hear it. Get lost. You are too late."

"Brent, you aren't your dad." Officer Cane met his eyes with a probing, caring expression. "You are a good man designed to help others, not rob banks."

Brent's mind went instantly to the batteries Dr. Nee was making. That kind of helping others seemed to draw him. Brent knew he would have to give up the dream before it became a part of him. This was the kind of helping he would have to do now. His mother's life depended on his ability to get that box. "I said, get lost. You are too late," Brent's voice was cold and determined. Focusing on the security camera trained on the bank door, Brent removed power from it. Only Brent knew it had been done. Sprinting across the ray of light cast by the streetlight, he flattened himself against the back wall of the bank.

Closing his eyes to steady himself, Brent leaned against the wall. His head pounded, and his tired eyes made it hard to focus. It took a lot more concentration than normal to keep the camera off. When Brent opened his eyes, Dr. Nee was in front of him.

"So they called you too? Oh, joy," Brent observed sarcastically. "What? Could the mayor not make it today?" Brent was irritated that his teacher had been able to get so close without giving himself away. He looked around and spotted Officer Cane who was standing a little ways from them.

"Brent, there must be another way." Dr. Nee's tone was both gentle and firm.

"Get out of the way. I don't want to have to hurt you," Brent warned.

"Would you?"

The question caused Brent to pause. "My Mom is in danger. John left without her, and this is the only way I know to help her. I'm going to do whatever it takes to get her free."

Dr. Nee was silent for several seconds. When he spoke again, his words were slow and thoughtful. "Are you going to break into all of the boxes and jeopardize everyone in town's security in order to find what you are looking for?"

"If it means saving my mom, yes." Brent turned the light on the keypad green and the door beeped.

"Yes!" Brent hissed softly. He went to open it, but the light was red again before he grabbed the handle. He tried to pull it, but it was locked. He tried again, but he could hear the latch re-engage before he could pull the door open. He would have to disarm it and pull at the same time.

"When you get inside, how will you get into the boxes?" Dr. Nee asked. "Those must be opened with a manual key."

Brent patted his pocket. "I have a solution for that."

"And how will you know when you have found what Cincher is looking for?"

The security light above the door allowed Brent to see the intensity in Dr. Nee's expression. Dr. Nee was right. There would be over a hundred boxes to try to look through. If he kept the valuable things, maybe he could make another life for himself somewhere far away.

"This isn't for you, Brent." Dr. Nee's statement broke through Brent's thoughts. "You must choose wisdom. If you break into the bank, you will step into a terrible cycle that will change your life. If, by some random chance, you aren't caught now, you will spend the rest of your life running or hiding like your dad. You are better than this, Brent. God has good plans for you."

"God?" Brent's eyebrows lifted momentarily in surprise. "Look, Dr. Nee, I'm trying to rob a bank with a ridiculous amount of witnesses. You can save the sermon for another day."

"You may not have another day." Dr. Nee pointed out.

"Do I look like I care about that?" Brent demanded. "I have to get my mom out of this. I take the box, give it to Cincher, Mom will marry John, and this will all blow over."

Officer Cane approached them. "This is where the security box is, isn't it?"

"You cops are awfully slow." Brent was glaring at him.

"For your information, Brent. There are seven different banks in this city." Officer Cane stood tall, meeting Brent's anger with calm authority. "As you might have guessed, none of those banks have a security deposit box under your dad's name. Not only that, but all of the banks in a one hundred mile radius have been contacted or visited by us "cops". You are running out of time. Either you start working with us and help us find your mom, or you keep up this foolish one man show and let her get killed."

Both Dr. Nee and Brent blinked at Officer Cane in surprise.

"I'm not going to treat you like a kid, Brent. I tried to tell you nicely before, but what you need is a good dose of the cold, hard truth. You have wasted too much time trying to do this on your own. And I have the feeling we are dangerously close to a deadline you have kept to yourself.

"Telling you would be signing Mom's death sentence." Brent was losing his nerve. Exhaustion muddied his mind, making it hard to think.

"You have to understand how criminals work. This may be hard to take, but Cincher is already planning on killing your mom. The only reason she is still alive is because she gives them the leverage to get you to do what they want. There is only one chance of out-smarting them this far into the game."

"And what's that?" Brent demanded defiantly. "We all pray and hold hands?"

Officer Cane's eyes were still locked on Brent's. "You are wasting time we don't have, Brent. Either we work together, or you make a stupid move and rob a bank trying to find one box out of hundreds." Officer Cane was not pulling his punches.

Dr. Nee stood silently off to the side, letting the officer do his job.

If Officer Cane had tried to baby Brent, or convince him with sob stories of his future, Brent would have easily been able to shoot down his arguments. This was different, and Brent knew it was no use arguing with the facts.

"When is the deadline?" Cane asked.

"Sunrise," Brent blurted, giving no further explanation. He looked longingly at the keypad by the door. It must have had some kind of extra backup power source because the one inside the bank had been so simple to disable.

Cane touched his watch, and the face shone pale green for a split second. "So we have got about six hours. That's better than I thought. What else do I need to know?"

Brent hesitated, his jaw working. He knew Officer Cane

was right, but it still felt like he was betraying his mom by telling. "Cincher wants the deposit box that belonged to my dad." Once Brent started, the information flowed from him. "Some guy stopped me to tell me that he had a secret Roland Macintyre didn't want to get out. He said something about a deposit box dad set up ten years ago. I wasn't interested and told him so. I guess the guy sold Cincher the information about what was in the box because the next thing I knew, Cincher was breathing down my neck trying to get my dad's deposit box. Another guy named Ace is helping him," Brent paused, remembering. "Ace saved my life, or at least made me feel like he did. It could have been part of an act to get me to trust him." Brent's hand went to his neck. "It sure felt real."

"It probably was real." Officer Cane interjected. "Brent, Cincher is a very dangerous man with a quick temper. You are lucky he wants something he thinks you can get. That, and Ace stepping in, are probably the only reasons you are still alive."

"So Ace is a good guy?" Brent asked. He felt the lock picking kit in his pocket and knew the answer.

"No, Ace Maguire is definitely on the wrong side of the law," Cane answered. "His teenage son was killed last year, following in his footsteps. There's some talk about him going soft, which is probably why he's working for a low life like Cincher." Cane looked thoughtful. "This morning, when you were jumped, was it Cincher and Ace who roughed you up?"

"No, I don't think it was them. These guys were bigger. I think there were two of them, but they were hitting me so fast that it was hard to tell. At least two."

"Okay, and I have to confirm. You do not know what deposit box they want, only that it is in this bank, correct?"

"They are sure it is here. Honestly, I don't even know if there is a box." Forgetting his bruises, he pressed his hands against his tired eyes. With a moan, Brent dropped his hands to his sides and laid his head back against the side of the bank. “It’s hopeless.”

“Not yet.” Officer Cane pulled out his phone and called the chief. After a brief conversation, he switched his radio to a more secure channel. “Alright, here’s the plan. We don’t know where the box is, but Cincher doesn’t need to know that. We’re going to stage a…” He stopped, his hand dropping to the Glock at his side. Someone was coming.

CHAPTER 25

Violet sat on a threadbare couch watching Ace move around the tiny apartment kitchen. "Ace, we don't have the key for the box. You know that," she pointed out. Cincher was out again. Ace had warned him that the police were too close, but Cincher hated being holed up. Violet preferred it when Cincher was gone. His fiery temper scared her. Roland's temper was terrible, but he had never hurt her physically. Ace was the only reason Cincher had not killed her already.

"It's late. Why don't you hit the hay?" Ace suggested. "Nearly 1 a.m. already. I bet that's past your bedtime."

Violet ignored his advice. "We don't even know what is inside the box. Or even if there is a box. Roland never mentioned it, and I never even saw a key."

"Don't let it get to you. Your boy will come through." Ace's face grew somber, and he looked away. "He'll come through," he repeated.

"But why would Cincher bring it up after all these years if he doesn't want anyone to know what is in the deposit box? Why not simply let it rot away?"

Ace glanced over at her. "Maybe it's not as unknown as you think." A noise outside caused him to stiffen for a moment. Dismissing it, he went back to getting a plate from the cabinet. "It's better if you don't ask questions, Mrs. Macintyre. Why don't you do one of those sewing things there to pass the time?"

Violet glanced down at the basket of yarn and sewing supplies Ace had brought a few days ago. "I find it very hard to knit when I'm scheduled to die in the morning."

"You might not die. Your kid seems like a smart boy. He will find a way to get it."

"Today," she paused thoughtfully. "I guess it was yesterday now," she corrected, "was Brent's sixteenth birthday."

"Many happy returns," Ace said absently, scraping mold off of the last piece of cheese.

She decided to try another tactic. "I guess helping Roland's men when they got injured wasn't enough to earn my life," Violet reminisced, watching him assemble his sandwich. "Does your leg still give you trouble?"

Giving her a half smile, Ace brought over his plate and sat on one of the two straight backed chairs that flanked the heavily scuffed table. He laid his gun on the table and shoved a forgotten newspaper out of the way to make room for his plate. "That was a good try, Ms. Macintyre. I do appreciate you helping get the bullet out of my leg all those years ago, but a guy's got to eat. I stood up for your boy out there and gave him another chance. That was my way of paying you back for you and Macintyre patching me up that day." He picked up his thin meat and cheese sandwich and took a bite. "Crazy how a guy can drop through the ranks like a rock into a pond. One minute, I have access to all the cash I want. And the next, I'm working for a guy I never even bothered to talk to while slowly starving to death. I've got a little money," Ace reassured her around his second bite. "But I'm here with Cincher, and I can't chance being seen. That leaves me stuck here eating moldy cheese sandwiches. While the honest guy out there slaves all day to make fifty bucks and is free to eat as much as he can buy."

"Small choices add up, Ace. Choices lead to habits, and habits shape who you are."

The door opened, and Cincher walked in, tossing his oily hat on the table. "What is this? Some kind of picnic?" he demanded. "Ace, I told you to watch the bank."

"And who's watching her?" Ace asked around his sandwich.

"Just tie her up if you are going out. You are losing your touch, Ace, getting soft."

Violet saw the anger in Ace's eyes and quickly spoke up. "Cincher, we don't know how to get the deposit box or even what is in it. Why go to all this trouble to bring attention to it after all these years?"

"For your information, Ms. Macintyre, this particular bank has a policy on deposit boxes." He went to the kitchen, checking cabinets as he spoke. "If they are left ten years without being accessed and no contact can be made with the owner or a known relative, the box is opened and the contents are reviewed by the bank board."

"Wouldn't they send some kind of notice in the mail?" she asked, glancing at Ace, who was staring distastefully at his food. The angry fire had gone out of his eyes.

"Yes, and you would be the one to receive it. Unless of course, the address given was incorrect. Why isn't there any food?" Cincher growled, closing the refrigerator door.

"Why don't you try buying some for a change?" Ace tossed his half eaten sandwich onto his plate. "You seem to enjoy going out."

Cincher turned on him, his thin cord seemed to appear out of nowhere.

"The notice would come to the last known address," Violet said softly to herself.

Both men looked at her.

"The notice would come to the last known address," she repeated, speaking louder. "We have moved several times over the years, and I'm sure Roland did not update the address. I've never seen a statement from the bank here. I never even dreamed he had any connection with this bank."

Cincher's face darkened. He had not thought of where the notice would have gone. "You lived in the little white house on Cherry Street ten years ago."

Violet frowned at him, remembering his visit.

"Ace, go there and check for the notice," Cincher commanded.

"That's five hours away," Ace complained.

"I'm paying you, aren't I? Cincher's look was menacing.

"Not that I've seen." Not having any decent food to eat had rubbed Ace the wrong way. He was in the mood for a good fight.

Cincher reached into his jacket and pulled out a roll of cash. Counting off four hundred dollar bills, he slammed them down on the table. "Happy?"

"If they are real." Ace picked one up and examined it in the light. He did not miss Cincher's stealthy switch of one bill for a new one. "But where am I supposed to spend them? The police have notices on TV with our faces on them asking for tips."

"That's not my problem. I said I would pay you, and I have. That's your down payment. We get the box tonight, and you'll get a nice fat wad of money to sit on."

"And you want me five hours away when this thing blows up?" Ace knew the answer.

"Skip the trip," Cincher growled. "I might need you to deal with the lady once she's taken care of.

"You came to the house on Cherry Street ten years ago," Violet remembered aloud. "You came very early on the morning after Brent's sixth birthday."

"Ten years ago today," Cincher agreed, something hateful in his expression. "How time flies."

Officer Cane's handgun came up out of the holster as the footsteps came closer, but the barrel of the Glock remained pointed at the ground. When Jimmy rounded the corner, Officer Cane relaxed visibly.

Brent groaned in disbelief. "What's he doing here?"

"Wow, I didn't expect to find all of you back here." Jimmy pointed half heartedly at Dr. Nee. "Just him, well, actually I thought he would be out front."

"Head on home, Jimmy," Officer Cane slid his gun back into the holster. "We have this covered."

Jimmy hesitated.

"Maybe he can help you gun someone down while I rob the bank." Brent had pushed himself off the wall and was glaring at Jimmy.

"This is not the time for this." Officer Cane pressed his radio button. "I need a car for this party that's gathering behind the bank. I have a couple of people I need to get out of harm's way."

"Ten four," the radio crackled in response.

Cane pointed at Dr. Nee and then Jimmy as he spoke, "You and you. Get out front and into Burk's car. I don't want to see either of you until this is over, understand."

Jimmy opened his mouth to protest.

"Come on, Jimmy." Dr. Nee moved toward the front of the bank.

Officer Cane was on the phone again, getting the latest update from the chief. It wouldn't be long before the area was crawling with police.

Jimmy glanced at Officer Cane before turning to Brent. "Look, I know you hate me, and you have a good reason to. It doesn't mean anything now, but I'm sorry."

"Save it." Brent put his hands on either side of his head, trying to relieve the building pressure. "I have to tell you, there was this guy. Short and kind of blocky. I saw him from your building. He was looking around, like he was scared, but I lost him when I got down to the street. If you see him, follow him. I think he's the weak link."

Officer Cane turned and saw Jimmy was still there. He raised an eyebrow, and Jimmy put his hands up in surrender before hurrying after Dr. Nee.

"Looks like John Starclish showed up at the Cornshaw place a little while ago. He wants to see you." Officer Cane watched as Brent's face contorted with emotion. Cane gestured for Brent to lead the way down the side street between the bank and the real estate office next door.

"He's in Brandon's car. He'll pick you up as soon as you get out there."

"I don't want to see him."

"Give it a try. You might learn something helpful." Checking the street, Cane nodded at the unmarked vehicle, and Officer Brandon pulled it up to the curb where they stood. Before he could protest, Brent was helped into the car, and the door was shut behind him.

John looked over at Brent. Over the last few days, Brent had imagined what he would do when he caught up with John, but in his imagination, John never looked so awful. He looked like he had not slept in a week. His eyes were red rimmed, and he had not shaved for several days. A wide, purple bruise above his left cheek bone had spread up under his eye. His lip was split, and his knuckles were bruised.

"Burk got held up at domestic case. Said he'll come when he can," Officer Brandon informed Cane as he stepped out of the driver's side, locking the car behind him. He stood just outside the car, talking with Officer Cane in low tones, giving Brent and John some time alone. Brent saw several more police cars pull to a stop outside the bank. He frowned darkly. Was this Officer Cane's plan? Cincher would know in a heartbeat that Brent had informed the police.

Violet's face flushed with passion. "You killed Brent's birthday puppy. The one he had been waiting for weeks to get. He was heartbroken."

"He got over it," Cincher answered carelessly.

"But Roland didn't."

Cincher narrowed his eyes at her.

"He was livid when he heard what you had done. After the puppy had been buried, Roland stalked out of the house without a word."

"That's enough," Cincher spat angrily.

"Roland was gone for most of the day. I thought he needed time to cool off." Violet's eyes widened with understanding. "You came that night to hide out. My husband set a ten year time bomb at a bank five hours away with evidence you wanted to keep hidden. He knew that no matter what happened to him, that box would be opened because none of us knew about it."

Cincher was glaring at her. "I said that's enough."

"Roland was an incredibly patient man, Cincher," Violet informed him without fear. "Even if you kill me at sunrise, that box will still be opened, and you will face the consequences of whatever that box holds."

CHAPTER 26

"Brent, I'm so sorry." John's voice was thick with emotion.

"Sorry isn't good enough," Brent shot back. "Why did you leave her?"

"I didn't leave her, Brent. Not willingly. I'm not a fighter," John looked down at his hands. "They grabbed us right outside the airport. It was dark and not many people were around. A car pulled up, and a couple of guys got out. I guess they knocked me out then, because the next thing I remember is being tied up and blindfolded. Your mom was whispering for me to keep still and quiet. When they untied me to take me out, I managed to twist out of their grasp. Catching them off-guard was the only chance I had. I got in a few solid punches before they knocked me out again. When I came to, they had moved her, and there was not a scrap of evidence to prove they had ever been there."

"So you left."

"I spent days asking anyone who would listen if they had seen her," John corrected. "I reported her kidnapping to the police and checked back with them so often that they started shaking their heads 'no' as soon as I walked in. They were working on it, but had no leads. I spent days tracking down people who might know other people who might have some information for me. No one knew anything helpful. Or else they would not admit it. I couldn't find any trace of the kidnappers or your mom. Now and then, something hopeful would came up, but each time it turned out to be a false lead." John hesitated, "I didn't know what else to do, Brent. I came here because I thought maybe you would know where they would have taken her."

"Couldn't you describe the kidnappers to the police?" Brent asked.

"Only one. I only remember one man." John's face clouded with the memory. "A gaunt man with terrible eyes and thin wispy hair. They already had a picture of him on file. It's the one on the TV notices."

"I haven't exactly had time to watch TV." Brent did not bother to ask for more details. It was Cincher.

"They took my wallet and everything else. I had to borrow money to get back here. I thought maybe you would have heard from her or know someone who would know something." For a moment, he rested his forehead in his palms. "I can't think straight anymore. I didn't know where else to go."

"Why should I help you? You aren't anything to me," Brent asked without emotion. "You ran away like a coward, leaving Mom to take the heat." A strong insult was a good way to start a fight, and with so much out of his control, Brent felt like knocking someone around. He pulled the handle of the door to give himself more space, but it did not open.

"Great." Brent muttered, trying to catch the attention of one of the officers outside. Both skillfully ignored him.

"Brent, I would give my life to save her from these guys."

"Right." Brent tried the handle again with the same result. "Did you try praying?" Brent knew it was a low blow, but he wanted someone to yell at, someone to hurt like he had been hurt.

"I haven't stopped praying."

Brent was shamed by the man's soft answer. "Good." He mumbled awkwardly. He would not admit it, but he longed for what John had.

“Aren’t there any of your Dad’s old friends who would know where they have her?” John was getting panicky.

“Calm down,” Brent instructed coolly. He felt anything but calm himself.

“Were we supposed to get in somebody’s car?” Jimmy was standing awkwardly beside Dr. Nee in the dark.

“I believe he mentioned the name Burk,” Dr. Nee confirmed. “Maybe he is still on his way.”

“The only car is the one over there that they put Brent in.”

“Then I suppose we wait here.”

Jimmy shifted. He glanced down at Dr. Nee and shifted again.

The older man waited, amused.

“How do I fix this with Brent?” Jimmy was looking off in the distance.

“This, as in the trouble with Cincher, or the trouble involving your lie about your father?”

“The second one,” Jimmy muttered, glancing over at the unmarked car that held Brent. “I know I screwed things up. Big time.”

“You were the cause of years of unnecessary pain, Jimmy. A wound that deep will take time to heal.” Dr. Nee told him seriously. “What makes you want to make it right now?

Jimmy was quiet for a long minute. “I gave my life to Jesus about two weeks ago. Just before all this blew up.

Dr. Nee smiled up at him. “I’m glad to hear that, Jimmy.

“Yeah, but the problem is, now I can’t get rid of this pressing feeling that I need to tell Brent the truth and make it right. And with you cutting in with that newspaper article, things sped up a lot faster than I had planned.”

“That was not my intention.”

"I know. It's weird. Mom became a Christian several years ago, but I didn't really care about it until after I started doing Brent's challenges. That made me see how hard it is to do what is right on my own. Stuff started coming up that I knew I needed to let go of or change, but I couldn't seem to do it. I talked to my mom, and when she explained how Jesus had paid for and conquered sin, it all made sense, you know?"

Dr. Nee nodded.

"The weird thing is that, apparently, Brent's mom has been meeting with my mom for lunch once a week for months without either of us knowing about it. Don't tell Brent that yet."

"God has an incredible way of working things out."

"I guess so. But I'm still stuck with my problem. So what should I do?"

"Ask God for wisdom. Tell Brent you are sorry, change your behavior toward him, and show him you mean it by consistency. It will take time, and there's no guarantee that he will forgive you. But that is all you can do."

"I guess you are right." Jimmy paused for a moment before adding, "Hey, have you noticed how many cars have passed at that intersection down there? It is, what? One or two in the morning. Why are so many people out?"

"If my hunch is right, those are not civilian cars."

"Do you want to go see where they are going?"

"Do you enjoy being shot?" Dr. Nee's eyes shone with mischief.

"You want me to get you an empty deposit box?" The bank president had been awakened out of a sound sleep and despite his crisp suit, his face betrayed his sleepy state.

"Yes. Now that we know it is at your bank, we need to get Cincher to believe it's the box he's been waiting for. We needed it two hours ago. So we will need to head over there right away," Chief Davis informed him. "I'll give you a lift to the bank. The boy is waiting there."

"Isn't this a bit dangerous to send a teen into a hostage situation with an empty box?"

"Only if word gets out that it is not the real box," the Chief told him meaningfully.

"No fear of that from me," President Rodsworth assured him.

"Besides, it won't be empty," Chief Davis smiled. "I'm having our records department pull a few key newspaper articles involving Cincher that we can put inside.

"I hope it works. I'm ready when you are."

"Good. My car is right outside." As they walked out to the car together, the chief silently acknowledged the officer stationed outside the banker's house. The man gave a slight nod in return.

"I appreciate you being so cooperative," Chief Davis unlocked the car and slid into the driver's seat. "I understand it is very late, or rather very early for someone used to banker's hours."

Rodsworth smiled good-naturedly at the subtle jab. "If it gets that poor lady free, it would be well worth the inconvenience."

"I think so, too," Chief Davis agreed.

"Okay, Brent, here's the plan." Officer Cane had opened the door from the outside, and he crouched on the curb where he could look Brent in the eyes. "It is super dangerous, and we could lose everyone involved if something goes wrong."

"Great lead in," John said from his side of the car.

"I'm giving it to you straight because it is your decision in the end. We could offer a trade and wait around for Cincher to bring your mom to us."

"But he won't because the box has something he doesn't want the police to know about." Brent interjected.

"Correct," Officer Cane looked pleased. "If you take a deposit box and go to him, three things could happen. One, you give them the box and walk away free with your mom. Two, Cincher gets suspicious, and our men step in before anything gets ugly."

Brent glanced over his shoulder at John. "Or three, we all die."

"Yeah, but we are shooting for one of the first two."

"That seems like a big gamble to stick Brent into a situation like that," John observed.

Officer Cane shifted so he could see John better, "If you have any better ideas, we are open to that too. Our main problem is that we only have about four hours left."

Brent frowned and would have corrected him, but John spoke from beside him.

"He's right Brent. Cincher is a time bomb waiting to blow. If it gets too close to morning, he might panic and try to get as far from the box as possible if he thinks he can't get his hands on whatever is inside. The bank doesn't officially open until nine, but some business happens before or after business hours."

"We can know what box it is." Brent spoke slowly as the idea came to him. "All they have to do is look at which box is ten years old and up for review."

Cane looked pained for a second. "How did we miss that?"

"We didn't know it was at this bank until tonight," Officer Brandon pointed out. He was standing watch at the door. "We were looking for a deposit box under Roland Macintyre's name. Something that did not exist."

"Do we dare let him bring the real box then?" Officer

Cane asked.

"That's for the chief to decide."

"What do you think they are doing?" Jimmy had seen Officer Cane crouch down to talk with Brent. The open car door hid them both from his view.

Meanwhile, another car pulled up, and Wilson Rodsworth got out. Jimmy knew the bank president by sight because he sometimes stopped by the commissioner's office where Jimmy worked. He was a professionally dressed man who combed his thin hair over to hide his balding dome.

Dr. Nee and Jimmy watched with interest as the man walked quickly to the front door of the bank. He glanced around and pulled out a key.

As if on signal, Brent stepped out of the police car and walked toward the bank. His steps were purposeful, but his face was scared.

"Let him go," Dr. Nee warned when Jimmy started to move toward the bank. "The police have this area surrounded and are doing their best to help his mom. They don't need us to interfere before our time."

"I don't see anyone."

Dr. Nee smiled, "That is the point, Jimmy. I believe they call it a stakeout."

"You said before our time. Does that mean you are planning on helping?" Jimmy asked curiously.

"If I can help, I will," was Dr. Nee's vague reply.

Brent followed Rodsworth into the bank, and they waited in silence for him to reappear.

CHAPTER 27

"That's the little man!" Jimmy whispered fiercely, drawing Dr. Nee's attention to the stubby man who had just hurried across the street. "The man I saw from the factory roof. He's involved. I don't know how, but he is!"

"Calm down, Jimmy." Dr. Nee instructed firmly. "He will hear you. Stay here and keep an eye on him. I'll let the officers know." Dr. Nee walked off before Jimmy could respond.

For a moment, Jimmy did nothing, watching in silence as the stubby man hurried on. Then he remembered Dr. Nee's comment about helping. This was something he could do.

Jogging in the direction the man had gone, Jimmy glanced back to see Brent emerge from the bank holding a deposit box.

The time for action had come.

"Brent, he's getting away!" Jimmy called to him without slowing his pace.

"I have to go now, or Jimmy might lose him." Brent stuck the old, dusty deposit box under his arm and ran after Jimmy, leaving the bank president staring after him in disbelief.

"What was that about?" Chief Davis came jogging over from where he had been talking to Dr. Nee. He was a big, imposing man who had very little reason to run.

"He said he had to go, or Jimmy might lose him," Rodsworth answered, scratching his head. "Was this part of the plan?"

"No, I think the plan just changed." Chief Davis got on

his radio and called all units to move south and keep an eye out for two teens on foot and a stubby, boxy man." He imagined the smiles the last description would bring to the faces of his men.

"What was that?" Officer Cane joined them, his face displaying his concern. "We were supposed to tail him."

"He grabbed the box and made a run for it." Rodsworth was using a neatly pressed handkerchief to wipe the sweat from his forehead.

"Do you think he crossed us?" the chief asked Cane seriously.

"I hope not," Cane shook his head in frustration.

"Drive around ahead of them and try to cut them off," the chief instructed. "I'll see if we can locate the real deposit box."

"You gave him a decoy box?" Shocked and angry, Officer Cane looked from one man to the other. "He trusted us. I gave him my word."

"Cane, listen."

"I don't have time to talk about it. Cincher's going to kill them all when he finds out it's a fake." Cane sprinted to his cruiser. The car's tires screeched on the pavement as he shot off down the street.

For a moment, everything was quiet, and then Chief Davis sighed heavily. As chief of the police department, he had to make a lot of quick calls. Tonight he wondered if he had made the wrong one. He could only hope that his men would be able to locate the boys in time to make it right.

"Mr. Rodsworth, I need to take a look at your bank records. We need to get our hands on the contents of the real box before Cincher realizes the one he has is not the real deal. Once that happens, if he is lenient, we may have to trade whatever evidence is in that box for two Macintyres. I want to have the contents logged and photographed before that happens. I've got a team on the way.

“Yes, Sir. Right this way.”

“Brent?” Jimmy pulled him down behind the waist high hedge that grew around the walkway to the apartment. “He went in there.”

“That’s where we used to live.” Brent searched the windows. They were all dark. “The room must be on the other side, unless they are keeping it dark.”

“You brought the box?” Jimmy asked incredulously. “I’m impressed.”

“My mom’s life is on the line, Jimmy. Of course I brought the box.”

“Is it the real thing?”

Brent looked sideways at him. “Of course it is. Why would the police give me a decoy and not tell me?”

“I don’t know.” Jimmy shrugged. “Let’s go in.”

“You are sure he went in there?”

“Positive,” Jimmy assured him. “He went in and upstairs, but I don’t know how many, just that he went up.”

“Why did you stop me? I could have followed him in.”

“He was already in by the time you got here. You would have met him on his way back down.”

They both thought about what that would have meant and said nothing more.

“Cincher, you gotta skip town.” The short, jittery messenger spotted Violet and ducked his head, pulling up the collar of his jacket to hide his face from her. “The police are swarming the area around the bank. I got in as close as I could. This classy guy in an expensive suit let the Macintyre kid into the bank about fifteen minutes ago. There was way too much activity around that area tonight."

"At the bank, huh." Cincher's face grew dark. "Only about four more hours and their time is up. I thought that kid had more sense."

"What else did they say, Stub?" Ace asked from across the room.

"It's getting expensive to travel," the messenger whined. "You would have walked into their trap without me."

The killer's wrist flicked, and the dreaded cord was in Cincher's hand. "Ace asked you what they said, Stub." His eyes were deadly.

Stub instantly forgot about hiding his identity. Putting his hands up, he backed away. "Never mind the money, Cincher, I'll tell you. One of the officers mentioned the boy bringing the box alone. They said they hope he makes it and you stick to your end of the deal."

Cincher was still glaring, but no longer at Stub.

"Seriously, Cincher, what's a little information between friends? You can forget the whole thing." He laughed nervously as he pulled open the door and checked the landing outside. Cincher's rope flashed across his vision, and the messenger grabbed at it as it cinched around his neck.

"No, Cincher, no. I came to help you," he pleaded desperately.

"You came for cash," Cincher corrected, his voice chillingly calm.

"I'm living off the streets. We all are now that Macintyre is gone, and the cops are breathing down our throats. You kill me, and you'll be helping the cops out. Plus then you will have two bodies to dispose of."

Cincher drew the cord tighter for just an instant. "If anyone finds me here, I'll kill you." Releasing one end of the thin rope, Cincher shoved the messenger away in disgust.

Stub stumbled in his haste to put distance between himself and Cincher. For a bold moment, the jittery, dirty man, hesitated, his eyes on Cincher.

Pulling out a crisp hundred dollar bill, Cincher dropped it to the floor. Turning, he re-entered the apartment, closing the door behind him.

Outside, he heard Stub's timid footsteps as he retrieved the money, and the quickly retreating steps that followed.

"So they want to play dirty and pretend to send the boy alone." Cincher was still toying with his cord, moving it through his hands like it were a living creature with a mind of its own. "Looks like your time has run out, Mrs. Macintyre."

———

"Anything?"

Officer Richardson shook his head. "Not a thing, Chief. She's here in the city, that we know, but we can't find anyone who has seen her or even seen anything suspicious." He sighed heavily. He was several hours past his shift and had already put in a double.

"What about the boys?" Chief Davis signaled for the banker, who had stopped to listen, to continue looking through the old records.

"We know the general area the boys are in and have created a perimeter," Richardson answered. "I've got some men walking the streets looking for anything suspicious. We could do a full out search, but Cane is afraid it will spook Cincher, and we will lose them all. Chief, we are running out of time."

"Don't you think I know that, Richardson?" Chief Davis turned his attention back to the bank president who was studying the records from ten years prior. "Can't you remember what name he used, Rodsworth? Macintyre was a very forceful and memorable person. Surely you remember him."

Rodsworth looked up, annoyed by the interruption. "I don't believe I ever met or even saw the man."

"But he did have a deposit box here?"

"Yes." Rodsworth frowned at the memory. "Well, at least I think so. It was a long time ago, and I had forgotten about it altogether. These records brought it back. I was at a meeting of the trustees when he came in. My employees told me later that a man came in who was in a terrible rage. He met with one of our new clerks privately. Come to think of it, I never followed up about what that meeting was about."

"Do you have his name?" Davis asked.

"The clerk's name?" Rodsworth nodded, still flipping through the papers. "Of course we do. We are a bank. Records are very important."

Chief Davis cut him off. "Save it, Rodsworth. What's his name?"

"I would have to look it up. He quit that same night. Knowing what I know now, I wouldn't be surprised if Macintyre threatened him or paid him off."

"Probably that guy who started this whole thing by selling secrets," Richardson pointed out. Davis nodded sourly.

"From what I heard of him after his death," the bank president went on. "Roland was a forceful man and was used to getting what he wanted. All I can do is look through these old files and hope the clerk logged his work properly. That takes time."

"That's the one thing we don't have, Mr. Rodsworth."

"Here he comes," Brent whispered, ducking.

Jimmy kept his head just high enough to peer over the hedge. Stub was looking around, scared. He turned sharply to cut through the hedge where they were hiding. Brent shook the bush slightly, hesitated, and shook it again.

"Who's there?" Stub whispered fearfully.

The boys were silent.

Stub moved around nervously and finally decided against cutting through the hedge. He looked back at the apartment building once more before scurrying off in the opposite direction like a rat, with fearful angry glances behind him.

"Alright, here's the plan." Brent whispered, rising enough to watch the short man hurry away. When he was out of sight, Brent turned to Jimmy, barely able to make out his features in the deep shadow where he crouched. "You go up the street that way a block or so. There's one of those new emergency call stations. Call the police and let them know where we are, and any other details that would be helpful. Get them here as fast as you can."

"While you go up and take on the bad guys alone?" Jimmy protested, careful to keep his voice low. "No way."

"Jimmy, this isn't a game. I have to try, and I have to go now, alone, before the police come. You gotta trust me." Brent looked up at the apartment, preparing himself for what he had to do.

"Man, I'd hate to see you die. Can't I come help you in some way?"

"Call the police." Brent felt strangely calm. "That's the most important thing you can do."

"Alright."

"Jimmy," Brent hissed.

Turning back at the far end of the hedge, Jimmy looked back, his face questioning.

"Thanks."

Jimmy gave him a worried smile and sprinted off down the street.

Brent thought of John and Dr. Nee and hoped they were

still praying.

CHAPTER 28

"Cincher, no." Ace stood ready, the table between himself and the killer he was working for. "You gave her boy until sunrise. He might still work it out. Kill her now and you have nothing."

"Going soft, eh, Ace? Don't want to see the Macintyre family squirm? They deserve it, and you know it."

"At sunrise, but not yet." Ace stood his ground. "Stub said the boy was bringing the box. Give him some time to get it here.

"With the whole police force tagging along. I say she dies now." Cincher was searching Ace's face for any sign of betrayal. "I told her kid not to go to the police, but he did. The deal's up."

"But if he couldn't get it without them..."

Cincher's hard laugh cut him off. "I'll get the box and her. He doesn't have to know she's dead. That teller could have been bluffing about what Macintyre put into that box, but this family has cost me a lot of time and trouble."

"I do."

They both turned to look at Violet who had been silent until now.

"You do what?" Ace asked for them both.

She met their stares boldly. "I know what is in the deposit box."

Cincher's eyes narrowed. "Go on."

"When Roland came home again the day you killed Brent's puppy, he was strangely calm. I asked him what he had done, and all he would say is that he had set you up to get what was coming to you."

"You are stalling for time," Cincher growled.

"There's evidence in that box," Violet finished. "Evidence that will put you away for life." She could tell by the flash of anger in his gaunt, ugly face that Cincher knew what the evidence was.

"He thought he was clever, but it will cost you," Cincher threatened. The end of the cord lashed angrily through his fingers as if it too felt his wrath.

"How will another killing help, Cincher? Think this through," Ace warned. "You gotta get out of here while you can. The police are too close. Even if you get the box, what's keeping them from raiding the apartment and getting it back?"

"I'll get out. But not before I kill her." He moved toward Violet, intent and cruel. "It's the only way I can get even with Macintyre."

Ace's gun barked, and Cincher instantly cradled his right hand. Falling to his knees on the dirty carpet, he leaned over, holding his wounded limb close to his chest. "You didn't even have the decency to kill me," he growled, his teeth clenched against the pain.

"You don't deserve that kind of death," Ace retorted. "Too many people have suffered for you to escape so easily." He turned his gun on Violet. "Trust me, this is the easiest way."

———

"Chief, we just got a call from someone named Jimmy. He said the Macintyre boy has located Cincher in the Broad Vista Apartment just south of here."

"Contact Cane, Spencer, and Brandon. Tell them to

create a perimeter and move in quietly. This may be our last chance to get her out alive. An all points bulletin over the radio would be too dangerous right now. If my guess is right, the Macintyre boy is already in up to his neck.

"Ace, please don't shoot me." Violet's calm quiet voice seemed out of place.

Ace stood looking at her, undecided. He was not a killer, but Cincher would kill her if Ace didn't do it first.

A light knock interrupted the tense moment. It was repeated, louder.

Keeping Cincher and Violet in sight, Ace moved to the door. "Who is it?" he asked softly.

Brent's voice came through the door. "I have the box."

Standing painfully, Cincher wavered, caught himself, and made his way to the kitchen.

Ace turned the lock and stepped away, still keeping Violet covered. Brent pushed open the door slowly. He stood on the threshold, his eyes locked on the gun in Ace's hand.

"Ace, please don't hurt her," Brent begged. Ace did not look at him or move.

Seeing the blood on the carpet, Brent looked at his mom for any sign of injury. She sat on the couch, stiff with fear. "I have the box," his voice trembled with his hands as he held it out.

"And a gang of police down below," Cincher growled, pulling a towel from the cabinet. He looked pale, but determined.

"No," Brent corrected quickly. "The police aren't here yet."

"Open the box," Cincher commanded.

"I don't have…" Brent stopped. Moving into the room, he shut the door behind him. "Where do you want it?"

"On the floor there. I enjoy seeing Macintyre's on their knees." Cincher, groaned in pain as he struggled to wrap a kitchen towel around his injured hand. Tucking his wounded hand inside his jacket, he cradled it there with his good arm.

Brent knew the blood on the carpet belonged to Cincher and glanced at Ace. The man stood steady, still pointing the handgun at Violet.

"It's in my pocket," he informed Ace.

The man nodded his consent, moving the gun to cover Brent.

Kneeling, Brent pulled the lock pick kit out of his pocket and set to work on the lock. He had only practiced one night, and his trembling hands made it hard to move the pins. After several minutes, the lock turned, and Brent looked up expectantly at Cincher.

"Open it," he growled, coming toward Brent.

Lifting the lid, Brent revealed a little stack of newspaper articles dated ten years ago. Brent saw the name Nelson beneath the picture of a worried looking man being crowded into a courthouse.

"Macintyre will pay for this," Cincher growled angrily. "He may be dead, but I'll make him pay."

"But isn't this what you wanted?" Brent glanced at Ace, confused. "This is the box. The bank president said it was the right one."

"You think I'm dumb, Little Macintyre? You think I don't have a brain?"

"No, I don't understand. This is the box they gave me. The clippings have your name on them." Brent grabbed a handful to show him. "Maybe my dad thought that together these would give the police a clue. Maybe he wasn't as smart as he thought."

"Do those papers look like they have been in a box for ten years?"

Brent was starting to panic. He knew the police would come soon, and then it would all be over. "I don't know. This was the box. The bank president got it for me."

"Stay where you are, Cincher," Ace commanded. The gun barrel swung back to where Violet sat, weeping silently.

Brent stood frozen. "Ace, please," he whispered, afraid any sudden move would push him to action.

"Ace, he brought the box. Please let him go," Violet begged.

"Be quiet, woman," Cincher spat. He stumbled to the chair by the table and sank into it, his gaunt face as pale as death.

Ace had not moved, but his breath was coming faster now.

"It's not too late," Violet repeated. "You can give yourself up."

His head was shaking 'no' almost imperceptibly.

Cincher slumped forward onto the table, his good hand sliding into the newspaper that had been tossed aside on the table.

They heard a noise downstairs. The police had arrived and were moving in.

Brent's warning came too late as Cincher righted himself. The handgun that had been under the newspaper was now in Cincher's hand.

The room went dark, and Brent saw the burst of flame leave the gun barrel. The room burst with light once more, and his eyes darted to his mom. She sat on the couch where she had been, staring in disbelief as Ace crumpled to the ground.

"Get down!" Brent shouted, plunging the room into darkness once more. He leapt forward, tripped on the open deposit box and slammed into the table. Cincher leapt back, disoriented by the second burst of light. The gun went off again.

Something whizzed over Brent, who was scrambling to his feet. It struck Cincher's bad arm causing him to cry out and crumple to his knees. Brent wrenched the gun from Cincher's weak grasp. Looking back, Brent saw Jimmy standing triumphantly on the threshold. His arm was drawn back ready to launch the second rock.

Brent did not have time to think. The room flooded with police, guns drawn. Cincher cried in pain as the officers pulled him from the floor. Checking for weapons, they cuffed him and moved him toward the door, leaving only the dreaded cord laying lifelessly on the table.

Allowing himself to be patted down, Brent searched for his mother in the confusion. When he spotted her, Officer Cane was helping her up from the dirty carpet. She had dove to the floor at Brent's warning.

Without asking for permission, Brent went to her.

"Oh, Brent, I was so scared he would kill you!" Violet hugged him tightly. She had been brave during her captivity. Now that she knew her son was safe, the emotions welled up unchecked.

Brent let her weep against him.

Officer Brandon stooped to check Ace's wound. Standing again, he shook his head. He was gone. Once the apartment had been cleared by the other officers, Officer Cane radioed in and updated the chief.

"They found the box." He met Brent's confused frown without looking away. "I didn't know they hadn't found it." He explained softly. "I never would have sent you in if I knew it was a fake."

"It doesn't matter now." Brent was too happy to have his mom safe to be mad at Officer Cane.

Officer Brandon took charge of the situation. "You three, head downstairs and don't let anyone in or out of the building. Richardson, you cover the landing on this floor. No one is to come out of their rooms until we have the Macintyres out safely."

The men moved to obey. There was nothing they could do inside the apartment anyway. The chief was sending over a crime detail. They would have to photograph the scene before anything could be moved.

For the first time, Officer Brandon noticed Jimmy who was still standing to the side, watching everything unfold. "Rocko, you take the Nelson boy home and after that you go home. You're done for the night, got it?"

Rocko nodded gratefully.

Reluctantly, Jimmy followed Officer Rocko from the room.

Brent watched over his mom's shoulder as Officer Cane scanned the room. His gaze stopped on the couch where Brent's mom had been sitting. Frowning, he crouched by the couch and felt the cushion. Brent guessed it was still warm. Catching Brent's eye, Officer Cane pointed to the bullet hole in the upholstery. It was right where Violet Macintyre had been sitting only seconds before.

CHAPTER 29

"Hey Brent," Jimmy kept his distance.

Brent kept his eyes on the train passing loudly on the track below.

Shoving his hands into his pockets, Jimmy waited.

The last cars slipped under the bridge and out of sight before Brent looked over at Jimmy. "I'm sorry for what I said about your dad, Jimmy."

Jimmy shrugged. Coming a little closer, he leaned his arms on the rail of the bridge a few feet from Brent. "I should have told the truth."

"I haven't seen you in over a week. Is everything okay?"

"Yeah. They had my dad on trial again. You know, with the new evidence from the deposit box. He always claimed he didn't shoot the man at the gas station. Now everyone knows he was telling the truth."

Looking over at Jimmy, Brent asked, "What happened that night? The night your dad was arrested?"

"I guess you deserve to hear it." Jimmy sighed. "I was six and a half that day. My mom liked to celebrate little things, so we were having my half birthday party that night. Dad called and said he was on his way home, but had to stop for gas." Jim's face grew serious. "He never came home. Mom told me and my brother that it was because the police thought he had done something bad. The kids at school told us our dad had shot and killed the gas station man. He was a nice guy, and we all knew him. He had a candy bowl for the kids and knew our names. All that made it hard for anyone to move on. School was torture for us after that.

After they arrested him, Dad used his one phone call to tell us he hadn't killed Mr. Randy. He said that we should go ahead and celebrate because the police would sort it out, and he would be home soon." Jimmy paused. "I haven't talked to him since that night."

"But how did they mix him up with Cincher?" Brent had seen pictures of Jimmy's dad on the news at Ornstein's. He was tall and had dark red hair like Jimmy. There was nothing similar between him and the gaunt killer.

"The cameras were down that night." Jimmy responded. "Cincher probably cut the wires before he killed Mr. Randy. However it happened, Mr. Randy was the only one who saw his murderer that night. Someone saw dad come running out after the shooting. They never found the murder weapon, so all the evidence they had pointed to him."

Brent looked down at the tracks below. "It was my dad's fault that your dad had to be in jail for so long."

"It was pretty clever of your dad to stash the murder weapon and an evidence letter like that. I mean, if you don't consider my dad's situation," Jimmy corrected quickly. "Your dad had ten years to change his mind. And, if something ever happened to him, he knew Cincher would get what he deserved."

Brent shook his head, "He should have given it to the police right away, so your dad could have gotten what he deserved, his freedom."

"And given himself up, and blown his cover as a mastermind criminal?" Jimmy shook his head. "That's not how smart criminals work."

"How would you know?" Brent eyed Jimmy with a suspicious side look.

Shaking his head, Jimmy dismissed his comment.

"John said the fingerprints on the gun were Cincher's." Brent observed. "How did they get fingerprints after so many years?"

Jimmy's eyes lit up with interest. "They talked about that at the trial so the jury would understand. The gun was in a protected place. There was no weather or other people to mess up the prints. The police were able to lift several of Cincher's fingerprints from the gun. There was even a partial print on the trigger. That, and the fact that the rifling on the bullet that killed Mr. Randy matched the lands and grooves of Cincher's gun, proved my dad was innocent." Seeing Brent's confused frown, Jimmy explained. "Rifling is the marks the bullet gets from the gun as it passes through the barrel. They can use that to track down the manufacturer or match the bullet to another shot from the same gun."

"Wow."

"It was a pretty interesting trial." Jimmy shoved his hands into his pockets and fell silent.

"It's good that your dad is coming home, right?" Brent could see Jimmy was struggling with something inside.

"Brent, I treated him like he was dead for ten years. I didn't talk to him when he called. I never even went to see him." Jimmy looked away, collecting himself. "I would hate me if I were him."

"Maybe he doesn't hate you. Maybe your dad is like Dr. Nee and John. You know, someone who believes in God and forgives people." Brent paused. "Is he?" he asked hopefully.

"Mom said he got saved in prison years ago. She asked Jesus to save her not long after that. She was always telling me that he was a different man because of Jesus." Jimmy's face was sad. "I never went to find out. I was so ashamed of him." Jimmy kicked at the rocks at his feet. "I wouldn't believe him. Now I don't know what I'll say to him. The trial was the first time I've even seen him since I was six. I still haven't talked to him." Jimmy wiped his eyes with his hands. "It's just awkward."

"You are one of them, too, aren't you?" Brent asked after several minutes of silence.

Jimmy looked over at Brent with a confused frown. "One of who?"

"A Christian."

Hesitating, Jimmy nodded. Amusement tugged at the edges of his mouth as he looked away and added, "Thanks to your dumb bed making challenge."

Brent did not respond to the quip. "I could tell." The quiet way Brent said it, made Jimmy uneasy.

Instead of speaking, he waited.

"You changed." Brent gave him a half smile, "In a good way. It wasn't like the old Jimmy to try to help me out. And then you saved my life with whatever that was you threw at Cincher even after I slammed you and your dad."

Jimmy was silent.

"Jesus makes a big difference, doesn't He?" Brent fiddled with a piece of peeling paint on the rusty red bridge rail.

"Yeah." There was a joy in Jimmy that shone like happiness through his eyes. "I never understood how bad off I was, and how good He is."

Brent could tell that Jimmy was trying hard not to be pushy about his new faith.

"I know about it John told me and my mom before that, but I've never made the leap. I guess I wanted to wait and see if it was real."

"So, is it?" Jimmy was watching him.

Brent evaded the question. "Tell me how you did it."

"Well," Jimmy looked thoughtfully out over the scenery below them. "I just told God that I believed that Jesus came to earth and lived here without breaking any of God's laws.

That He died an innocent man, to pay for my sins, and rose from the dead because He is God. I told Him I knew I had broken God's laws, and needed to be saved from the punishment of my sin. Mom explained all that a lot of times over the years." Jimmy added. "So then I asked Jesus to save me." Jimmy glanced over at Brent. "Kinda rough, but I don't think the words are as important as the choosing to believe. There's a verse that says, "If you confess with your mouth that Jesus is Lord and believe in your heart that God raised Him from the dead, you will be saved."

"Look at you, knowing Bible verses!" Brent grinned, impressed.

"Impressive, isn't it?" Jimmy pretended to polish his nails on his shirt.

Brent rolled his eyes good-naturedly.

"Actually, I learned it last week, so I could say it to you." Jimmy confessed. "This is a big deal, and I wanted to explain it right." He looked expectantly at Brent.

"What?"

"Well, are you going to do it?"

Brent shifted uncomfortably, "What? Talk to God?"

"Sure. You believe Jesus is God, right?"

"Yeah," Brent felt a tingle of excitement building inside.

"And you know you have sinned, right?"

"Right."

"And you believe Jesus paid for your sin. True?"

A smile pulled at the sides of Brent's mouth. "True."

"So why not tell Him?" Jimmy crossed his arms and leaned against the bridge rail. "Brent, you gotta let God be in charge and stop trying to do everything on your own."

When Brent hesitated, Jimmy studied him. "You know, if you aren't ready, that's okay. This is a for life decision. Not some random thing you do and then forget about it."

Chewing his lip thoughtfully, Brent met Jimmy's eyes.

"I am ready."

"So, what's stopping you?"

Brent tried to suppress his smile. "Nothing except this guy I know who won't be quiet long enough for me to talk to God about it."

Laughing, Jimmy put his thumb and index finger together and made a big show of zipping his mouth closed and tossing away the key.

Brent laughed, "That's better."

Taking a deep breath, he let it out slowly. Leaning his forearms on the bridge rail, he looked out over the scenery. "God, I'm a pretty lame guy," Brent spoke aloud. "I've got a bad temper and a bad track record." Brent glanced over at Jimmy and added, "Jimmy calls it sin." His attention moved back to the expanse below them, and his face grew serious. "Whatever it is, I've got it. So, I'm asking You to forgive me. I believe Jesus paid for the bad things I've done. And I believe He's the only one who can actually forgive me and make me a new person. I need that. I know Jesus was, I mean, is God. And I believe He never sinned even though He lived here as a man for a while." Brent frowned thoughtfully. "That doesn't really make a lot of sense to me, but I guess since You're God, you have all that part figured out. Anyway, I'm asking you to forgive me. " He fell silent. He hadn't felt any big fireworks of joy, but something heavy seemed to have been lifted from him.

"That was good," Jimmy told him after a few minutes.

Turning to look at him, Brent opened his mouth in mock surprise. "You were eavesdropping, weren't you?"

Laughing, Jimmy stooped and picked up a handful of little stone chips from the side of the road. "Maybe a little," he confessed.

"You know what I can't believe?" Brent quickly changed the subject. He didn't want Jimmy to ask how he felt. He knew he would not be able to explain the feeling of rest he felt inside. He did believe, and now he knew for himself that Jesus really did make a difference. Somehow Brent also knew that this step was only the beginning.

"What can't you believe?" Jimmy asked absently, he was carefully lining up the bigger chips of rocks on the bridge rail.

"I still can't believe they sent me in with a decoy box."

Looking up from his project, Jimmy considered Brent's statement. "Maybe they thought if you believed it, Cincher would too."

"Well, I'm glad the gun and the letter were enough to prove your dad was innocent. Even though it was done wrong, it's the only good thing my dad ever did."

CHAPTER 30

A commotion on the far side of the running track caught Brent's attention.

"What's going on?" Henry asked. They had been eating lunch at a table with a couple of the other guys.

Not bothering to answer, Brent clambered out of his place between Henry and Clive. He was fairly sure he knew who he would find in the center of the disturbance.

Racing straight across the oval of the track, Brent approached the ring of guys ahead. As he predicted, Jimmy's red head was in the center of the ring. He already had a black eye and a slight bloody nose. Marvin didn't look much better.

"Break it up," Brent commanded loudly.

A few guys forming the outer ring stepped back automatically, not realizing the command had not come from a teacher.

"Duck!" Brent shouted and Jimmy did. Marvin's fist missed its target by mere inches.

"You stay out of this, Macintyre," Marvin warned. "Maybe you are too poor to have a TV, but the rest of us know who Jimmy's dad is."

"Oh, you mean James Nelson? Isn't that the man they just proved was innocent?" Brent was looking each of the guys in the eyes, making them squirm. They were only half hearted in their support of Marvin. "Let me get this straight. You are trying to beat up Jimmy because his dad didn't commit a crime?"

The ring was getting looser, and a few guys simply walked away.

"Why don't we beat up Peter?" Brent asked, looking around the ring of guys. "His dad didn't do a crime either. Or Seth. His dad is a baker. That should be a 'crime free' occupation. Let's beat up Seth next."

Seth and Peter looked at the other guys uncomfortably.

"I said get lost." Marvin growled.

"Make me." Brent stood tall and defiant before the bulky bully. The stragglers turned back to see how it would end.

Marvin spun, and his fist flew toward Brent's middle. Brent dodged, lessening the impact of the blow. "You are going to get suspended, Marvin." Brent warned, dodging again and throwing a punch of his own. Marvin jumped back, putting some distance between them.

"What? Are you two friends now?" Marvin sneered, catching his breath.

Brent looked over the other guys at Jimmy who was using his shirt to wipe the blood from his nose. "Yo, Jimmy. You want to be friends?"

Jimmy shrugged, "I suppose I could stomach it, if you can." His response was for the benefit of the other guys, but Brent saw the pleasure in his eyes.

Locking eyes with Marvin, Brent nodded. "Yeah, we're friends."

Marvin's top lip curled in disgust. He had hoped to rile his opponents. Instead he had accidentally united them.

"We'll make a truce." Jimmy offered. "You don't hit us, and we won't hit you."

"How about we stop hitting each other like school kids and grow up," Mrs. Gram suggested. She was picking her way through the grass toward them, her high heels slowing her progress.

Brent and Jimmy shared an amused glance.

"All of you back inside. The whole mess of you are in so much trouble. You know how Mr. Bond feels about fighting." She turned to pick her way back to the school without waiting for the boys to obey.

"I wish you didn't have to get into a fight two days before the wedding, Brent. You will be all purple and blue for the pictures." Violet's voice was muffled behind the fitting room door. It was her final fitting of her wedding dress, and she had asked Brent to come along.

"Too late for that, Mom." Brent was feeling very out of place in the bridal store. A mom and her daughter were browsing the rack behind where he stood, exclaiming over the silks and lace like they were in a candy shop. "I'm already yellow and gray from the fight with Cincher's guys."

"You might have to wear makeup."

"Not a chance, Mom." He had heard the smile in her voice. "Are you almost done? The wedding will come before you get into that dress if you aren't careful."

"Brent Macintyre!" she exclaimed with a laugh. "Never rush a lady."

Brent laughed and took a seat on an uncomfortable cushioned bench nearby. He thought about what she had said. It was not the lady advice that caught him, but his name. Macintyre. It had marked him as long as he could remember. The name Macintyre earned him undeserved respect as a child from men he had never met. After his dad was killed, it brought shunning and contempt. Now he had the chance to change it, and for some reason he had been struggling with the decision for days. John had offered to adopt him. Brent would become Brent Starclish instead of

Macintyre if he agreed.

"You are awful quiet out there," Violet observed.

"Maybe I fell asleep," Brent quipped half-heartedly.

Violet opened the door and stepped out. Smiling at his open mouthed stare.

"Mom, you look amazing!"

She blushed. "The high neck and three quarter length sleeves aren't really trending for the young brides." She leaned toward him and added, "That makes it cost less."

"Well those girls would look better if they picked one like this." Out of the corner of his eye, Brent saw the young bride-to-be pause and look over. Smiling mischievously, Brent went on. "I like how there's nothing revealing or distracting to pull people's attention away from your radiant face!"

"Oh, stop it." Violet walked across to the mirror and smoothed the front of her long skirt.

Brent got up and walked around her. "You could make a second dress from all that cloth dragging on the ground!"

"Brent. You stop that," she laughed. Putting her fists on her hips, she tried to be serious.

"You got teeny little beads all over it!" Brent pointed out. "Too bad they made them white. They blend in."

"Okay, okay. Seriously now. Do you like it?" Violet searched his face for his true feelings and found only admiration in his eyes.

"I love it. I'm proud to have such a gorgeous person for a mom."

Violet flushed with happiness. "I'm so glad you like it."

The lady who had been helping Violet came over and straightened things here and there, asking how it felt and if Violet was satisfied.

Once that was settled, Violet disappeared into the fitting room again.

"Have you decided what you will do? About John's offer?"

Violet asked through the door. "I know you were thinking about it because you got very quiet after I said your name."

"What do you think about it, Mom?" Brent took his post on the hard white cushioned bench again.

"You will always be my son. The name doesn't change anything in our relationship."

"Not ours, but it will change other people's relationship with me."

"You think so? Maybe it will be different after we move," Violet offered.

"Dad's work was pretty expansive. Besides, after the trial with Cincher and Jimmy's dad was all over the news, the name Macintyre will be fresh in their minds. Without dad's reputation hanging over me, I could make some friends and maybe get a decent job." Brent fiddled with the scratchy lace that bordered his perch.

"That makes sense to me."

Brent could hear the rustle of fabric inside. "You don't think it would be…" He stopped himself.

"Disowning your dad?" Violet seemed to be able to read him even though she could not see him.

"Yeah."

"Brent, your dad did a lot of things without thinking of you and what it would cost you. I don't think he should be the deciding factor. If his name will keep that hurt fresh in your mind, you should take John's. Even if you don't keep his name, you can still remember the good things about your dad."

"I think he's hoping I'll tell him tomorrow after school. He asked me to meet him at Bill's. Did I tell you that Bill gave me my job back?"

Violet emerged with a grin. "Only about seven times today." As if on cue, the lady came and took the dress.

Putting her arm through Brent's elbow, Violet smiled up

at him. "You are a good man, Brent."

Brent noticed that she left off his last name. That was for him to decide before tomorrow.

"Mom?" Brent licked his lips nervously. "There's something I need to tell you."

She grew serious and turned to face him. "Okay."

"Can we get in the car first?" Brent needed more time.

"Of course." She signed the paperwork the helpful lady had ready at the counter.

"It is all yours!" The lady's voice was soft and excited. "I hope your day is perfect!" she said as she handed Brent the long garment bag.

"It's not my day," Brent told her without thinking. He took the bag, holding the hanger up to keep it from touching the ground.

Once the dress was safely laid across the back seat of John's car, Brent and Violet got in. They sat in silence for several minutes. Brent, kicking himself for opening his mouth, and Violet praying he would have the courage to say what he needed to say.

"I killed dad," Brent finally blurted without looking at her. He didn't want to see the shock and hurt he knew would be in her eyes.

"What do you mean?" Violet asked slowly. "You shot him?"

"No, Mom. I.." Brent rubbed his face with his hands, the pain felt good somehow. As if it were deadening the pain inside. "I was the one who got the police's attention. I'm the reason they found and killed him that night. I…" he choked up, unable to speak.

Reaching over, Violet squeezed his hand.

He nodded, his eyes closed. "I saw him kill the bank teller, Mom. Dad's face was so evil."

"Oh, Brent." She was tearing up, hurting for him. Turning in her seat, Violet pulled him into an awkward hug, "You have carried that alone for too long." She held on to him, and he let her. "You did the right thing." She whispered. "I love you, Brent. I always will."

He laid his head on her shoulder, and for the first time since his father's death, Brent let himself cry.

Chapter 31

"Mind if I walk with you to work?" Jimmy asked, catching up with Brent after school.

"Don't you have to be at your job?" Brent was not used to having Jimmy as a friend yet.

"No, the commissioner is on some important trip. His secretary said he won't be back until tomorrow night. Which means I won't be needed in the office until Monday," Jimmy gloated. "I've got a whole Friday of freedom."

"It is too bad that you don't enjoy your work as much as I do mine." Brent gave him a lofty, condescending look.

"Oh, high and mighty are we?" Jimmy momentarily stuck his nose up at Brent. "I do enjoy my job. And I also enjoy a little relaxation now and then."

A police car drove by with the other traffic, triggering Brent's memory. "Hey, your dad comes home tomorrow, doesn't he?"

Jimmy's jubilation faded. "Yeah."

"Have you figured out what you will say?"

Jimmy put his hand behind his neck and looked up as if trying to get rid of a neck pain. "It's going to be so awkward."

"Just talk about your black eye," Brent suggested, trying to look serious. The ice from the school nurse had done very little to stop the bruising of Jimmy's eye. "You look like John. Only fresher."

"You are one to talk." Jimmy answered. "Your bruises may

have faded, but they are definitely not gone. I wish I had a mirror so I could show you your smug mug."

Officer Cane waved at them from across the street as they passed. "Happy Birthday, Brent." He called with a grin.

Brent thanked him with a confused frown.

"I thought your birthday was a couple of weeks ago." Jimmy looked back at Officer Cane and saw him put his index finger to his lips. He checked to make sure Brent had not seen the signal.

"It was. It was a pretty eventful day. Maybe he forgot." Brent looked back, but Officer Cane had turned to chat with Seth and Peter and appeared to be getting a rundown of the fight between Marvin and Jimmy the day before.

"Can I tell you something," Jimmy asked after a few minutes of silence. "Since we are friends and all that now."

"Sure."

"I go by Jim now," Jimmy told him awkwardly. "At work at least."

Glancing over at him, Brent smiled in amusement. "Growing up, huh?"

Embarrassed, Jim studied the front of Second Trust Bank as they passed. Brent fell silent as well. There were so many memories tied up in this area now.

After a few minutes, Jim sighed. "It's going to be weird, you know, having Dad home again after ten years."

"Try getting a new dad altogether." Brent kept his eyes on the sidewalk ahead.

"The wedding is pretty soon then?"

"Tomorrow. It's like double dad day."

"A dreaded double dad day," Jim agreed. He picked up a small smooth rock from the shopping center's decorative flowerbed they were passing. Tossing it up, he caught it easily. As they walked, he tossed the rock from hand to hand. Now and then, he arched it high and caught it on the way down. "Do you want them to get married?" he ask, sending the rock up in a high arch.

"Yeah, I do." Brent reached over and caught the rock before Jimmy could.

"Hey, get your own ammo," Jim protested, taking the rock from Brent's open palm.

Brent shoved his hands into his pockets. "Anyway, I think it will be good for Mom to have someone steady who can actually provide for her. I can't get a full time job for a couple of years still. With John, she won't be always pinching pennies to scrape together enough for the rent each month."

"But do you like him?" Jim tossed the little stone back into the last flower bed on the property as they passed.

"I wasn't sure at first," Brent answered honestly. "But the whole situation with Cincher showed me how he does under pressure. I can tell he really loves her, Jimmy, uh Jim, I mean. All that he did to find her and protect her, it was cool." Brent ran his fingers through his hair. "I guess that sounds pretty lame, but I had never seen that kind of love before."

"No, it makes sense. He comes through at work fairly often, and he seems like a good guy. Everyone respects him."

Brent sighed heavily.

Jim hit the crosswalk button, and they stood waiting as the traffic drove by. "So why are you going to Bills' to work on cars instead of helping with the wedding stuff?"

"John said he wanted to meet me at Bill's after school."

They crossed together when the traffic light changed.

"You didn't ask why?" Jim asked, walking backwards so he could study Brent's face.

Brent shook his head.

"Any ideas?"

Taking a deep breath, Brent let it out slowly. "John told me a few days ago that he would like to adopt me and give me his name. I would be a Starclish instead of a Macintyre. We will be moving once he finishes up his job here. Dr. Nee has a research lab up near where we are going, and John found a good position there that he's happy about. He wanted me to be able to continue my studies with Dr. Nee. All that to say, with a new name, I could start over. I wouldn't have to be the son of a killer anymore."

"Wow, that's a big decision."

"I know. I've been praying about it." Brent glanced at Jim, expecting to see him laugh.

Instead, Jim nodded. "Good call."

They turned the corner and saw John standing outside of Bill's Auto, looking pleased.

"There you are!" he called to them. He gave a thumbs up to someone behind them.

They turned in time to see Dr. Nee close the door of his car. "He was sending me as a rescue party to see if you were coming," Dr. Nee explained cheerfully.

"You know you can't just park in the middle of the road, right?" Jim asked with a grin.

"Thank you, Officer." Dr. Nee bowed slightly to Jim. "Brent, John has something to show you." He walked past them toward John. The mysterious excitement of the two men was contagious.

"Okay," Brent followed him. "You coming, Jim?" he asked.

"He can come only if he stops criticizing my parking." Dr. Nee looked back at Jim, his eyes sparkling with fun.

Jim laughed and put his hands up in surrender.

Dr. Nee, Jim, and Brent walked together to the auto shop.

John called into the garage, and Bill emerged a moment later, wiping his hands on a rag.

"I know how much you love cars, Brent. So John and I got together and got you a beauty!" Dr. Nee led the way around the side of the shop.

"No way!" Jim exclaimed. "They got you a car. You are

only sixteen."

Bill, grinning widely, joined the little parade.

"There's some kind of catch, I can tell." Brent stopped short. There, sitting up on blocks, was the frame of what had once been a sleek car.

"Your new wheels!" John announced grandly.

"It has no wheels," Jim observed.

"Nor does it have an engine, or interior panels, or anything else for that matter." Bill laughed. "Every perfect starter car begins with a sturdy frame. And, to top it off, I put in a good word for you with my cousin. He's got an auto shop there that's bigger than this one. John says it's only about twenty minutes from where you will be living. Anyway, my cousin has agreed to train you how to use his tools in exchange for you working for him a couple of hours after school each day."

"That would be great!" Brent exclaimed.

"Is this some kind of joke?" Jim looked at Brent sympathetically only to find him staring in joyous awe at the frame.

"I could make this, like, my own car." Brent met Dr. Nee's shining eyes. The professor nodded, knowing Brent's deeper meaning. A car he could use his gift on. Maybe even remotely. The car he had only dreamed of making until now.

"You're happy about this?" Jim asked incredulously.

Laughing, Brent reached out and shook John's hand. "Thank you so much!"

John smiled. "You are very welcome. To be completely honest, though, the car wasn't my idea. It was Dr. Nee's, but I'd love to work on it with you."

"Not to be a dream crusher, but how are you going to move it?" Jim was walking around the frame trying to see value in another angle. "Your 'car' doesn't have any wheels."

"I've got a friend with a trailer who will be passing through next week," Bill answered. "He'll bring it up with him."

Jim scratched his head with a confused glance at Dr. Nee.

"I still don't see why this makes him so happy."

Bill went to examine the frame with Jim, leaving them alone.

When John spoke, his words were thoughtful. "Have you thought about my offer?"

Brent knew he was referring to the adoption and new name. "I have."

"There's no rush. No matter which name you choose, Brent, I still want to be part of your life."

Brent nodded.

They stood together for a few more minutes, enjoying Jim's exclamations of bewilderment.

"I'd better get back to help your Mom," John was still smiling. "I'm glad you like the 'car'. I was half afraid you would think it was a bad joke."

"It's perfect."

"I'm really glad." He turned to go. "I'll see you back at the house."

"John?"

John faced him expectantly.

"I've thought about it," Brent started slowly. "And I would like to have your name. To be a Starclish." Brent looked down at his shoes and added, "I want to be a man like you."

"Brent Starclish." John grinned. "It has a good ring to it."

The wedding was over, and the happy couple had pulled away down the long drive of the church his mom had been attending. Brent stood staring after them. It was hard to believe it had happened. It had been him and his mom for so long. Now they were three again.

"You okay?" Dr. Nee came to stand by him as the crowd of well-wishers started to clear.

"I'm happy for them. But a lot will change."

"Change is often a positive experience." Dr. Nee stooped to pick up some of the flower pedals that had been thrown.

"You really should publish a book, Dr. Nee." Brent's expression gave away his joke before he said the punch line, but Dr. Nee went along anyway.

"And what would I find to write about?" he asked, cupping the pedals gently in his hand.

"You could call it Wise Words of Dr. Nee and other Chinese Proverbs."

Dr. Nee shook his head with a smile. He was about to respond when Officer Cane approached them.

"Congratulations, Brent." He offered his hand, and Brent shook it.

"Thank you."

"It was a beautiful wedding." Officer Cane was in full uniform, having taken some approved leave during his shift to attend the wedding. His radio chattered, and he turned it down a little. "The cake was exceptional. That totally made the day perfect." His radio chirped again, and he frowned. "Excuse me." Stepping away, he adjusted the volume, cocking his head to listen.

They watched as his face grew serious. "Roger that," he radioed back.

"There's a time bomb at the commissioner's office. Pray." he told them, sprinting toward his squad car.

"You can help them." Dr. Nee looked Brent in the eye.

"What?"

"Come with me." He hurried toward his car, half jogging to the parking lot with Brent keeping up easily. "It is time to use your power for more than turning on and off lights, Brent. You can help them."

"With a bomb? Dr. Nee, I don't know anything about bombs."

"The timer is electronic, Brent. You can stop it. You can stop the electrical current that ignites the explosives."

Brent stared at him dumbly. "They have a bomb squad for that, Dr. Nee."

"Times of great danger can also be times of great strength." Dr. Nee opened the driver's door of his car and slid behind the wheel.

Brent raced around to the passenger side and hopped in. "I don't know anything about bombs. What good will my gift be if I get blown up?"

"What good will your gift be if you do not use it to help others?" Dr. Nee countered, pulling onto the street. "You won't get blown up." He was speeding up, handling the car like a race car driver instead of a science and electronics teacher.

CHAPTER 32

"You are going to get a ticket!" Brent was grinning and bracing himself as they rounded the corner. A few more blocks brought them to the edge of the danger zone. The police were evacuating several blocks around the building. A good number of pedestrians were milling around along the police line hoping to catch sight of some of the action.

"Find Eddie. He needs you," Dr. Nee instructed. "I'm wanted elsewhere."

Sensing the urgency in his tone, Brent sprang from the car as soon as it stopped. Running toward the line, Brent was stopped by Officer Brandon.

"Brent, haven't you had enough excitement?" Brandon raised his voice so all the people around could hear too. "All of you get clear of this area. There's been a bomb threat at the Commissioner's office."

"That's two blocks away," someone protested.

"It's a bomb, Sir." Officer Brandon was trying to be patient. "The size has not yet been determined. You could be in the blast radius."

A lady screamed, and people scattered, pushing and shoving in their panic to get out of harm's way.

Brent looked around. Dr. Nee's car was already gone.

A lean stranger with tight curly hair approached Brent in all of the confusion. He was calm and purposeful. "Brent?" he asked meeting Brent's eyes with a serious, searching look.

Brent nodded.

"Dr. Nee said you were the man I needed to talk to about disabling the bomb inside."

"Are you Eddie?" Brent asked uncertainly.

"I am."

Officer Cane pulled up in his police cruiser. He looked at Brent. "How did you?" He gestured with his thumb in the direction of the church they had all been at a few minutes before.

"How long do you have until the bomb blows?" Eddie asked Officer Cane.

Cane consulted his watch. "From the time of the tip, about seven minutes and fifty-six seconds."

"That's perfect."

"Cane, I need help." Even though the threat was two blocks away, Officer Burk looked scared. "This lady fainted."

"Get out of here, Brent," Officer Cane instructed, running to help Burk.

Eddie turned to Brent. "I need you to stop that bomb."

"How do you know I can disable a bomb?" Brent kept his voice low.

"I don't know," he answered with a slight smile.

Something Dr. Nee had said to him during one of their sessions popped into Brent's head. "God has a tangible way for you to use your gift to help others. Your job is to find out what it is."

"I'll give it a try," Brent agreed. "If you can get me in."

"You'll need this." The stranger's green eyes shone with anticipation as he held out a black vest marked with big bold letters that read, "Bomb squad."

Brent stared. "Where did you get that?"

A mysterious look was his only answer. "There are gloves in the left pocket and tools in the right. Follow me, I'll get you inside."

"Okay." Brent slipped into the vest as he walked beside the man. It was as if they were invisible. Police were all around, but no one seemed to see them.

"This way." Eddie lifted the caution tape for Brent to duck under.

Brent glanced at the officers, but no one protested as he ducked under and jogged with Eddie toward the building where Jim worked. Brent was thankful his friend had been at the wedding and not at work.

"Tell me what you know." Brent kept up easily with Eddie.

"The bomb squad had a call across town, and my bomb guy can't get here in time." As they left the chaos of the evacuation line, Eddie gave a thumbs up to a man who was obviously waiting for him. Brent saw the man put a phone to his ear to pass on the update.

"The commissioner is inside the building," Eddie went on, quickening the pace slightly. "My guess is that he discovered the bomber before the man was ready, and the guy knocked him out. Worst case, the commissioner is already dead. Either way, my team will get him out while you disable the bomb. People say, 'no pressure.'" Eddie looked over to see how Brent was handling the information. "This is the opposite of that. People's lives are at stake, and we are all depending on you."

Instead of anxiety, Brent felt a strange confidence. "Do you know the exact location of the bomb?"

"Yes, the bomb's location has been confirmed with an aerial infrared scan of the building. From the information we have, it is in the commissioner's office near the desk. The catch is that the commissioner's body also appears to be near the desk." Eddie was setting a quick, steady pace. His breathing remained calm and regular as they put the first block and a half of buildings behind them. The commissioner's office was just ahead. "From what Andy can see, it appears to be what is known as a time bomb."

"One that is run by electricity instead of a lit fuse," Brent frowned. "It could be on a timer or set to be detonated remotely."

"Right. My guess is a detonator. That could be good or bad, depending on what kind of bombs you are used to."

Brent did not feel the need to tell the confident stranger that this was his first bomb. His mind worked quickly. All he would have to do is pull the power, and the bomb could not be detonated. After that he could work out how to disassemble the bomb. He had done something like that during his private lessons with Dr. Nee. Only now he knew what he had been working with.

As they neared the building, Brent slowed his pace to give himself time to focus. This was the biggest power pull he would do since the streetcar incident. He had to keep power from every part of the building until they were able to confirm the location of the bomb.

"Have you been inside this building before?" Eddie asked as they slowed to approach the door.

"Once." Brent struggled to focus as he remembered the last time he entered. He had been clutching the newspaper Dr. Nee had given him, and seething with anger at Jim. The anger was gone now.

Two men of similar build joined them. One looked like he was from the Middle East with olive skin and dark hair. The other man was tanned by the sun and had short brown hair.

"I'm Vince. This is Andy," the olive skinned man informed him. "Thanks for coming."

"He's a well-dressed Bomb Guy," Andy pointed out as Eddie pulled open the door with a gloved hand.

Looking down at himself, Brent realized he was still wearing his suit from the wedding. "You pay a little extra for the classy version." He quipped. Sweat was already beading on his forehead.

Despite the tense situation, Andy and Vince shared an amused look as they followed Brent across the lobby.

The whole building was dark inside. Brent wasn't taking any chances.

"Why don't you wait outside?" he suggested.

"We are here to get the commissioner out. If we can get him out before it blows, that's even better," Vince told him seriously. He pulled out a hand gun, and Brent stepped away instinctively.

"The guns are only a precaution," Eddie reassured him, keeping the barrel of his Glock low. "If the bomber is still inside, we need to be ready."

Brent saw that all three of them were carrying. He licked his lips nervously. "Okay."

Pulling out flashlights, they clicked them on. Unaware of the slight pointed shift in power that allowed them to come on. Brent was now pulling electricity from the building while producing enough to light the flashlights. He would need to find the bomb before something broke his concentration.

Brent followed as they lit the way to the commissioner's office. Their movements were quick yet calculated. The lights swept over the room as they made sure that the bomb was the only immediate threat.

"It's clear." Andy stated stepping aside to allow Brent to enter.

Brent easily located the important man's desk. There were papers strewn over the floor and desk. Brent guessed that the commissioner had come in to put the packet of papers on his desk. Instead, he had startled his would be killer, and now lay limp on the floor. Brent approached the desk, looking over the desktop first. There was nothing big enough on top to hide a bomb.

Moving in fast, Andy, Vince, and Eddie hefted the big

man and carried him out, leaving Brent alone with a single flashlight and the bomb.

Because he was already disabling the electricity in the building, Brent could not look for the bomb using the electricity it emitted. Pulling on the gloves that had been in the pocket of his vest, Brent set to work. Moving quickly, but methodically, he seared through the desk one drawer at a time. Nothing.

The time ticked by, marked by the imposing but elegant antique grandfather clock. Laying on the hardwood floor, Brent found what he was looking for. The explosives wedged up under the base of the large desk were enough to cause serious damage to the structure of the building. If the bomb had gone off as planned, the commissioner, Jimmy, and anyone else who happened to be in the blast radius would have died.

Making sure there were no trip wires attached, Brent pulled the detonator out from under the desk. Allowing the power to return to the rest of the building with a few convincing flickers, Brent kept the commissioner's office dark. With the flashlight balanced on a partially open drawer to give him light, he worked quickly and confidently. He was the one controlling the power, so Brent knew he had all the time in the world to get it right. That kept his nerves in check and his fingers steady.

Brent guessed that by accidentally interrupting the bomber, the Commissioner had actually saved his own life and the lives of his staff team. Knowing the bomb would be discovered and removed before the next morning, the bomber must have decided it was better to detonate the bomb now and kill the unconscious commissioner. But why had he waited long enough to let Brent get inside? And how did the police get the tip so fast? Was the bomber trying to draw the attention of someone specific? Or had Brent pulled the power before the man had the chance to detonate the bomb? Questions flew unanswered through his mind.

The tools in the 'Bomb Squad' vest Brent wore proved to be exactly what were needed. He disengaged the detonator from the explosives. When he was done, Brent stood with a sigh. His eyes moved to the clock. A little over five minutes had passed since he entered the room. Brent couldn't help smiling. It was not bad for his first try on a live bomb.

"You handled yourself very well." Eddie's voice made Brent jump. "You might want to work a little more on awareness of your surroundings," Eddie joked with an amused smile. He had been standing by the door, watching Brent work.

"What are you doing in here?" Brent held up the detonator in his hand. "This could have killed you."

"And you," Eddie pointed out. "I don't ask men to go into dangerous situations without backup. You looked like you knew what you were doing. I'm always looking for gifted people like you who can keep their cool under pressure."

Brent smiled, enjoying the praise. "What now?" he asked.

"Do you mind taking off a couple of pieces? That will keep whoever it was who set the bomb from returning and resetting his death trap before the police arrive?"

Moving to the desk, Brent sat in the commissioner's chair.

"You don't know who set this?" asked Brent. Pulling the tools from his pocket, he put the little handful in a pile on the desk. Brent had not restored power to the room yet, so Eddie came over to hold the flashlight so Brent could see to work.

"No, I don't know who it is. Not yet."

Brent liked the determined way Eddie added 'not yet'.

"Whoever it was, has been planning this for a while. I don't want him to get cocky and come back in behind us." Eddie went on. "The bomb squad disabled the bomb they were working on across town. Andy told me just before I came back in that another bomb was reported on the west side of town. It was in a closed factory building, but for some reason it never went off."

"Must have been a faulty job," Brent observed.

Eddie did not answer right away. "It could have been." He obviously knew something Brent did not.

"Is the commissioner okay?" As a last measure, Brent was clipping the wires in several places leaving nothing long enough to reconnect the device.

"Yes. He's unconscious, but he's alive. Vince and Andy will drop him off and return the car."

Brent glanced up. "The car wasn't stolen right?"

Eddie frowned slightly as he shook his head no, but his eyes told a different story.

Eyeing him for a moment, Brent was not sure what to make of the strange answer. Standing, he surveyed his work. "That should do it."

Eddie selected a piece from the desk, tilting his gloved hand to get a better look at it. After a moment he nodded, satisfied. "Good work." Slipping the piece into a zip topped bag, Eddie headed for the office door.

"What do we do now?" Brent remained where he was. He had hoped the police would come in and see that he had done something good to help the law. Maybe then they would believe Brent wasn't like his dad.

"We leave." Eddie looked back in time to see Brent's surprised expression. "No fingerprints, no evidence. Only a disabled detonator on the desk, and a breathing commissioner who is being delivered to the hospital now."

"But don't you want them to know that you saved him? And that I disabled the bomb." Brent felt foolish for saying it, but this man didn't know how hard he worked to prove he wasn't a crook.

Cocking his head, Eddie studied Brent. "It would be nice, wouldn't it, Brent? No, I don't stay to take the credit. That's not why I do it."

"You use your gifts to help the other people God created." Brent's words brought a smile to Eddie's face.

"That's one way to put it. The police force works very hard at what they do. I like to let them get a little more credit now and then to help boost morale. Plus, I enjoy getting one step ahead of the bad guys so the cops can pick them up." Opening the door, Eddie looked back at Brent. "Come on, they will be here soon."

"Do you always take a souvenir?" Brent wondered if he should have taken one. After all, it was his first bomb to disable.

Eddie's laugh echoed softly in the hall. "No. I don't. I need to know where he is getting his parts. Three bombs in one day isn't normal. All three being disabled before they blew also isn't normal."

"I was wondering that, too. Why would he tell the police about all three?"

Eddie stopped and pointed down the hall, "This way. We will use the back." He seemed to be very familiar with the layout of the building. Brent considered turning the hall lights on, but thought better of it. If Eddie wasn't turning the lights on, there must be a reason.

Brent followed, intrigued. "So how does the piece help you?"

"If I can find out where he is buying his stuff, I might be able to get information on who he is." I have a couple of months to piece this together."

"What happens in a couple of months?" Brent felt like a little kid full of questions.

Eddie grinned mysteriously. "I've got an appointment to keep." He paused, looking at Brent with that same searching look. "This bomber isn't done, and I'd like to have another bomb expert in this area. I have the feeling that this guy is a part of something bigger and that he will strike again soon. Would you be interested in being on call if something comes up?"

"Yeah, I can help. I'm still in school, but I think I can get away if it's an emergency."

"Good. In the meantime, stick with Dr. Nee. He's a man of many talents."

Brent could tell Eddie was ready to leave, but he had one more question he needed answered. "Eddie, why do you think the bomber didn't set off the bomb right away and kill the commissioner?"

"I don't know. I can think of two possibilities: that he was still getting out of range, or that he is a part of something much bigger." Eddie frowned thoughtfully. "We have two months to track him down and find out." Pausing with his gloved hand on the crash bar of the exit door, Eddie looked over at Brent. "You will have to keep all this to yourself. Are you okay with that?"

Brent wavered for a moment before nodding seriously. "I'll keep it to myself."

Checking outside to make sure the coast was clear, Eddie pushed the door open.

"Welcome to the team, Brent." His green eyes met Brent's, and Brent knew he was stepping into something much bigger than himself. He was taking on the low profile, high action life of a super hero, and he already knew he would love it!

Strength of Silence

Eddie stayed where he was, listening. In the distance, a motor started up. He waited until it had faded before he stood. Dizziness washed over him, and he steadied himself against the counter. Still moving unsteadily, Eddie removed the floorboards and laid them aside. He heard something out front and froze. If the police caught him here, there would be no end of trouble. Moving toward the back door Eddie pushed it open. Outside, trash cans and a variety of other things littered the yard. A car motor rumbled toward him, and Eddie ran.

Jason Roper

Infused with invincibility and trained for greatness, Jason Roper is set to fulfill his father's dreams. But when Roper deviates from the instructions he is given, he stumbles upon an expansive criminal network. Determined to use his power to help those in need, Jason Roper discovers that there are times when invincibility alone is not enough.

Is Jason Roper destined for greatness as he has been told, or is his life just a front for a larger, more sinister plan?

Other Books by J. Alspaugh

Roper Returns

Jason Roper's second mission is clear-cut. He moves in with confidence, feeling invincible and unstoppable. But things are not what they appear on the surface. Even his invincibility has limits Roper did not know.

With no one to turn to, Roper finds himself sinking into a darkness he does not have the power to evade.

The Man Behind The Melody

The unexpected death of his twin sister threw Mark into a whirlwind of change. Disowned by his stepfather, Mark set out with only one goal in mind, to get as far away from the hateful man as possible. He clung desperately to the last link with his sister, her saxophone. Wandering the streets, Mark's path crossed with a stranger who could see potential no one else could see. Mark, an unwanted orphan, was offered the chance to become more than he had ever dreamed. But could the stranger be trusted?

THE STRIKER OF CHOI

The health of the Striker is the health of Choi. If he goes hungry, the town of Choi will grow hungry. If he is injured, the townspeople will suffer injury. He must be protected at all costs and must never leave the town of his birth. If he were to leave, the curse of the town would be in the hands of strangers.

Striker knew the legend well, but was there more to the legend than he had been told?

THE SWORD OF JUSTICE

His mission was to eliminate those who had received the death penalty from the king. Justice was a King's Man. A man who had sworn allegiance to the king and who was backed in power by the full authority of the king himself. A man hated by every criminal in the king's realm.

Would Justice's loyalty to the king and skill with a sword be enough to protect him from his enemies?

www.ingramcontent.com/pod-product-compliance
Lightning Source LLC
LaVergne TN
LVHW091119080826
845145LV00008B/1975